HEIST

The Trilogy:

1. THE HEIST. 2. GOOD COP BAD COP.
3. THE END RESULT.

RADCLIFFE

PUBLISHERS

Published in the UK in 2022 by Radcliffe Publishers

Paperback ISBN: 978-1-7395823-0-2
eBook ISBN: 978-1-7395823-1-9

Cover design and typeset by SpiffingCovers

HEIST

The Trilogy:

1. THE HEIST. 2. GOOD COP BAD COP.
3. THE END RESULT.

RICHARD POOLE

I would like to dedicate this book to my wife, Andree, for her help in checking facts out, and patience.

Also to the memory of my late twin brother, Dave.

BOOK ONE

HEIST

PART ONE

CHAPTER 1

Christmas 2008

Cat was on the roof, pulling up foam-insulated gas-type bottles. He looked across and could see the Boss parked a hundred yards down the road; another gang member was parked about a hundred yards further down. Cat lifted one bottle up and carried it towards the intake air vent on the roof; he gently undid the nozzle, directing the contents into the vent. As he went back for the second bottle, he saw another gang member giving him the thumbs up. He directed the second canister into the air vent, then bound the whole of the vent with industrial cling film, to stop any gasses escaping. He waited five minutes and, making sure he was out of line of the cameras, he eased himself down between a telegraph pole and the wall, headfirst, in a style he had developed. He looked through the top of the office window clearly seeing the three guards slumped, heads on table, as though sleeping. He tapped on the window, the guards didn't move, he hit it harder, still no one moved. He went back on the roof, unpeeled the cling film, packaging everything up. He signalled to the other gang members, and lowered the cylinders down to Guy, before climbing down himself.

"All clear inside, all sound asleep."

Cat and Guy made their way to the front gate, meeting the Boss and Joe.

The Boss said, "Cat, that outside door is on a security chain, get over and undo it, the door should be open with the guards inside, but chained. When you get in, switch the reverse airflow switch on, it's on the left, just inside the door. Get the keys, in the cabinet between the screens. Shut the door when you come out, let some of the gas escape, then open this gate."

Cat was over the gate in a flash and back in less than a minute, opening the gates for the other three members of the gang. Locking the gate behind them, all four went into the main office. They all were wearing overshoes, boiler suits and masks – all made of a disposable material – and rubber gloves.

Guy checked the guards. All were injected with a further knockout mixture. He said, "That should keep them quiet for about five hours."

"Right," said the Boss, "this way." He led the way from the main office to a smaller inner office, and using the keys from the cabinet he let himself in. "Joe, you sit in here for five minutes before every hour, on every hour and don't move. On the hour the guards are supposed to do a routine check with HQ. They use a daily codeword and say *Nottingham One in order*; today's codeword is *Draughts.* Keep your eye on the time and call on time. These are the security alarm switches, including the strong room area. They switch them off for ten minutes every hour during the night to check the whole building, the log says the next one is in two minutes. They call HQ before and after every check. We'll wait in here for two minutes, then switch off."

The Boss was Bob Teal. At 42 years old, he was the oldest member of the team, an architect and careful planner, with a vicious streak in him. He had no convictions, and was wealthy in his own right, after the careful planning of earlier jobs. He also ran a highly lucrative investment company, as well as his architect business.

Cat, real name, Jerry Morton, was an expert climber, hence his nickname. Bought up in the Gorbals area until 12, then the East End of London where he learnt his trade. He lived on violence and was afraid of no man. He insisted on being tooled up on any job he did – he carried a small snub-nose revolver in his overall pocket and a sawn-off shotgun strapped to his waist, like a cowboy. Every member had objected, but he had insisted he came like that or not at all. He won. His convictions were all for violence.

Guy Salmon, ex-public school, former rally driver and expert mechanic. He knew his cars inside out and joined the team 12 months ago, after their last driver died whilst racing a police Jaguar up the motorway. He was very strong, loved the high life and fast cars. He had one previous conviction. He and Cat had been attacking a strong room in Essex, he had got caught, Cat had got away. It cost him five years but earned him a big reputation in the criminal world. The strong room was at Teal Investments.

Lastly came Joe Andrews, an electronics expert and electrical engineer. He loved a challenge and had been with the Boss for a number of years, trusting him implicitly.

The phone rang. "Right, that's HQ ringing Joe, the codeword's *Draughts*," said the Boss.

Joe picked the phone up after three rings, waited and said, "Draughts, Nottingham One in order, alarms off." He hung up.

The Boss said, "Set watches, when Joe's done his bit, we'll all meet back here. Guy, you come back to the strong room with us, Joe will look after the office side. Joe, give us a shout on 19 minutes."

They all made their way to the strong room area. Joe set his equipment up, plugging into the vaults electronic system, working the clock to its opening time. The others busied themselves in a well-trained manner, arranging tools and bags.

There was a whirring noise as Joe began to slow the clock down, until there was a loud click and it stopped. He reached for the wheel, turned it easily and opened the vault door. "Now let's earn our keep. I'll shout you."

The others stood looking in awe at the amounts of cash lying on the shelves, some in boxes, with various names of banks, building societies and brand-name stores attached to the bundles.

"It won't shift itself boys," said the Boss. "Cash boxes and bundles only, no jewellery, we've got eight minutes this time, let's go."

They grabbed a box each and began forcing them open, putting the contents in the sacks.

"Fucking 'ell," said Cat. "I've never seen so much cash."

The plan was to fill four sacks each, with an extra one each if they got time.

"How we doing, Guy?" shouted the Boss.

"Better count to 30 then lock up this time," he shouted back.

"All finish now," said the Boss. "Cat, Guy, bring that big box with you to the office, we can sort that there while we are waiting."

Joe came back in, resetting the clock and alarms.

As he returned, the phone rang. He let it ring three times, picked it up and said, "Draughts Nottingham one in order, alarms on."

"Good. Guy, check the guards. Cat, let's have a coffee."

"OK Boss."

Whilst Guy went next door, Cat poured them all a mug of coffee and a tot of rum.

"As it's Christmas, Boss."

"No more than that."

"Guards OK, Boss," said Guy.

"So far so good," said the Boss. "We've got 40 minutes to wait before we get back into the vault. That will do us then, I want to be out of here."

"What do you reckon we've got so far?" asked Guy.

"It's Christmas weekend, should be good for a couple of million I hope," said the Boss as he attacked the large box they'd bought out. As he opened it he sat back smiling. "Well someone's got a sense of humour." On top of the cash bundle was a Christmas card showing Santa Claus with a swag bag and mask climbing down a bank chimney. Inside it read, "Santa gets back what others take at Christmas."

"Not this Santa, let's fill the sacks," said the Boss.

They continued to fill sacks to a manageable level.

"I want each sack filled half to three quarters at least. It cost me plenty to set this job up, plus some for my expenses," said the Boss.

***

The Midland Express Security building was situated in a residential area of inner Nottingham. It was square-shaped, having been built about ten years earlier as a warehouse. The security firm had had it about five years and had turned it into a secure cash storage premises, with large vaults. It was a Saturday, Christmas Eve. The vault was stacked with cash from various large business premises throughout the city, including some banks and building societies. Shops had done a booming Christmas trade, and as banks wouldn't be open for at least three more days, the cash wasn't going anywhere. Bob Teal had seen the premises whilst on a business trip some three years earlier. He had been with the architect who had been responsible for the alterations to the premises, and had even managed to obtain a copy of the plans with every detail he wanted on them. They were locked in a strong safe in his London office, along with many other plans of premises throughout the country, so he wasn't afraid of snoopers. Since that time he had been putting this plan onto paper. He was a divorced man, living on his own, and often away on business, although he did entertain at his flat. This time he was on his way back from a business trip to Scotland, stopping off at his cottage on the outskirts of Derby, not too far from a motorway junction. The others had booked separate hotels, not known to the other gang members, although they were to keep in touch by mobile phone, just in case. The plan was to all meet up on the following night at a London hotel, around the corner from his flat on Park Lane to sort out shares of the job. In the meantime, all the sacks would be sealed with plastic pull-ties and each member would take some with them. If any of the sacks were tampered with or missing, that member would have a tough time, even death, as Cat had stated at the planning stage. He would have done it to whoever, no matter who it was. He looked round at the others filling sacks and tying them together to enable them to carry them yolk-style to the cars.

"Three minutes before I ring," said Joe.

"Guy, check the guards again before he rings," said the Boss.

He came back moments later. "Still flat out, Boss."

***

Their watches showed 2am as Joe rang. "Nottingham one in order, draughts." Before ringing off he said, "Merry Christmas to you all at your end, thanks mate." Putting the phone down he said, "If they knew what kind of Christmas I was having, and they were going to get, he'd have said something stronger."

"Right, Joe, get back to the vault and let's get on," said the Boss.

They all made their way back to the vault area, where Joe opened the vault as he had done earlier. "Let's get this job done," said the Boss.

In no time they had another eight sacks loaded and ready. "How long have we got, Joe?" shouted the Boss.

"Seven minutes," he shouted back.

"One more sack each, then I want everything back in the vault before we shut it. I don't want them to know we've been in until the vault opens on the clock."

They managed four more sacks before the Boss shouted, "That's it, no more."

Anything they weren't taking with them was dumped back inside the vault, the door shut and reset. All the sacks were tied up and tagged, ready for loading in the cars. "Make sure we've left nothing lying about, I want out after the next phone call."

***

"Get up on the roof, Cat, check we are OK outside. Guy, leave your car where it is for the time being. If it's clear, bring Joe's car in first, in case anyone rings we need Joe to be here. I want this to be over after this next set of alarms are off. And remember gentlemen, all shoes, overalls and gloves in the plastic bin liners before you get in your cars. And all sacks on the plastic sheets in the boot. I don't want any forensic in the cars. Understood?"

Cat was quickly up on the roof and signalling the all-clear. They let Guy out, quickly relocking the gates after he had driven back in, in Joe's BMW. He and Guy loaded four sacks in the boot. Cat signalled the all-clear and they let Guy out. He returned a few minutes later with his own Jaguar, locking the gate behind them. They went through the same procedure, putting four sacks in the boot, before, on Cat's signal, he drove that out, returning moments later, the gate being relocked.

Cat came back into the office and said, "Christ, it's getting colder out there." He took the rum bottle out and began to take a drink. "No more, I said," said the Boss.

Cat looked at him, took a swig without taking his eyes off him, put the top back on and sat down.

"Don't push it, Cat," said the Boss.

"Christ, what's that?" said Guy, as a bell sounded in the office.

"It's the outside gate bell, there must be someone there. Put the guard's coat and hat on and go and see, we can't leave it ringing," said the Boss.

Guy walked in the office, put the coat and hat on and went outside. He nearly choked when he saw the glint from the police sergeant's helmet. Regaining his composure, he went towards the gate and said, "Good evening officer, all the best for the Christmas and New Year."

"Same to you mate, where's Harry, is he in tonight? I said I'd call by," said the officer

"He's booked the night off, the crafty old bugger. Saw there was four of us on duty so booked it off, we can manage with three but no less."

"Are you new here then?"

"I'm over from the Lincoln depot to cover for him. I don't mind, it makes me some extra cash for Christmas."

"I see, well I'll call by later in the week and see Harry," said the officer.

"Call back in about an hour if you want, we should be brewing about then if you want," said Guy.

"I'll see what time I get. All the best, cheers goodnight."

"Goodnight officer, all the best to you and yours," replied Guy.

He went back inside. Cat said, "Why the fuck don't you invite him in to fucking help us, we could use some police transport to get away in."

"Bollocks, only being polite."

"OK that's enough, let it go," said the Boss.

The phone rang, Joe picked it up and said, "Nottingham one in order, alarms off. Oh sorry, draughts. OK cheers."

They began to sort out when the phone rang. Looking at the clock, it wasn't a scheduled call. Joe picked it up and said, "Nottingham one." A moment later he said, "Who do you want, love?" He put his hand over the mouthpiece and said, "There's a bird on asking for one of the guards."

"Tell her he's on the bog and ring back in 15 minutes to avoid the call from HQ," said the Boss.

"Hello love, he's on the toilet, ring back in a couple of minutes. No hang on, ring in about ten minutes after HQ have rang, bye." He returned the phone to its cradle and sat back. It rang again straight away. After three rings he picked it up and said, "Nottingham one." Pausing, he said, "Sorry pal, one of the lad's wives just rang to say happy Christmas. We're alright here, alarms on, draughts. Call you soon, cheers."

"Right let's move. Cat, on the roof, make sure it's all clear and you've left nothing up there, on the all-clear. Guy, fetch my car in, then Cat, let's get out quick."

All three nodded to their boss.

A couple of moments later they got the all-clear from Cat. Guy fetched the Boss's car, his quota was loaded into the boot, and driven out. Cat's car was bought in, loaded with his share of sacks, the foam-covered gas tanks, and driven out.

"Guy, you go now, we'll meet up as arranged tomorrow at the cottage, and don't be late. Joe, you leave last in case the phone rings. I'll meet you round the side. Cat can lock the gate after Joe leaves, put the keys back in the office, and go back out over the roof. Wait for him to give the final all-clear."

Cat came off the roof and, following instructions, locked the gate behind everyone, before putting the keys back in the office. He climbed back up onto the roof, giving them the all-clear.

Joe and the Boss would give him a couple of minutes and pick him up on the corner to take him to his car. The Boss had insisted all cars must be hire cars, of their own choice.

As they walked towards their cars, Joe said, "Nice little tickle Bob, no problems, smooth as clockwork."

"So far, let's get away first."

They both turned their heads at the sound of the first bang, quickly followed by another one.

"Christ if that's what I think it is," said the Boss, as Cat came running towards them holding the shotgun. "That fucking copper was round the back when I came off the roof, he was watching you walking away and was on his radio asking for some help. He heard me coming down the pipe and grabbed me, so I let him have it."

"You fucking idiot, let's go. I knew you were itching to use that fucking shotgun sometime, you twat." The Boss was grabbing him angrily and pulling him towards the car. "See you at the cottage, Joe."

He got Cat into his car and drove away carefully. He could hear the approach of cars being driven at speed, and see blue lights flashing off the sides of buildings as they got nearer. He dropped Cat off round the corner from his car.

"If you don't get rid of that gun by tomorrow night's meet, you are in deep shit mate."

Cat snarled back, "I've been in it before." And shut the car door.

CHAPTER 2

As they were disappearing round the corner, a police dog van and traffic car were pulling up at the front of the premises, closely followed by the night CID officers and a couple of panda cars.

They were ringing the front gate bell and getting no response.

"I'll go over the gate," said Dick Jones, an ex-marine, a capable no-nonsense detective sergeant with ten years' service in the force. He quickly scaled the door and went to the lighted window where he saw the guards still slumped over. He banged on the windows and, getting no response, tried the door. It opened on the chain. He shouted to the officers at the gate, "Have a look round the outside, looks like the guards have been drugged or something."

Reaching through, he slid the chain out of its socket and entered the office. He checked the guards and found them all to be breathing, but not conscious. Using his police radio he called the control room.

"DS Jones, I am at the premises of Midland Express Security Offices on London Road, the guards are unconscious, unable to locate Sergeant Peters at this time. Can you inform senior officers and get key holders for the premises as soon as possible? Also require ambulance and medical assistance. Other officers are searching the outside perimeter. Have you got that?"

The Control Inspector said, "Yes, can you tell us if the

place has been attacked at this stage?"

"Not at the moment I can't, I'm trying to find the gate keys. Hope you have started a log, inspector."

"That's in hand, DS Jones, you do your bit, I'll do mine."

Dick found the keys he thought were the main gate keys, and was unlocking the gate when his partner said, "We've found Sgt Peters, he's up the road with his brains blown out."

"Have you notified the control room, John?"

"Dog man's not done it, I think it's blown him apart, and my radio is in the car, I'll do it."

"No John, I'll do it, you watch the front gate a minute." Dick got onto the radio.

"Duty Inspector, we have found Sgt Peters, I'm afraid he's been fatally wounded. Can you call the circus out and get me some uniforms here asap?"

The control room replied all was being done.

Dick went to a uniformed PC who had just arrived at the gate, out of breath after running to the scene, and told him to stay on the gate and let no one in or out unless he, or John, was satisfied who they were. "No one," he hissed.

Dick said to John, "What was Sgt Peters' last radio message, do we know?"

John said, "He radioed up to say he thought something was suspicious and he was checking it out. I didn't catch where he was, control room must have done though."

They walked round to where Sgt Peters lay on the ground, a large pool of blood around what was left of his head. "Poor sod, never stood a chance," said Dick. The PC nearby was about to put a blanket over the body.

Dick said, "No blanket, get a plastic sheet out of the box in the back of our car, it's clean, put that over him and stand by him till the police surgeon gets here. Don't leave him, OK?"

"OK Dick," replied the PC, glad to be out of the way for

a few minutes.

"Poor sod," said Dick. "No way to end up at Christmas or any other time, he must have disturbed some bastard coming off the roof, looking at his head injury and foot marks on his greatcoat."

The dog handler came back to them and said, "I picked up a trail down to the next corner, near that cutting, but lost it. I think they got into a car there."

"Is anyone at that scene?" Dick asked.

"No," said the dog man. At that moment, the uniformed officer came back with the plastic sheet, another PC and the Night Inspector. "Can I borrow the PC sir? I want him to guard a possible escape route the dog man's picked up."

The Inspector nodded, still looking at his mate, Sgt Peters lying under the sheet.

Dick directed the PC to where he wanted him to stand and instructed him not to move until further notice.

"Sgt Peters is dead sir, shot in the head from close range, never stood a chance. I sent for the circus, the guards inside are either drugged or something, alive but unconscious. I don't know whether we are too early to stop a job, or too late."

Inspector Hill said, "Thanks Dick, we are too late for Trevor. Let's hope we can salvage something. PC Wright, you stay with the body until I order you elsewhere, understand?"

"Yes sir," came the meek reply.

Dick walked back to the main gate with John and the Inspector, nodding to the PC to open the gate for them. "Dick," said the Inspector. "Have you asked for the mobile incident room to come out?"

"No," replied Dick. "I've asked for the circus, I presume that comes with it."

"OK, John, you stay at the front gate and keep a log until it comes, get onto control room and ask for it on my behalf."

"Yes sir."

Dick and the Inspector walked into the office; the three guards were still out cold. The phone started to ring, Inspector Hill picked it up. "Hello, this is Inspector Hill of the Notts police." After a short pause he went on, "I don't know any codeword. Is that the Security HQ control?" He then went on to state that he had had a police officer shot near to the premises and that the guards were unconscious.

The voice on the other end confirmed it was HQ and asked if the vault had been attacked. "Not sure yet," said Inspector Hill. "It's certainly not open."

The HQ operative said, "We have had regular contacts with the guards all shift so far, when did this happen?"

"Not sure ourselves yet," replied the Inspector. "Can you leave this line open and call out whoever we need from your end, to meet us here asap?"

"Yes, press the hold button, when you want to get back press it again, someone will be here. I'll contact our local director, a Mrs Henderson, she comes from Bingham."

Inspector Hill pressed the hold button down and said, "Dick, can you organise some knocking on doors? I know it's late, but let's start anyway, someone might have seen something, and the gunshots might have caused someone to look out. The gaffer will want to know what's going on."

"I'll sort that out sir."

As he walked to the front gate, he saw Det Supt Dee and Det Insp King talking to the PC on the gate. "It's alright Pete, they are on our side, sorry about that sir, I thought John Mills might have seen you sir."

Supt Dee replied, "I did see him. I've got him organising the control unit up, we logged in but didn't stop, he suggested we speak to you. What's gone off, Dick?"

"Well sir, it appears that Sgt Peters disturbed someone climbing either onto the roof or off the roof and took a couple of barrels through the head. He's round the back. I checked the main office before we found him, all three guards are unconscious, doped or something. Nothing out of place as far as I could see. I don't know if he disturbed the attackers before or after anything's happened. I've got a couple of lads guarding where Sgt Peters is and the dog man did a track to where he thinks a getaway car was. I'm just about to set another couple of lads on door-knocking. I've asked the control room inspector to call out the circus. Now you are here, I'll join John in the control unit, if that's OK."

"That's fine, just stay available. The Chief Supers on his way, no doubt we might get some top brass out as well. Some extra staff are being called out to Trent Station for a briefing, I want you there. You say it appears alright inside, the vaults not been done?"

"As far as I can see, apart from the guards being knocked out, nothing looks out of place. Insp Hill is in the office, he's spoken to their security control, they're calling their local director out from Bingham, he's keeping an open line to them," said Dick.

Supt Dee said to DI King, "Colin, go in the main office and get an open line to our control room, and make sure the right people are being called out. Dick, take me to Sgt Peters."

Dick and Supt Dee walked down to where the body of Sgt Peters lay, now covered with a plastic sheet, a uniformed PC standing nearby. "Where did the dog man track to?" he said.

"Over here sir," said Dick, leading the way down the road and through a small alleyway, guarded by another uniformed PC. "We think there might have been a getaway car parked about here but we don't know what it was or where it went."

"Right, before you go back to the control unit have a quick briefing with the lads doing the door-knocking, then see me back at the main office inside."

"Yes sir."

Supt Dee walked slowly back to the front of the building, deep in thought. Why shoot an officer if you haven't done a job? If you've done a job, where's the trace of it? It didn't make sense. What made Sgt Peters suspicious, although that might now never be known?

Getting back to the main office, he was met by DI King, who introduced him to Stephanie Henderson, local director of the security firm. "Nasty business, Mrs Henderson. We have a dead officer, you have three unconscious guards, and we still don't know if anything's been taken. Can we get into the vault anyhow?"

Henderson replied, "Not until the timer switch activates in about four hours' time."

"Can't it be opened sooner?" asked Dee.

"Only if we get an engineer out of bed."

"Well get one out asap, we'll send a squad car if we have to, get with it, woman."

She sat down at the side of one of the still unconscious guards and began dialling for an engineer. As she did so she saw another man enter the office and heard him say, "What have we got then, Fred?"

Supt Dee turned and saw his boss, Det Chief Supt Ron Belling. Quickly, and without missing much out, he informed him of what had happened and what was being done.

By this time Mrs Henderson had got off the phone and was introduced to Belling, who said to her, "What's likely to be in that vault, Mrs Henderson?"

"Anything from two to six million in cash, maybe more, plus safety deposit boxes, it's got Christmas takings from shops, banks and building societies. Until I can get into the vault, I don't know. I have managed to get an engineer to come out, he'll be about an hour or so."

"Good, at least we can get on. Fred, can we get these guards taken out and to hospital, send a couple of uniformed lads with them in case they come round, let's get Scenes of Crime Officers in to start dusting, and don't forget the roof. Colin, get on to our control, and get some extra lines operating from Trent Station. Do any of you know Sgt Peters' wife?"

"I do," replied Insp Hill. "Josie, nice lass, couple of kids, I'm godfather to one of them."

"Get yourself a relief, I want to go and inform her of what's happened, will you join me?"

"Yes sir, let me ring my wife, she can help us out, they're good friends."

"Meet me in the incident room when you are ready," said Dee, and walked outside, where he saw Mrs Henderson. As they walked towards the main gate, he asked her how many guards were normally on duty.

"Normally four, but we can manage with three. They sometimes have to travel to check local properties and stuff like that, we like to keep at least two in the depot."

"Where's the fourth guard tonight then?" asked Belling.

"Harry Young should be on, but looking at the guards' log in there, he's booked it off."

"Have we got an address for him?"

"I can get one."

"Good, leave it in the control unit, we'll need to speak to Mr Young," said Belling.

***

At the control unit, Insp Hill was waiting for him. "Ready sir, I've spoken to my wife, not told her much, but she will be ready."

Belling relayed to the officer there that he and Insp Hill were off to inform Sgt Peters' wife, and if they were needed, ring him on his mobile.

Whilst they were driving, Belling said, "What kind of man was Sgt Peters?"

Insp Hill replied, "A good copper, liked uniform, had a nose for things and wasn't afraid of getting stuck in. A family man with two children, who he adored, we joined together, and saw each other socially with our families."

Pulling up outside his house, Insp Hill said, "Won't be a minute."

Letting himself in, he was met by his wife. "What's happened?" she asked.

"Sorry to drop this on you Lesley, but Trevor's been shot dead. I'm with the Det Chief Super, he wants to tell Josie. I thought you could help, and stay with her."

His wife looked into his face and said, "Shot dead?"

"Yes love."

"Good god, poor Josie and the kids. Let me take some brandy with me." She returned with a full bottle and joined her husband. Getting into Belling's car, he said, "Sorry about this Mrs Hill, thanks for helping us out."

She said, "Can you tell me what's happened, because Josie will be asking me what I know about it."

As they drove, her husband outlined what had happened, and what they knew so far. That Trevor had been shot outside a security depot, but didn't know if the depot had been attacked or not. They were waiting to open the vaults, until then, who knows.

"It's that one there, sir," indicated Insp Hill. "The one with the Fiesta on the drive."

They parked outside a detached house with a well-presented front garden. "Trev liked his garden," said Lesley.

They walked up to the front door. Lesley pushed the bell, two long rings, before an upstairs light came on. They could see a figure through the frosted front glass coming downstairs. A voice asked, "Who is it?"

"It's Lesley and Mick, Josie, open the door."

The door was opened, and Belling saw an attractive woman in a floral dressing gown, blonde shoulder-length hair, dishevelled through sleep. She looked at Lesley, saw Mick's uniform and a stranger in a suit. She said, "It's Trevor, isn't it? He's had an accident, what's happened, where is he?"

Mick said, "Josie, this is Detective Chief Superintendent Belling. Trevor has had an accident. Can we come in?"

"What's happened, he's alright isn't he, he's not dead is he?"

Lesley guided her to a chair in the front room and reached for some glasses from the nearby coffee table. "I'm sorry to have to tell you this, Mrs Peters, but your husband disturbed someone this evening near to a security depot. We don't know the full details yet, but I'm afraid he was shot and died at the scene. There was nothing anyone could do to help him, I'm sorry."

Ch Supt Dee's voice was near to breaking. He had been a policeman for nearly thirty years and had never got used to this face-to-face stuff, telling someone their loved one was dead, especially a police colleague, and it being Christmas was even worse.

"No, no!" she screamed. "It's not true, Mick, tell me it's not true, it's not Trev, it's someone else!"

"I'm afraid not Josie, I'm sorry, there was nothing we could do."

"Lesley, it's not Trevor is it?"

"I'm sorry love, it is. I'm so sorry."

Josie Peters sat stunned. She took the glass of brandy without realising what she had got, and took a drink. She coughed and said, "What am I going to tell the kids? He was coming home to play Santa, what am I going to tell them?" She dropped the glass and flung herself at Lesley, sobbing uncontrollably. Lesley looked up at her husband and Belling and said, "Leave her with me, I'll stay with her, you get back, but I'd be obliged if you'd send the police doctor round with a sedative or something if you see him."

Belling said, "Thank you for your help, Mrs Hill. I'll make sure that's done. Once again, Mrs Peters, I'm sorry." She didn't hear him.

Letting themselves out and on the journey back, neither spoke until they neared the depot. Belling said, "Inspector, I am grateful to you and your wife for that, but I would like you and your men to stay on duty. Can they manage that? I'll get them off as soon as I can."

"I think you will have to order them off duty over this one sir. Trev was a popular bloke with most of the shift."

On arriving back at the depot, the police surgeon, Dr Carter, was there, at the side of Sgt Peters. "Nasty wound Ron, straight through the top of his head. He wouldn't have a clue what hit him, poor devil. I've managed to see the guards before they went, looked like they were drugged the way their sleeves were undone. We'll know better after some blood tests. I'll arrange that. Your lads are busy inside now, that engineer bloke's come."

"Thanks Doc, send me your statement. The pathologist should be on his way. We'll leave Sgt Peters here, he likes to see them at the scene. Before you go, can you go to the control unit, see Insp Hill? He'll give you Sgt Peters' home address, we've just been and broke the news, she may need a sedative or something."

Belling looked down at the still form of Sgt Peters; a shudder ran through him. There but for the grace of god go I, and many other police officers, he thought.

He was pulled from his thoughts by Dick Jones saying, "It was maroon or dark brown, sir."

"What was, Jones?" he asked.

"The car parked down where the dog man did a follow-to. A couple out walking saw a car there when they first went out. It was moving away when they first saw it, then when they came back, it was parked up again. And another bloke out walking his dog said he saw what he thought was a silver Mercedes car backed up to the depot gates before he went to bed. I've spoken to him, he reckons about 1.30 ish, maybe a bit later."

"That's about an hour or thereabouts before Sgt Peters shouted up, isn't it?" he queried.

"Not far out, sir," said Dick. "I've sent him to Trent Station for someone to take a statement from him whilst it's still fresh."

"Good, how's thing inside?"

"I don't know sir, not been in since SOCO arrived."

"Let's go see then," said Belling.

They met Supt Dee inside. He said, "According to what SOCO have picked up so far, it looks like they have had a go at the vault, there's glove marks all over it, scuff marks on the floor outside it, but until it's opened, we won't know. SOCO have found some evidence that someone was on the roof and at the air vent up there, and scuff marks on the pipe near where Sgt Peters was found. If it's been done, they are professionals, professional fucking murderers."

"Alright Fred, stay with it, if that engineer comes, no one in that vault apart from SOCO, OK? Come on Jones, with me to Trent."

CHAPTER 3

About twenty miles away, Bob Teal was cursing Cat. "You fucking crazy idiot, we've got enough cash to last a lifetime, and you put even more pressure on us by shooting a fucking copper."

Cat hurled back, "I didn't fucking mean to, he was just there, I couldn't avoid him. It was a shock seeing him there, looking up at me coming down."

"Shock, it's a fucking shock now. There'll be fucking thousands being offered for information, one whiff it's us, and life inside here we come. Fucking hell, how many times have I told you? No shooters, but no you have to have it your way. Well, if it comes down, you take this fucker on your own, I'll make sure of that. After we've shared out, this gang's finished, I'm away, and I suggest you do to. Get packed and fuck off out of my sight."

Bob Teal had dropped Cat at his car and instructed him to follow him, but not to cancel his hotel. He had rung Joe and given him the route to his cottage, telling him to meet them there. Bob Teal was renovating a large country cottage, set back off the road in two acres of land on the outskirts of Derby. Guy had not answered his phone but had been given the route to the cottage.

Cat had begun to gather his stuff together from his car. Bob Teal said, "Joe, you can drop him off at Derby railway station and leave him there. I don't care what time the next train is, leave him there. Cat, you leave your share here and your car, we'll sort it. And leave your weapons, you can't get checked with them."

Cat turned round and said, "I'm taking them with me, and some of my share, whether you like it or not." He turned back to carry on packing.

"Cat," said Bob Teal. "Turn round."

Cat turned round and his face went white. "You see, you are not the only one who has a gun." Cat was facing a sawn-off single barrel shotgun. "You do as you are told, or you don't leave this room breathing."

Bob Teal's hand was as steady as a rock on the shotgun. He was looking straight into his eyes, "You do as you are told, do I make myself clear?"

"You haven't got the nerve, Boss," Cat said, as he began to walk across to where his own guns were. "You haven't got the fucking nerve. It takes guts to pull a trigger, you ain't got any." As he reached his bag, he heard a click and froze.

"I'm warning you Cat, touch that bag and you're dead."

Cat looked at him again, a brief smile on his lips. He thought he could see fear in his eyes, sweat on his top lip, he said, "You couldn't do it, I could to you, but not you to me."

The Boss said nothing, just stood his ground. Not moving a muscle. Cat's hand crept towards his own shotgun, his fingertips touching the weapon he so loved and knew he could use again tonight if he had to. He began to spread his fingers wider, still looking his boss in the eye and smiling. He saw the shotgun move slightly in the Boss's hand then heard the explosion. His gut took the full blast, he was thrown against the wall, the smile vanished, a look of surprise took its place, he was dead before he slid down the wall.

"I've got guts Cat, you haven't."

No one moved for a moment. Joe reached out and took

hold of the gun. "Let it go, Boss. It was you or him, he knew the odds and he wouldn't back down, he'd have done you sooner than look at you."

Bob Teal sat down, letting Joe take the gun, "Get me a brandy," he said. His voice sounded like he had a mouth full of pebbles.

He took the brandy from Joe and took a deep drink. He closed his eyes, then opened them again. "Thanks Joe, sorry about that."

"It's OK, Boss, we'd better get things sorted here and get rid of him."

"There's an old well at the far end of the garden, all overgrown, I'm going to fill it in anyway and put a false bucket thing on top. He might as well go down there, and his guns as well, there's plenty of rubble to chuck down, he won't be found, don't worry."

Cat's body was easily lifted between them, out into the long back garden. With a bright moon it wasn't too difficult to make things out. There was an old wheelbarrow near the shed, they put the body on to it and wheeled it down towards the bottom end, which was still somewhat overgrown.

"Careful Joe, it's here somewhere, it's covered by an old board. Here it is." He lifted up some rotting old board and peered down into darkness.

"Ready Joe."

"Ready Boss."

They lifted the body out, rolling it onto the rim of the well, which stood about two feet high, and then pushed it over – a bump, a thud, then quietness. "Sorry it ended like that old son," he said into the well, "but you wouldn't listen. Give me the guns, Joe, and get the tanks and stuff from the boot."

Joe passed Cat's shotgun and revolver to the Boss. He threw them down after Cat. "Now let's get some rubble down there. Before we do that, get the gas cylinders from his car, chuck them down as well."

"OK. I'll go through his car, you sort out the stuff in here."

Joe went out to Cat's grey Mondeo. The first thing he noticed was the ignition had been ripped out and it was hot-wired. He took Cat's sacks of cash into the cottage, then bought his bag of disposable clothing and gas cylinders in. "Good news and bad news. Good news, there wasn't much stuff to sort out; bad news, it looks like Cat stole the car to do the job in, it's been hot-wired."

"Fucking hell, now a stolen car to get rid of as well. I told everyone to hire cars. I've lit the wood burner, burn what you can, anything he took into that depot burn, leave the rest, we'll put it down the well."

They pushed gloves, overshoes, canvas holdall, credit cards and papers with Cat's name on, into the stove. It left a thermos flask and a bottle of rum, and gas cylinders.

"Clean the flask out, wash the rum bottle out, they can all go down the well." He put the shotgun cartridges and bullets to one side, next to the leather pouch the guns were carried in.

"What about the car, Boss?" asked Joe.

"We'll have to get it up onto the moors and torch it. I don't think they will think it's connected to the job. By the time they get to it, it will be completely gutted. You sure it's clear, boot and all?"

"Positive."

"Let's get that done before too much daylight comes up. I want this place cleaned up when we get back."

CHAPTER 4

Back in Nottingham at the Trent Police Station, Chief Supt Belling was briefing the Assistant Chief Constable (ACC) Alan Langley, as well as Chief Constable Robbie Shelford, who had taken everyone by surprise turning up on Christmas morning. He was saying, "Is everything in full swing Ron, everything possible?"

"Everything has been set up that we can do at this time. We're still waiting for the engineer to arrive to sort out the vault, we'll know then whether we have a robbery and murder, or a murder sir."

"I want us to put our man first," he said.

"Yes sir, hopefully one will come with the other, whatever's happened," said Belling.

"Obviously," said ACC Langley, "but if they've done a job, the MO could tell us something, sir."

"That's true Alan, but I'm more concerned about our man's death. Does his wife know, Ron?"

He was thinking, here we are, two fucking top brass, think a click of the fingers will turn up something, they hadn't looked at a crime between them in twenty years.

"Ron, has his wife been informed?"

"Oh, yes sir, just thinking about something else. I went up with Insp Hill, his wife is with her. I've asked the doc to drop by with a sedative if she needs one."

"I may call by later with Mr Langley, to show my face you know. Keep me informed."

She will be dead chuffed I'm sure, thought Belling.

***

At the security depot, Stephanie Henderson was saying to Superintendent Dee, "Not much longer by the looks of it."

The engineer was adjusting some equipment on the clock. "Another couple of minutes should do it," he said.

Dee could see that the vault door had already been dusted by fingerprint men, and clearly showed many, many glove marks on the outside. These had matched up with some found in the office area.

"That's it, guv," said the engineer, and pulled the wheel round two full turns to open the door.

Henderson let out a gasp. "They've done us, Christ they've done us."

Looking in, the inside was as though a bomb had gone off. Bags were ripped open, empty boxes were strewn around, even bundles of notes were lying around.

"Don't go in," bellowed Dee. "Hawkins, in here fast and bring your assistant."

DCI Hawkins, Senior SOCO, came in with his assistant, both carrying their forensic bags with them.

Hawkins looked in, then turned to Dee and said, "Can you get everyone out of here? Leave this to us, put a PC on the door, no one to come in until I say so. Anything we get we'll call you in, sir."

Dee went back into the office, picked the phone up and asked to be put through to Ron Belling. "They've done the vault Ron, done it well at first glance. Hawkins is in there doing his stuff. I'll get things set here and join you in a short while."

"Thanks Fred. I'll inform Shelley and co. By the way, has the pathologist arrived yet?"

"Yes, he should be with Sgt Peters now. I've got the undertakers standing by. Where do you want him taken to?"

"QMC or the City, whichever suits him. Get DC Miles to travel with them to do the necessary at that end. Can you get back here, 6am for a briefing, Fred?"

"See you there," replied Dee, and made his way to the control unit to relay instructions.

CHAPTER 5

In the cottage, Bob and Joe had just got back from Stanhope Moor where they had left the Mondeo parked in the lay-by burning furiously. They heard a car pull up. Joe looked out. "It's Guy," he said, and let him in.

"Where's Cat?" he asked.

"Unfortunately, Cat wouldn't listen to reason, so I've put him down."

"What do you mean, put him down?"

Joe said, "The Boss shot him, he would have shot the Boss otherwise, we've put him down the old well."

Guy said, "You had better tell me what's been going on."

Bob said, "I'll tell you all about it later. I want us all to stop here tonight, let things calm down a bit. Bring the sacks in from your car, Guy, give him a hand Joe. And any other stuff we need to get rid of, and let's get this place tidied up."

They went into the garden, tipped the cylinders, flask, empty rum bottle and the rest of the gear down the well. They got the wheelbarrow, took it back towards the shed where a large mound of bricks and rubble were piled up. They took it in turns to wheel it to the well and empty the contents down. Some old lino and carpet followed.

Bob said, "That should be enough for the time being, I'm going to fill it in later and put a bucket on it. Let's sort inside now."

They cleaned traces of blood off the plastered wall and the floor tiles with soap and water. As far as they could tell there was no trace.

"That wall's got to be skimmed again and the tiles buffed and sealed, that should do it," said Bob. "Put the news on, see if anything is out yet, Joe."

Joe turned the stereo on. It was just coming up to 6am, the main headline was read out by the newsreader. "Police in Nottingham have started a murder enquiry after a police officer was shot whilst on patrol on Christmas Eve. They are searching the Meadows area near to the scene where the officer was shot dead, near a cash security depot at about 3am this morning. At this time it's not known if the depot has been attacked. There will be more on this story in our main bulletin at 8am." The newsreader then went on to other news.

"Right, let's get some rest, until about 8am at least," said Bob. "You can take the front and back rooms upstairs, I'll stay down here. I'll let you know what I'm thinking later."

"OK Boss."

He felt himself being shaken and opened his eyes, it was Joe. "Sorry Boss, must have dropped off longer than we needed, it's nearly 11am, the news is coming on again." He passed a mug of tea to him.

The news jingle went off, taken over by a sombre sounding newsreader. "Police in Nottingham are searching for a gang who attacked the Midland Express Security Depot in the Meadows area of the city overnight, and escaped with what is thought to be a large amount of cash in used notes. During the course of this raid, a uniformed police sergeant, Sergeant Trevor Peters, was shot dead by the gang. Police have set up an incident room at Trent Police Station. Chief Superintendent Ron Belling is heading the investigation. We can now go over to the incident room."

"Mr Belling, can you tell us any more on this incident?" asked the newsreader.

"It would appear that during the course of this robbery, Sgt Peters in some way disturbed the gang. He was shot at point blank range and died at the scene. We have gained entry to the vault and it appears that a large amount of cash, in mainly used notes, has been stolen. At this stage, that value is not known. The guards were incapacitated somehow, we won't know until medical checks are completed. What I can tell you is that the security company have put up a staggering one-million-pound reward, for information leading to the arrest and convictions of this callous gang. They showed no mercy to an unarmed police officer and deserve none back, not even from the criminal fraternity."

"Was Sgt Peters married?"

"Yes, he was a married man with two children. His wife is being supported by a fellow officer's wife. Can I get back to this incident? We will not give up on this enquiry, no matter how professional they think they were, we will track them down, and hopefully lock them away for a very long time."

"Thank you for that, Mr Belling. Anyone with information is asked to contact Nottingham police or visit the mobile control room, near to the scene."

"That's one hell of a reward, Boss," said Joe, turning the radio off. "One million pounds."

"I reckon with that sort of reward on offer, we've got to tread very carefully." Already a plan was starting to formulate, which he hoped would save him at least. "Joe, Guy, get your money sacks in here."

"What are you thinking, Boss?"

"I'm thinking, no one apart from us three will know we used this place. I'm suggesting we take a small share each from one bag, put the rest down the well, there's a dry inlet down there we can use, then try and carry on our day-to-day life as best we can until a lot of the heat dies down."

Joe and Guy went outside and into the large double garage where their cars were. They bought all the remaining sacks in. Emptying each one out, they began to count them out into three separate piles of notes.

Bob then made three piles of £150,000. The rest was put to one side.

"£150,000 alright to be going on with, Joe?" he asked.

"How long before I get the rest? I was planning on going away for a long time."

"You'll get it as soon as I can arrange it, don't worry."

"£150,000 OK for you Guy?"

"I wanted to get back to London today and with my full share."

"Full share-out later."

"Good, let's get it down that well."

It was a clear day. A cold wind was blowing off the peaks, but apart from that it was dry. Bob tied a stout rope round the nearest tree, another around the sacks. "When I get down there, lower them down to me, Joe."

He began to climb down the well shaft until his feet touched the rubble at the bottom. When he had settled, and was able to locate the inlet he shouted, "Lower away, Joe."

Joe began to lower the sacks steadily down the shaft until he heard a shout of OK. He could feel the rope moving in his hands and getting lighter as the sacks were taken off. About five minutes later the rope was totally slack, and he pulled it back up.

He climbed back up and joined Joe. "Should be safe down there for as long as we want."

Returning to the warmth of the cottage, Joe realised he was starving. "Have you got any food in this place?"

"In the kitchen pantry, there's a freezer full, sort out some steaks or something. Guy will no doubt want to eat.

There's some wine in there as well, we might as well stop another night here, at least until we know roadblocks will have come off, if they put them on."

Guy said, "Not for me thanks, I want to get back, if that's OK." He picked his holdall up containing his share, said his goodbyes and left.

"I think we had better keep an eye out for him you know, Joe. I've a sneaky feeling things could go wrong his end. Just a gut feeling."

CHAPTER 6

Chief Superintendent Belling was on his second briefing of the day, to his team of both CID and uniform. Shelley and his partner were sat at the table nearby. Don't butt in, he thought, you'll only sound like twats to the lads.

"Right lads, as far as we can establish, Sgt Peters called at the security office at around 12 to 12 30am. We don't know why, he just put security office 12 to 12.30 in his pocket book, see Harry, then the word, Neg. That is obviously Harry Young. He is being spoken to at this moment. So far he is saying his youngest son was rushed to hospital yesterday, that's why he booked the night off. From the house-to-house enquiries, two cars have been mentioned, one a posh maroon or brown one, no make yet, which was parked here." He indicated a map of the area behind him. "The other, which we believe was a silver Mercedes, was seen backed up to the gate, we think sometime before Sgt Peters called there."

A voice close to him asked if they could get an exact time. Turning round he saw it was ACC Langley. Twat, he thought as he answered, "Dealing with witnesses in matters like this take time, sir. We are doing our best."

A number of titters went round the room, as Belling said, "Sgt Peters was found at around 2am. The vault had been opened somehow, and around four million pounds has been stolen, in used notes." A gasp went up from the listening officers. He carried on, "I have given out various tasks, I do expect them to be carried out, I don't want any slacking on this enquiry. The night officers can stand down, I will see them back here at 10pm. You will be briefed about your duties this evening and it may be another long night. Thank you for your help so far."

Dick Jones was about to leave when Belling called him back. "Just to say well done, you managed to get things in some order at the scene, it could save us a lot of work. Well done. You will be staying on this enquiry, see me or Supt Dee when you come back on duty."

"Thank you, sir." He left the station, happy that he had had some recognition, but something was still not right he thought. On his way home he was going over the night, the way things had gone, and felt as though he had missed something out. Sgt Peters had disturbed the gang in some way. Two cars seen, one posh, one a Merc. What model Merc? What model posh car? Then it hit him – photos, show photos to the witnesses, identify the models. He turned his car round and went back to the incident room. Supt Dee said, "I thought you'd gone off?"

"I was on my way home sir, and suddenly thought about the car, the two cars. Have photographs been arranged so we can identify any models, do you know?"

"That's not been done yet, I think it's in the pipeline though. We are trying to get some photos."

"If you let me go home, wash and change, I can organise that for you. I used to collect car mags. I've got loads of up-to-date pictures and stuff, and can get some more. Besides, it will get me off nights." Dick winked at Dee as he said that.

"Alright, have a couple of hours, then come back. Thanks Dick."

CHAPTER 7

Dick Jones was back at work and with one of the witnesses in under two hours. He had established the posh car was a Jaguar XK8, saloon. The other was a Mercedes, the witness thought, a 320 model, in a metallic blue shade.

He was sitting at the desk when Supt Dee came back in. "Any joy, Dick?" he asked.

Dick related what he had done and had sat pondering how to do any possible traces on these vehicles. He had loads of contacts in the motor trade.

Dee said to him, "Well you started that enquiry, you might as well carry on and see what comes up."

Supt Dee sat down and began to write down a list of enquiries he wanted carrying out, in the areas the cars had been seen. CCTV, door-knocking, relevant times, and statements from the owner, and PC at the scene. All these had to be logged onto the HOLMES computer system, to make sure they got done. He also logged the checking of hotels adjacent to the motorway exits. He felt as it was Christmas, something might turn up, these could be done by a member of the incident room staff by phone. He sat back, deep in thought. "What sort of person shoots an unarmed police officer in cold blood. After all that planning they must have done dummy runs and what have you. They get spotted on the actual job, and a copper dies, bastards."

He noticed he had written CCTV for the areas surrounding the depot, in relation to spotting any cars around at the relevant times. He also wanted CCTV searches widened and checked a month back, if possible. CCTV was still in its infancy, so he wasn't sure how wide or capable it was. All he knew was that in parts it had vastly improved.

CHAPTER 8

Guy looked over at the blonde hair spread out on the pillow beside him. Julie, she said her name was. He had picked her up on his drive back to London, she'd been thumbing a lift. They had stopped for something to eat, and she had drunk half a bottle of wine. She told him she was a nurse, she was 23, and single.

She had told him she was visiting her sister, but she wouldn't be back until the day after tomorrow. She was going to find a bed and breakfast somewhere. Guy had suggested she come and stay with him for a couple of days, until her sister came back, there was plenty of room in his flat. She had jumped at the offer. She had also jumped on him in the bedroom. She began to stir, he leaned over and kissed her. They had made love hurriedly earlier, he wanted to take his time now. She opened her eyes and said, "Hello you."

He reached over for her and began to pull her towards him. She stopped him and said, "My turn now."

She pushed him back and began to kiss his throat, moving down his body, taking in both nipples. Moving lower she felt his erect penis brush under her throat. She eased it deep into her mouth, beginning to move slowly up and down, licking and sucking. At the same time, she began to move her body round, until she could feel his tongue licking at her opening. His tongue moving to her love button, she grabbed him even harder, as she felt the first shudder of an orgasm. She began to move even faster, up and down, and ground herself harder against his mouth, his tongue still finding her button. She gagged slightly as his hot liquid hit the back of her throat, feeling his body arching. She shuddered with another orgasm, then another, slowing down, and drinking him in, until she was quite sure there was nothing left. She pulled her mouth from him and lay with her head on his legs, happily exhausted. She slowly rolled off him and turned round putting her head on his chest.

"That was fantastic, you really knock me out," she said.

"You make me feel like an old man after a session like that, I'm knackered. What time is it?"

"Why, are you going out?"

"Yes," he said, "I have to meet a couple of colleagues over a bit of business."

"It's Christmas."

"Won't take long, make yourself at home, in fact if it's not too late when I've done, I'll ring you and take you out to the best place in town. Anywhere you want."

"Anywhere I want?"

"Anywhere you want," he said as he rolled out of bed and into the shower cubicle. He ran cold water over his body at first, then as hot as he could stand it. With the sex and shower, his body felt as though it was aglow.

He came back to the bedroom, she was still in bed. As he dressed he said, "Can you drive?"

"Yes," she replied.

"There's some keys on a hook in the kitchen, the Jags downstairs, it's a hire car, can you handle it?" he asked.

"Yes, my dad's had Jags before, I've driven his loads."

"Good, when I get back I want you to drive it. I want to take it back."

"No problem," she said. "Ring me and I'll be ready."

"Make yourself at home then," he said, bending over and kissing her left exposed breast.

He went down to the basement car park, and got into his own Red Jaguar XK 8 convertible, lowering the hood before he eased out into the traffic. It took him 15 minutes to reach the hotel near the Park Lane flat.

"You heard the news, Guy?" asked the Boss.

"Not properly, no," he replied.

"The security company have offered a million-pound reward for our capture."

Guy sat down. "A million-pound reward, fuck me."

"That's why we went back to my Derby place and left the stuff there."

"No more jobs, split what's left, go our own ways. I don't want any further contact with each other after that. For our own safety."

Guy looked at Joe and the Boss. "I'm stunned. Cat dead, a copper dead, we are all wanted for murder now no matter who did it. Christ, what a fucking mess."

"Look Guy, I couldn't avoid the shooting of Cat, he asked for it, him and his guns are out of the way. They will never find him unless one of us talks. I'm suggesting we either take our equal shares or leave it where it is for the time being, or you let me transfer it abroad. I have the facilities to do that. Then I can set up a bank account for you and Joe wherever you want."

"Where abroad?" asked Joe.

"I have business interests in the Cayman Islands, it won't be difficult hiding money over there, believe me. I could do my work over there."

"That's alright for you, Boss, what about me? I don't want to work over there, do you Joe?" Guy asked.

"If I went, I wouldn't work again, only enjoy spending it. I'm with the Boss on this, let's split it up over there."

"Look," said the Boss, "we've got £150,000 each. That's enough at the moment. I bought some back for Cat's missus, in case she turns up, but I can sort her out with some more if she wants it."

The Boss broke the plastic tie, emptying the contents onto the tiled part of the floor, bundles of fives, tens, twenty- and fifty-pound notes were in £100 and £500 lots.

All three began sorting them into piles of £5,000.

"Get us a drink Joe, a whiskey and ice. Do you want one Guy?" the Boss asked.

"Bacardi and coke, Joe please," he replied.

"Don't forget yourself Joe, make them large ones," the Boss said.

It took them half an hour to sort them into piles.

"£208,000 in this bag," said the Boss. "We must have close on three to four million with what's stashed in the well. I suggest we take £50,000 out for Cat's missus. I'll put the other in my safe for her if she wants some more. Agreed?" he asked.

Both men nodded in agreement.

"Can I use your phone Boss for a quick call?" asked Guy.

"Over there, next to the desk," he indicated.

Guy quickly dialled the number. "I'll pick you up in half an hour," he said. Putting the phone down, he continued, "My lodger for the moment, sweet young thing."

"It didn't take him long to get over Cat, did it?" said Joe.

"No, a £150,000 note in your hands makes most people forget. Get us another drink, I'll tidy up," said the Boss.

CHAPTER 9

The incident room at Trent Station was in full flow, desks had been arranged, typists were tapping away, phones ringing, maps and photos being put up, filing cabinets moved to the right spot.

Dick Jones, in the meantime, had been working hard trying to get a lead on the cars and was awaiting replies from a couple of hire companies. "Why are you so concerned on checking hire companies out, Dick?" asked a nearby colleague.

"I've been on to the PNC desk checking for any stolen Jags and Mercs matching our suspect cars, and none have been reported stolen, at least not matching ours. There are some outstanding, but different colours. I've asked them for printouts on matching cars, that will take some time. I can't see them re-spraying cars. False plates, yes, re-spraying, no. I don't think they'd use their own cars, would you? If they did, they aren't as professional as we thought. So I reckon hire cars. It's worth a shot, might be under false names, I don't know. I thought I'd try the major ones, they do executive cars, the boss has given me a bit of a free hand, might as well use it, before he gets me plodding about, door-knocking."

His phone rang. "Hello, DS Jones."

"Mr Ortez here, from Hertz car hire in London. I've checked our executive car hire list. We have a Jaguar on hire, out to a Mr Guy Salmon, a London address, he's hired from us before, no problems. Apart from that, nothing else."

"Can you fax details through to me please, Mr Ortez? By the way, you don't know what colour the Jag is, do you?"

"I'll make sure it's included. Anything else?"

"Not at this time, I'll get back if there is, cheers." Dick put his phone down and looked at the notes he'd made.

"Well it was worth a try," he was saying to himself when Superintendent Dee walked up to him. "How's it going, Dick? About time you went home, you'll be no good to me asleep."

"Just waiting for a couple of folks to ring me back sir, then I'm off."

His phone rang. "Excuse me sir. DS Jones, Trent incident room," he answered. "Yes, I've been waiting for your call." Putting his hand over the mouthpiece, he murmured, "Avis car hire, sir."

The caller said, "We have a few executive hires out at the moment, what was it you were looking for?"

"I'm looking at a Mercedes 320 or similar, silver colour, and a maroon or brown Jaguar. Who am I speaking to please?" he asked.

"Mr Kent, Executive Hire Manager at Avis. Looking down my list, we have a 320 Mercedes out, can't tell you the colour off this list. No maroon Jaguars, I'm afraid though."

"Who is the Merc hired out to?" asked Dick.

"To a company, Teal Investments, they are regular hires, they have offices in London and abroad, and I believe they are hired for visiting executives. They are due to be returned the day after tomorrow. In fact, they have a BMW out as well, to the same customer, Teal Investments."

"Who are the named drivers, can you tell me, Mr Kent?"

"One is for a Mr Robert Teal, the other Mr Joseph Andrews, the firm's address is in the Strand, very well known to us."

"Can you give me the registration numbers, I can check PNC for the colour, and can you also fax all the details to me please?"

"I can certainly fax details, it you want to hang on a minute, I should be able to get the colours for you."

"I'll hang on," said Dick.

As he was waiting, Dick was drawing a line through both enquiries on his pad, thinking, well I've tried my angle, but it's not paid off. He would run all the names through the computer anyway, as a matter of course. He heard the voice on the phone saying, "You still there, DS Jones?"

"Yes."

"The BMW is black, the Mercedes is a metallic silver. Do you still want me to fax details to you?" asked Mr Kent.

"Yes please," replied Dick. "Thanks for your help."

Putting the phone down he pondered, must be a coincidence, it must be. The cars might fit, but a reputable firm hiring regularly from Avis, I can't see it. I've got to follow this enquiry through, for Sgt Peters' sake, even if it's negative. Leaving his desk, he approached Supt Dee. "Sir, I've checked the hire companies. Godfrey Davis is negative, but Hertz and Avis have a couple of cars out on hire, might fit, might not. They are to a London firm, reputable so they say, regular hirers. What do you want me to do?"

"Put the details down for CRO checks and put the names into the incident room. If we need to speak to them, you might get a trip to London, but don't hold your breath. There's still plenty of work to do up here. Are you going home now?"

"One more phone call, then I'm off home." Returning to his desk, he picked the phone up and dialled a London number. A voice answered, "DI Richards."

"Paul, it's Dick at Nottingham, how are you?"

"Very well mate, and yourself?"

"Are we still on for our Spanish trip in a couple of weeks?"

"You bet."

The two had met on a CID course at Birmingham a couple of years earlier, and become good friends, keeping in touch by phone, or whenever they were passing through the area.

"I was, but we had an officer shot and killed overnight during a raid on a security depot, mucked all Christmas up for everyone. I was wondering if you could do me a couple of discreet enquiries down there?"

"Sure, anything to help. Fire away."

Dick passed on the information he had got from Avis and Hertz. He mentioned the names of the hirers, Robert Teal, Joseph Anderson and Guy Salmon.

"Guy Salmon, where did you get his name from?"

"Hertz car hire. Why, do you know him?" Dick asked.

"I nicked him when I was a DS on the squad. He's a bit of a whizz kid in motor sports and engines. He knows a bit about alarms and stuff. He got five years I think, it was for a safe job in Essex somewhere. Do you think he's involved in your job then, Dick?"

"I shouldn't think so, his name cropped up on the car hire check. What I'd like is for someone to have a quick nose round, see if there is anything there for us. To really yes or no them."

"Well I know Salmon, I got on quite well with him, I'll bump into him accidentally, see where he's been. Will tomorrow do sometime?"

"Paul, that's great, it won't cause you any problems, will it?" Dick asked.

"Not now I'm the gaffer here it won't. Speak to you later mate, cheers."

"Cheers Paul, one I owe you. Hope it won't upset our Spanish jaunt," Dick said, putting the phone down.

***

Down in London, DI Paul Richards sat back in his chair and looked at the names he had written down, and circled Guy Salmon. He had been caught after a tip-off doing a safe job at an office block in Essex. They had nearly lost him when he went across the roof after his partner, who got away. He refused to name anyone else and took the job on his own. For his sins he got five years for his first conviction. He had been a bit of a tough nut, but what police called a likeable villain. Richards had seen him on a couple of occasions since his release, and although he hadn't said what he was doing, he seemed to be quite well off and hadn't come to the notice of the police since, as far as he was aware. He rang through to the local records office, requesting a copy of his file be sent over to his office. He decided he would do a bit of digging for old times' sake. One never knows, old son, he thought.

CHAPTER 10

The morning after Dick Jones' request, DI Richards sat at his desk, reading the file on Guy Salmon. His eyes opened wide when he saw the name of the office premises he had been arrested at in Essex – Teal Investments. "Christ, what a connection," he said out loud.

"What's that, guv?" asked DS Greg Watts, putting a cup of tea down in front of him.

The DI explained to his colleague what had happened, and about the request from Dick Jones.

DS Watts said, "Are you still going to do a visit, or a look round?"

"I think I'll play it by ear when I get there. Get the car Greg, you can drive."

They drove out towards Marble Arch, into a mews area. DI Richards pointed and said, "Salmon lives in the top floor flat there, drive into the service car park area Greg, see what cars are parked there."

DS Watts drove the blue Rover in the area indicated. As he did, DI Richards said, "Stop at the side of that van, that's Salmon walking over to that red Jag, he's got a blonde girl with him, look."

Both men saw Salmon and the blonde girl walking towards a red Jaguar sports convertible. The girl went to the maroon Jaguar parked at the side.

"That's the hire car, Greg, looks like they might be taking it back. Follow them, but not too close."

"You're the guvnor," said DS Watts. "He's a nutter. He's got the bloody hood down. It's bloody freezing."

The DI said, "He likes to be noticed. I bet he leaves it down when she gets in as well. Pint on it."

"No, I bet he puts it back up when the girl gets in, you're on. A pint on it."

They followed the cars for about ten minutes, to the Hertz depot, where the blonde drove into the compound. Salmon joined her on foot and went into the office, both reappearing after a couple of minutes. He got into the red Jaguar, his blonde companion got into the passenger side, moving off slowly.

But as he was speaking, the Jaguar stopped, the hood started to go up. "Pint you owe me, guv," then it came down again.

"What were you saying Greg?"

"Pint I owe you I was saying."

"Stay with them for a bit, see where they go, I want that hire company spoken to."

DI Richards rang his office, passing some instructions to the officer answering. These were to contact the manager at Hertz, requesting him to keep the maroon Jaguar that had just been returned at that depot, locked and secured until further notice. Use his name and stress to them that it must not be cleaned or anything. He would be in touch with them later. If there was a problem, give them his mobile number to contact him. He further requested that they were not to contact the last hirer under any circumstances.

Whilst this exchange was taking place, DS Watts continued to follow the Jaguar at a discreet distance. It was a return journey, back to Salmon's address. They both left the Jaguar and went inside.

"Let's give them some time on their own, take me back to the car hire firm, I want to make sure that's done properly, then you and I are going to call on our Mr Salmon, see what feeling we get."

***

Inside Salmon's flat, he and Julie were having a coffee. She asked him, "Why did you hire a car, instead of using yours?"

"I needed a bigger car, I had some people to ferry round, mine's not that sort of car. Anyway, what do you want to do now?" he asked.

"To go into town for that posh meal you promised me," she replied.

"Get yourself dolled up then, I know just the place."

She went into the bedroom and began sorting out her clothes. The phone startled her, she then heard him say, "Just a minute love."

He came to the bedroom door and said, "Business call, Julie," and pulled the door to.

She picked the extension up at the bedside and heard him saying, "What are you ringing me for Hannah? What do you want?"

The female voice on the other end said, "I want to know where Jerry is, I've not seen or heard from him since he was going out with you the other day. He told me he would only be away one night. Where is he?"

"I don't know love, we went up north for work, and I haven't seen him since," which was true in a kind of way, thought Guy.

"I know what work he did. I know if it's to do with you, it's crooked. Has he been caught or what Guy? I've got a right to know. You did time for him. I know how you feel about him."

"Stay where you are Hannah. Are you ringing from home?" he asked.

"Yes," she replied.

"I'll be right over."

He put the phone down. As he did he heard a click, as though the extension had been in use. Looking from the phone to the bedroom door, he began to wonder. The phone rang again, he picked it up and gave his number. "Sorry, wrong number," the voice on the other end said. The phone was put down.

He went into the bedroom and was greeted by the sight of a naked Julie, towelling herself down. He grabbed her and said, "Washing or listening?"

Quickly she responded with a full kiss, replying, "Getting ready for you, do you want starters, or afters, or both?" she asked.

Letting her go, he said, "Afters. But I have to nip out first if you don't mind. Won't take long. Help yourself to whatever."

"I haven't got much choice, have I?" she said.

He left her there, still not convinced about the phone. If she had heard anything, she wouldn't know what it was about anyway.

He was in his car and away in two minutes. As he turned the corner at the top end of the mews, the blue Rover of DI Richards, driven by DS Watts, came in from the other end, without seeing each other. "His cars gone, guv," said DS Watts.

"Looks like it, let's give him a knock anyway."

Knocking on his door, they heard movement inside and the door opened. The blonde they had seen him with earlier stood at the door, with a towel covering what she could.

"Oh, I thought it was Guy coming back. Who are you?"

Showing their warrant cards, he said, "DI Richards, this is DS Watts. Guy said call in any time. And you are?"

"Julie."

"Is Guy in, Julie?" asked DS Watts.

"No, you've just missed him, he won't be long though. Do you want to come in and wait?" she asked.

"I'd like to ask you some questions if I may, Julie," said DI Richards. "Where has he gone?"

They had made their way to the sitting area. Wrapping the towel round her, she said, "I don't know, a woman rang, she said her name's Hannah. I know I shouldn't have, but I listened on the extension."

"What did she want?" he asked.

"She was asking something about where Jerry was. He and Guy had been working up north together a couple of days ago, and this Jerry bloke hadn't come back yet. She wanted to know where he was. He's gone to see her."

"What else did she say? Did she sound upset?" DI Richards asked her.

"Well she didn't sound too happy. She said something about Guy doing some time for Jerry, and she knew how he felt about him, whatever that meant. Is Guy in trouble then?" she asked.

"How long have you known Guy?" he asked, avoiding her question.

"Only a couple of days, he picked me up. I was hitch-hiking, he picked me up just outside Nottingham. I'm down to visit my sister, she'll be back tomorrow. I'll go to her place then. Guy's alright, honest."

"Has he had any other callers, or been out since you've been here?"

"He nipped out last night and we took a hire car back earlier, that's all," she replied.

"Why did he want the hire car, he's got his own car, hasn't he?"

"I asked him that. His is a Jaguar sports, he wanted a saloon to pick some colleagues up in, he said there was more room."

DI Richards paused before he asked his next question. "Has he told you what he does for a living?"

"No," she replied. "It must pay well though, he's got plenty of money, so until my sister comes back, I'll stay with him."

"Tell him I called, but not what we have spoken about."

"Why not?" she asked.

"He might not like people listening to his phone calls and telling the police what they heard. Would you?" DI Richards asked.

"No, I see. Who shall I say called?"

DI Richards handed a card over to her. "Give him this, he does know me. We'll see ourselves out. You can always give me a call if anything else crops up, you know."

As they were going down in the lift, D/I Richards said to his partner, "That was interesting, that woman mentioning he did time for someone whose gone missing, especially as they had gone up north on a job together. I knew he covered for someone on the Essex job. I wonder."

"Are we going to put a tab on him, guv?"

"Not yet. Let's do a bit more homework on our Mr Salmon, see what his reaction is to our visit."

CHAPTER 11

The visit to Hannah was not going very well as Guy was insisting he didn't know where Jerry was.

"Hannah, we were on a job, afterwards we split up and I haven't seen him since, honestly," he was saying.

She said, "Well he's not gone missing before, he's always come back."

"He's probably lying low somewhere, until the heat dies off."

"Why aren't you then?" she asked. "He always contacts me, at least twice a day, he hasn't even done that."

"Well I didn't shoot anyone." The words were out before he could stop them.

"What do you mean, you didn't shoot anyone. Jerry did?"

"Hannah, for god's sake calm down. Listen, sit down." he guided her to a chair. "I'll get us a drink and tell you what I can." He went to the cabinet and poured them both a large brandy, handing one to Hannah as he sat down. He took a deep drink, looked at her and said, "Hannah, you must listen. Don't interrupt me. We were doing a job, which has come in good, in cash anyway. Cat, sorry, Jerry was getting away and was disturbed by a police officer. Jerry shot and killed him. I only found out later. I've not seen him since, and that's the truth."

She sat stunned. "Jerry shot a copper? Are you serious?"

"Yes, it's not something I'd joke about, is it?"

She looked at him, eyes closing. "That one up north, Nottingham, that's been on the news?"

"Yes," he replied.

"The news people are saying that job was over four million in cash. They've put up a million-pound reward for your gang. Is Jerry hiding with the money?" she asked.

"In a roundabout way, I think he is, but I don't know where. I can give you some cash to be going on with, if you want some."

"You mean you can give me some of Jerry's share?"

"Hannah, leave it with me, I'll see the man tonight and see what he says. I'll ring you when I've spoken to him. I'll find out what I can about Jerry."

She said, "And I'll tell you what I'm going to do shall I? I'm going to give you until 7pm tomorrow to come up with where Jerry is or I shop you to the police, and I won't mention Jerry to them, you can do that if you want. Don't think I won't do it. At least I'll get some reward money."

"Hold on, Hannah, I can get you a quarter share of the cash, don't do anything until I get back to you," Guy begged her.

"So there was four of you, that's something else I can tell the police," she sneered at him. "Get out and get it sorted, your time's running out, Guy."

Guy got into his car, and drove straight over to Bob Teal's apartment, ringing the bell in long stabs until he answered. "Who's there?" Bob's voice asked.

"It's me, Guy, it's urgent," he said.

"Well, get your finger off the bell and come up, it had better be fucking urgent."

He went up in the lift to the penthouse flat. Walking in, he was met by Bob, Joe was sat on the sofa. He said, "Bob, we're in trouble, Hannah, Cat's bird, has been onto me about where he is. I let slip he was lying low, because he'd shot a copper, she guessed it was the one in Nottingham."

"Slow down, Guy, you say you told her he'd shot a copper?"

"Yes, I let it slip, she was ranting at me and it just slipped out."

"What else did you tell her?" he asked.

"She's heard it on the news anyway, she knows it was about four million taken, and that the reward is one million pounds. I've offered her some up front until we sort out the four shares."

"So you told her there was four on the job as well. Did you tell her our fucking names and addresses as well?"

"Don't be stupid."

Bob grabbed him by the throat. "Stupid I am not, I planned this job, it went off as planned till that little fucker shot that copper. You blab this and that out and call me stupid." He pushed him away. "I suppose you told her she can have the share yesterday."

Guy rubbed his throat, not having seen the violent side before. "I told her she would get Cat's share, but she would be sworn to secrecy."

"Guy, do you know what you have done, do you? Apart from us three, with Cat dead, no one had any idea we had done that job, until now. You have put us all at risk telling her about it. Why didn't you just tell her you didn't know where Cat was, and left it at that?"

"She only knows me, she doesn't know who you and Joe are," he said.

"What about when Cat doesn't turn up with a large bag of cash, what's going to happen then? Well?" he spat out.

"She did say that if Cat didn't turn up, or she didn't have the cash before 7pm tomorrow, she would go to the police. That's why I've come straight here."

"And if she goes to the police and informs on you, and tells them there were four on the job, are you going to take that copper's murder on your own?"

"I'm sorry, I wasn't thinking straight."

"Would you consider giving her Cat's share?" Bob asked him.

"Only if you and Joe agree to it," he replied.

"And how does she explain this sudden amount of money? We agreed to leave it where it is for the time being, it's quite safe. Now we have to travel back up north for her share. What about when Cat never turns up, he never makes contact with her, what happens then? Have you thought that one out?"

"I'm sure she'll keep quiet, once she gets some cash."

"Guy. How is she going to explain it? She'll have you by the short and curlies, us as well if she finds out. Every other big job that gets pulled, she's going to think it's your gang and she'll want some of it, even if it's nothing to do with us. No, Guy she doesn't get paid, she's to be got rid of, and fast. You started this with her, you finish it."

"You want me to kill her?" he asked.

"How else is she going to be kept quiet? Think of your future, and ours, she has to go."

"How?" he asked.

"Make it look like an accident, does she drive?"

"I don't know," Guy stammered. "Think so."

"Arrange to see her, if she drives or not, you will have to make sure she has an accident, a fatal one. Do you understand?" Bob accented the last few words.

"Yes."

"And no come backs, none at all. Get it done tonight."

Guy looked across at Joe for help, he turned away to help himself to another drink. He looked back at Bob and said, "I'll see what I can arrange." He turned and walked out.

"What do you think to that, Joe?"

"I think you were spot on. He's got to learn where his loyalties lie, I'm just glad it's not me that's all."

"Joe, I need an early night, do you mind if we call it a day?"

"No, I could do with one myself, I'll be in touch tomorrow, cheers Bob."

After Joe had left, Bob made sure the private lift was back on his floor and locked by the master control switch.

He sat down, thumbing through his diary, before picking the phone up and dialling. It was picked up at the other end. "It's Bob Teal here, is that Santos?"

"*Si* Mr Teal, how are you?"

"Very well and you I hope. Is the villa ready for me?"

"*Si* Mr Teal, it is ready."

"Good, I'll ring with the times of arrival, if you will pick me up, OK?"

"*Si,* will you be alone, or do you want the guest room getting ready?"

"Get it ready, just in case, see you soon, bye."

"*Adios* Mr Teal."

He cut that connection and dialled another number. The call was answered after four rings. "Hello."

"Hello, it's your friendly architect, how are things up there?" he asked.

"Hectic, but as far as I am aware, nothing has been found to identify anybody. The police are keeping in close touch with me. If I hear anything, I'll let you know."

"Fine, I'm off out to the villa in a couple of days, there's something I have to make sure is done first. Get out when you can, you know the number there, be careful how you use it."

"No trouble, be in touch."

He put the phone down. His contact would keep him informed.

***

Guy, had got back to his home, and letting himself in he heard Julie say, "Good, now we can eat."

"Not yet, I have to nip out again, it's urgent. Hopefully it won't take long, then we can eat, I've just called back for my briefcase." He went into his bedroom and pulled his briefcase from the bottom of his walk-in wardrobe, before joining Julie back in the lounge. She said to him, "The police have been to see you,"

He whirled round. "The police. What did they want?"

"A Det Inspector Richards and his mate, he said he knew you, was in the area, and had called in to see if you were about."

"Did you tell him I was out, where I'd gone?" he asked.

"He could see you weren't in, and I couldn't tell him where you'd gone, because I didn't know did I? He said to tell you he'd call back. Are you in trouble, Guy?" she asked him.

"No, at least I don't think so. I ran into him a couple of years back and he keeps calling. I wish he'd ring me first. Anyway, he'll call back you said?"

"He said he would, but not when. How long will you be this time? I'm starving."

"I'll be as quick as I can, I'm taking a taxi. I'll ring you when I've done, then you can pick me up, get a quick snack if you are hungry."

Guy walked out with the words, "Don't be long," following him out of the door.

CHAPTER 12

Dick Jones in the incident room at Nottingham had been given the task of background checks on the guards at the Nottingham depot. He had already sent their names through to records office, and was looking at the faxes from the hire car companies when his phone rang.

"DS Jones," he answered.

"Hello Dick, Paul here, still hard at it?"

"Not many, mate. Whoever this gang were, knew what they were doing. They must have had inside knowledge from somewhere. No prints, only glove marks. Whatever they bought in, they took out, we've found nothing in there, which shouldn't be there, nothing at all. Anything to report from your end?"

"I called round to see that Guy Salmon bloke, but he wasn't in. A young lady staying with him for a couple of days was quite helpful. Evidently he picked her up on his way back to London, just outside Nottingham, the day after the job. She's staying there until her sister comes back from wherever. I don't know what job he does, but his pad is very posh, and so is his car, he drives a Jaguar XK 8 sports car. I'll keep digging cause she dropped something out which might help. Something about him doing a job up north with someone who hasn't turned up back home yet, and his woman is playing hell with him. As I said, I don't know what's going on, but if it's anything to do with your end, I'll get straight onto you."

"What about the other two names?" Dick asked.

"Nothing on them. I've not seen them, but they appear to be straight. I'll be back in touch."

"Thanks Paul, cheers." Dick put his phone down.

CHAPTER 13

After leaving his flat, Guy had rang Hannah from a call box, arranging to meet her in an hour on the Embankment, next to Cleopatra's Needle, where he would pick her up at 10pm. He had told her the matter would be sorted out tonight. He hailed a taxi and asked to be dropped at Waterloo Station. From the station it was only a short walk to his workshop. His workshop was a large lock-up garage, which held a couple of cars he was preparing for a future rally, and his white transport van. He backed the van out, locked the workshop and drove to meet Hannah.

As he drove along the Embankment, he was pleased to see there was very little traffic about and hardly any pedestrians. He parked about a hundred yards away from the meeting place. Looking at his watch, he had a twenty-minute wait. He began to think about what he was doing. He had been involved in a cash robbery, which had been successful, then gone wrong because Cat had shot someone. Cat in turn had been shot and disposed of. The money was stashed away and was safe. As far as he was aware, apart from Bob and Joe, only Hannah knew Cat was involved with him. Now she wanted her share. It was, he supposed, his fault for getting involved with them both in the first place. He and Cat had done a few minor jobs together and whilst Cat had got caught in a stolen car and got four months, he had been round to see Hannah, and one thing had led to another. He assured her that once Cat was released, they had to stop seeing each other. If he found out, he would have killed them both. Then he had got caught after that safe job in Essex, at Teal Investments, and got five years. He had not informed on Cat, so it was only natural that when he was released he stayed at Cat's until he got sorted. Cat had been out for a couple of days, and he and Hannah had started the affair again. Eventually, he had sorted things out, and after a couple of jobs up north, had moved into his present flat. It was then that Cat had dropped the depot job on him. He had met some contact who needed a good, reliable safe man and was a good driver, if needed. Cat had put his name forward. When he realised the contact was Bob Teal, he didn't know what to do. On meeting him, they spoke about his knowledge of safes and vaults, and when Guy had told him it was him who had done his Essex safe a few years back, Teal had smiled and told him he had saved him a lot of money, and at the same time, made him a lot. It appeared that Teal had told the police there was far more money stolen than had been, and he had stashed the rest wherever, and his investors lost out. Teal had agreed to take Guy on, to pay him back for keeping his mouth shut. Now he had to sort out Hannah again.

He saw her walking down towards their meeting point, on the opposite side of the road, near to the kerb. She was looking around her, looking for him he thought. Starting the van up, he slowly pulled away from his vantage point. As he got within ten yards of her, he floored the throttle. The van leapt forward so fast, it almost startled him. He saw Hannah turn and look towards him, her eyes opened wide in recognition, her mouth opened to scream. The van hit her full on, throwing her onto the bull catcher at the front. He slowed and she dropped off, he drove over her. He felt two thumps, as both offside wheels drove over her body. Looking in the rear-view mirror, he could see Hannah lying in the road, silhouetted by the lights on the

Embankment. He drove the short length of what remained of the Embankment, before turning into a small side road and parking up. He walked slowly back to the Embankment, looking to see if anyone was about. It was still quiet. He made his way towards where Hannah was lying. He reached the still form, looking down he saw her eyes looking up at him, startled. He stepped back a pace, then realised the eyes weren't seeing, she was dead. He reached down and gently pulled her shoulder bag away, lifting it up and tucking it under his jacket. He was thinking, it might take longer to identify her, giving him some breathing space. "Sorry Hannah," he whispered as he took one last look and walked away.

Getting back into the van, he threw the bag on the seat beside him and drove back to his workshop. Once inside, he checked the van for any visible signs of damage. As it was to be used as a support van for his rally cars, he had fitted a small bull bar to the front. It was that that had taken the force of Hannah's body. He would check it in daylight to be certain no trace was left. Locking his premises, he made his way back to Waterloo Station, ringing his home as he walked. "Hello Julie, it's me, pick me up outside Waterloo Station, I'll wait there for you."

"OK," she replied. "Where are your keys?"

"On the desk in the hall."

"No they aren't, I'm at the desk now, they aren't here."

"Just a minute," feeling in his pocket, he realised he had a set with him. "Sorry, I've got them. There's a spare set in the cloakroom, hanging under the shelf at the back. You can't miss them."

"See you in ten minutes," she said, putting the phone down.

***

As Julie had been ready to go out for about half an hour, she quickly went into the cloakroom. She saw the keys hanging on a hook under the shelf at the back where he had said they would be. She reached for them. As she pulled them off the hook, she stumbled against a pair of his shoes. Losing her balance, she grabbed at a brown leather holdall hanging on a coat hook. As she grabbed it, the bag opened up. She stared open mouthed at the contents. Holding herself steady she lifted the bag off the hook, putting it on the desk, and opened it wide. "Wow," she said.

She had never seen so much money. It was full with bundles of bank notes. The ringing of her mobile brought her back to her senses. "Hello," she answered, her voice shaking.

"Hello sis, where are you? I thought you were coming to stay with me?"

It was Alice, her sister. "I'll ring you back in a couple of minutes," she told her, breaking the connection.

She began to take the bundle out of the bag, and had counted out £100,000, with still plenty to go. Suddenly she began to smile, and said to herself, "This man doesn't know me, who I am, where I live, or anything about me."

She quickly packed all her belongings together, put the money back into the holdall and walked to the door. She stopped, picked the phone up and dialled. "Guy, it's me, got held up, just leaving, see you," and put the phone down.

"Don't be long," he was saying, then realised the phone had been put down.

Julie walked out, flagged a passing taxi down, giving an address near to her sister's road. Dialling her sister, she said, "Hi Alice, it's me. I'm on my way. I've had a bit of luck. Tell you when I see you, bye."

Sitting back in the taxi, she felt a wave of nervous tension pass through her, thinking, "I've just pinched over £100,000, and he doesn't even know who I am."

***

Guy had waited for three quarters of an hour before he jumped into a taxi. He began to wonder if the police had called again and were waiting for him. He noticed his car was parked where he had left it. Paying the taxi off, he let himself in. The first thing he noticed were his car keys on the desk, and his cloakroom door open. He strode across, pulled the door open wider. "Julie, you bastard, you little fucking bitch," he shouted out loud.

He sat down, head in his hands, shaking his head. He tried to think about her, realising that all he knew was her name, nothing else. And she had helped herself to £150,000.

His hand was shaking as he dialled. "Bob, it's Guy. I've got rid of Hannah, she won't be any problem any longer, but I need some more cash. That fucking bird I picked up on the way back, she's nicked all my cash while I was out."

"Can't you go and get it back?"

"I would if I knew where she was, I only knew her name." Guy was hoping for some sympathy.

"Guy, why are you ringing me with your problems? You know what the arrangements are, you will have to wait," Bob told him.

"But I've got no money," Guy pleaded, "She's taken it all."

"Well how do you want the rest giving away, Salvation Army, student rag week, or what? Can't you get some from somewhere else?"

"Bob, don't rub it in, I've been stuffed."

"You fucking ought to be. Look don't ring me anymore, I'll ring you in a bit." Bob put the phone down on him. The mobile would be dumped this evening in the Thames. Bob purchased off-the-shelf mobiles for each job he planned; they were dumped a couple of days later. He would ring back Guy on another one. That would also be dumped before he went to his villa. Only selected persons had his personal number, Guy wasn't one of them.

He rang Joe. "Joe, problem, be here for about 10am, is that OK?"

"No problem." Joe knew better than to ask over the phone what the problem was. He and Bob had been pals for a number of years and fully trusted each other, to the point where they would do anything to help the other, no questions asked.

CHAPTER 14

Hannah's body had been found, and the area cordoned off with police tape. Lights had been set up and scenes of crime were checking the area around her. The police surgeon was leaning over her, and pronounced her dead. "Hit and run by the look of it, Inspector, not long ago either."

The uniformed traffic inspector followed him round. "Any ID, doc?" he asked.

"Can't find any. I'll look back at the mortuary when we undress her. The PM will be later in the morning."

The inspector turned to the staff present, giving out orders that all photos and scene examinations were to be completed, and the scene to remain cordoned off until a daylight examination could be made. He would forward a report for the morning shift uniforms and detective inspectors for information purposes.

CHAPTER 15

At about the same time the police were on the Embankment, Julie and her sister were eating a light supper in Alice's flat. Alice had just asked her what the bit of luck was she had had, saying, "I could do with some, I've just got back and a message on my answerphone from one of the girls at work says we've all just been made redundant as from next week. Looks like I'll have to leave here."

"Don't worry, this will tide us over," said Julie, tipping the contents of the holdall out onto the table.

"Julie, where's that from? How much is there? I've never seen so much money."

Alice looked at her for an answer.

"I pinched it," said Julie. "Off a bloke who picked me up when I was hitching down here. I stopped with him for a bit. When he went out I was looking for his cars keys and found this. And now it's ours."

"We can't keep it. He'll come looking for it, for you, he'll get the police."

"I don't think so Alice," said Julie. "One, he doesn't know anything about me, only my first name, not even my phone number. Two, I think he got it by foul means anyway."

"How much is there?" asked Alice.

"Not sure, want to help me count it?"

The sisters began counting the money into £5,000 bundles. "£150,000," gasped Alice. "£150,000, Julie, what are you going to do with it?"

"Keep it, let's go to Dad's place in Spain for a while. We can go anytime now you've been made redundant. You ring in, tell them to send your papers and wages to you in Spain. I'm not working anyway, let's go."

"Are you sure?" Alice asked.

"Positive, if we drive over, we can take the cash with us then."

"Let's live then," said Alice, throwing bundles of money in the air.

CHAPTER 16

Across town, Joe had arrived at Bob's apartment, drinking a coffee. He asked what the problem was.

"Guy. He's the problem. You know he picked a bird up on the way back from the job, she's been there with him since, well up until last night. He went out to sort Cat's woman out, and when he got back she'd done a runner with £150,000. He's ringing me up wanting some more."

"What did you tell him?" Joe asked.

"That it was his problem, and to sort it out. I told him I would ring him, not to ring me. I don't want him to keep ringing me. I've already dumped the job mobiles, by the way, yours and mine. I've got one to use, then that's gone. Do you know Joe, that he doesn't know anything about that bird, only her first name? I ask you."

"What do you intend doing about him? You could give him the £50,000 we put aside for Cat's missus for the time being," Joe suggested.

"To be honest with you Joe, I'm worried. This job went like clockwork, all the information I had was spot on. Since the job, it's going downhill, what with Cat, then his missus, then this, and the police have already called on him, for what I don't know. I only used him because Cat brought him in. He got done for doing my place in Essex, I find out later. I'm concerned they might connect his name to mine. I don't think it will be long before the police make two and two add up to the right number. Plus, that million-pound reward on offer, if that bird sniffs that the money is from that job, I just don't know. I think he's got to have an accident."

"The motorway type?" Joe asked.

"The very same, Joe," he nodded.

The two had used a method, three to four years earlier, to get rid of another person who they thought could damage them. Apart from his own Mercedes, Bob had a Range Rover Vogue. The rear number plate had been altered and hinged in a way that it could be moved aside by the push of a button. It could also be swivelled to display another number from a similar model in the north of Scotland. A person lying down inside the boot space would be able to fire a shot at any following vehicle. The front tyres would be the target, causing the vehicle to lose control. An accident, at high speed, on the motorway.

"I'll ring him," said Bob, "and arrange to meet him at Watford Gap this evening. Tell him to follow me to the cottage, you take the hire car back, then get a taxi to Smiths, pick the Range Rover up from service, and meet me downstairs at 7pm in the basement car park. Make sure it's tanked up. Are you OK for a trip abroad, the morning ferry from Hull? We'll get the cash and get it to my business contact in Belgium. The sooner we get it away the better. Then we drive down to Spain. I'll take my hire car back and walk back. OK with that?"

"Suits me," said Joe. "Gives me time to pack."

Bob picked the mobile up and rang Guy's number. "Guy, it's Bob. Can you meet me at Watford Gap Services at 9pm tonight? I have to travel up north for tomorrow, I can get some cash for you on the way up, you'll have to follow me. Is that alright?"

"That's fine, what about Joe?" asked Guy.

Looking across at Joe, Bob said, "I've put him in the picture, but he's OK with it."

Bob didn't want Guy to know Joe was with him and listening.

"How much can I have?" Guy asked.

"You will get what's due. See you later. 9pm Watford Gap, cheers." Turning to Joe, he said, "Pick me up here at 7 then, I'm trusting you to have everything ready."

"Can't see any problem," replied Joe, "See you later."

***

At 8.45pm Bob pulled his Range Rover onto the north side of the M1 at Watford Gap Services. Finding a parking space near to the entrance, he switched the engine off. "No sign of him yet, Joe," he said. "Is everything OK with you?"

"Fine, I checked, the gears are working perfectly. And I've already swivelled the number plates."

"Good, keep well down, I want him up to about 90, then I'll give you the word. He's just pulling in now, hang on."

Bob flashed his lights at Guy. Pulling up alongside, he leaned out. Looking down at him, Bob said, "Follow me up, I'm in a bit of a rush, so stay with me."

"That will be easy, in that thing you'll be holding me back. Ready when you are." Guy pulled in behind the Range Rover as they left the services.

Heading north, Bob held his speed at a steady 75mph, moving between the centre and outside lane. Checking his mirror, he could see Guy was matching him, and about 40 yards behind him. As they approached the downhill slope past the Loughborough turn off, Bob moved to the inside lane and gradually increased his speed up to 90. The motorway traffic was not very busy. Bob gave the shout to Joe when he was ready. Joe looked out through the spy hole at the side of the rear number plate and could easily see Guy's Jaguar, holding back about 30 to 40 yards. He shouted to Bob that he was ready and lowered the number plate. Joe had fixed his pump action shotgun on a swivel in order to keep it steady and loaded it with one ounce lead slugs. Taking aim, he fired at the front offside wheel of Guy's car, pumping another shot straight in, firing almost instantly. The car seemed to buck up at the front, swerved into the central reservation, before bouncing off it, somersaulting onto its side, then its roof. It followed them down the motorway in a shower of sparks, like a giant sparkler. Rolling onto its side again, and then over and over, breaking up as it rolled, before it finally smashed into one of the overhead gantry supports at the side, wrapping itself round it and bursting into flames. Bob had kept his speed at 90 and was pulling away, shouting to Joe, "Well that's that problem sorted. Get sorted out back there and come up front. We aren't stopping."

Guy had been concentrating on his driving, making sure he kept up with Bob, when he noticed the rear number plate of the Range Rover drop down. He thought at first that it was dropping off, was about to flash his lights at Bob as a warning, when he saw a flash from the hole left by the number plate. He felt a thump under the car and the steering wheel pull sharply to the right as though his front tyre had burst. He pulled the wheel over to his left, when he felt another thump, the car had then flipped over onto its roof, the hood collapsing in on him. He screamed out loud, but then they died off. He was dead before he hit the overhead gantry.

CHAPTER 17

The following morning, DI Richards sat at his desk going through the reports and crimes generated overnight, as was his usual practice, looking for anything warranting CID attention. He came across the report on the hit and run on the Embankment, noting an unidentified female victim. Shouting a DS in, he said, "What do we know about this job yet, anything?" showing the report to the officer.

"Nothing at this minute, let me make a couple of calls, then I'll update you, guv."

"Keep tabs on it. If there's anything they want us to do, let me know. Make sure what's been done, has been done properly. Photos, prints, the usual stuff. You know the drill."

"Leave it with me, guv."

"Is Greg in yet?" he asked.

"On his way in, guv. He had to get some prescription for his wife, he won't be long."

"I'll update Greg when he comes in. Have a look at that Town Road burglary for me as well, will you?"

"No probs, I'll get back to you if there's anything for us. Oh by the way, you know that bloke you went to see the other night, the one with the Jag?"

"Guy Salmon, you mean?"

"Yeah, that one. He got wiped up on the motorway last night, crashed his car, killed outright. I saw it on the uniform pad. The motorway police wanted a check at his address by our lads. They've been round but no one's in."

"Get me the details on it, that's interested me for some reason."

The DI sat back thinking about his meeting with the young woman at Salmon's flat the other night, and what she had said was starting to niggle at him. He decided he'd look further into this man, just in case. He picked his phone up and dialled an internal number.

Putting his phone down – he'd been on the phone for nearly three quarters of an hour – he sat back and looked at his notes. "Greg!" he shouted out into the outer office. "In here!"

"What's up, guv?" he asked.

Handing him some paperwork, he said, "I've been onto the Intelligence boys about our friend Salmon, he was killed in a motorway accident last night by the way. When he was released from prison he went to stay with a Jerry Morton and his common-law wife, Hannah Bell, at this address. Get round and check it out, see what she says. On your way, call in at the Intelligence Unit and pick up some papers for me. When you've done that, I want you to call into the traffic boys dealing with Salmon's accident. Get his keys from his property and come back here. I've already squared it with them."

"On my way."

CHAPTER 18

Bob and Joe had made it up to the house in Derbyshire without any further problems and were sitting drinking wine after their meal.

"I think that now Cat and Guy are out of the way, we should get the money moved as soon as possible. I have been onto a couple of contacts on the continent who can help us out, they will get rid of the Range Rover as well. What do you reckon?" asked Bob.

"I have no problems with that, providing they don't rip us off."

"They will exchange the money for a fee of five per cent, and I've told them I will throw the Range Rover in, so no, we won't get ripped off."

"What do we do then?" asked Joe.

"We load all the money into the Range Rover and catch the ferry across to Belgium. Our contact there will take half and then travel with us to Geneva, where we get rid of the rest. The Range Rover is driven back by him, you and I fly out from there to Spain. The money is bank transferred whilst we are with him, and the paperwork for the car is signed over to him. When we get to Spain we sort out transfers to any account you want to put your share into."

"Can't we do that in Geneva?" Bob asked.

"If that's what you want, and your account is set up, yes."

"Let's get loading then," said Joe.

"The ferry is booked for tomorrow night, so we'll load up tomorrow. I want the Range Rover cleaned out, stripped of our gadgets and put back to normal before I part with it. Tonight we relax."

CHAPTER 19

Greg had done all his running about and was back in the office with DI Richards. "No one in at the woman's flat, the neighbours haven't seen her for a couple of days, which they say is unusual. One neighbour had a spare key and she let me have a quick look round, when I told her we were looking for some contact address. I managed to sneak a photo of her and I think that Jerry bloke from the bedroom. I found an address book next to the phone. I've got that as well. It's got Salmon's number in it but I'm not sure whether it's up to date or not. I've also picked up his keys."

"Right," said the DI. "Let's get round there, see what we can find. I've got a bit of a gut feeling on this one, I don't know why, but I have."

***

An hour later, both men sat on the couch in Salmon's flat. DI Richards was looking through the address book and had found Hannah and Jerry's address and phone number in it, as well as one for Bob Teal. "Why would he have Teal's phone number in his book, he had robbed him. They weren't friends were they? Ring it and see who answers."

Greg picked the phone up and dialled the number written down. The tone gave an unobtainable signal. "Unobtainable, guv."

"Right, what about this one marked 'workshop', try that."

"That's ringing, guv. An answerphone cut in. Some bloke saying, 'Sorry, Guy can't get to the phone, please leave a message and I will get back to you asap'."

"I want a check on that phone number and an address for it. I want a check on the Teal number, see how old that number is. You stay here, I'll go back to the office and send another couple of lads over here. I want this place checking for any records, bills, photos, keys, anything which might help us. Anything."

Paul decided to give Dick a quick ring in Nottingham and updated him. "Let me know if we can help any further, mate."

CHAPTER 20

Bob and Joe boarded the ferry without any customs checks, and after the overnight crossing, arrived at a small village called Aalst, about halfway between Ghent and Brussels. They went into the village square and ordered coffees. A short while later, Bob's contact turned up, a small swarthy Frenchman. Bob introduced him to Joe as Petr, and Joe as Adam. They had done business before and had both come out of it well. Bob explained what he needed doing, Petr said no problem and he was ready to go. They followed him to a reasonably sized lock-up on the outskirts of the village, where an electric shutter was raised, both drove in and the shutter closed. It was spotless inside.

Joe said to Bob, "What does he do here then?"

Bob said, "He is an investor, that's why he can get the money sorted."

They unloaded all the cash sacks onto a large table, where it was counted.

Petr said, "A lot of money Monsieur Bob."

"Can you handle it, Petr?"

"Certainly I can. Do you want it all doing now?"

"Well we were thinking about doing half here and half in Geneva," Bob told him.

"I can do it all here, save any more carting it about, as you English say."

"Do it all here then. Can you sort the Range Rover out as well?"

"Most certainly, that will be out of this country by this evening, let's get this cash sorted."

The total on the table was £3,940,000.

"OK," said Petr. "Where do you want it to go?"

Bob said, "Put it into an account of yours then when it's cleared link me up to the bank in the Cayman Islands, you've got those details already."

Petr quickly linked into an account of his, transferring all the money. "I have good contact with them, they will accept it, don't worry."

Ten minutes later, the transfer had gone through.

Joe asked how they could do it, with the money still in front of them. Petr told him, "Good contact, now I get your link to the Cayman Bank."

Once that was established, Bob took over. "I'm transferring £3.5 million, the rest is yours Petr, OK, and the Range Rover."

"Suits me, for a few minutes' work."

"That's done then. Can you run us to the airport?" Bob asked.

"Let me lock this cash away first, Then I will."

All the cash was bundled back into the sacks and placed in a huge disused commercial fridge, but more secure with an electronic lock fitted.

"OK, airport here we come."

Whilst the cash was being sorted, Joe had been onto the airport and organised flights leaving in two hour's time to Spain.

Later, at the airport waiting to board, Bob said, "Joe, is one and a half million pounds OK as your share? Only I still have some other expenses to pay out."

Joe said, "Yes, that's OK. You can transfer it over when we get to Geneva."

CHAPTER 21

Back in Nottingham, the incident room appeared to be at full throttle. DCS Belling was reading through what had come in and discussing what actions should be raised. These were enquiry forms issued by the HOLMES computer team, for individual enquiries to be allocated to the enquiry teams, to be returned when the action requested was fully completed.

Dick Jones walked into the office, saw Belling and said, "OK Boss?"

"Yes Dick, getting sorted."

Dick said, "I know it's probably the wrong time, but I have some leave booked next week. It's been booked since October last year, with my mate from the Met. I can cancel if you want me to."

Belling said, "No, take it, we should be well in with this job by then, a break should recharge your batteries. Where are you off to?"

"Only Spain," Dick said. "In fact my Met mate has been doing some enquiries down there on the QT and come up with something. You know I checked car hire companies. Well two of them hired a Merc and a BMW out, another one a Jag. Funnily enough, they all seem to tie together somehow. The one that hired the Jag out picked a girl up hitching down to London from Nottingham, day after our job. His name is Guy Salmon and he has a bit of form for doing a safe job. He has just been killed in an accident on the motorway. Also, another contact of his has gone missing, and this contact's wife was killed in a hit and run. Another thing, Salmon did the safe job at a firm call Teal Investments in London, and funnily enough, the other two cars are hired to that company. I think it's worth a trip to London, to get the whole picture."

Belling sat back, looked at Dick and said, "Well it's worth a look I suppose. Put it all down to be actioned to you, and DS Jim Harrison. I suggest you take him because he can carry anything on whilst you are away. Get your bag packed, you are off to London for a couple of days. I'll speak to Jim."

"Let's hope we can get a result," Dick said.

Dick went to another desk, picking the phone up to ring London. "Paul, it's Dick, we are on our way down, me and a DS. Can you book us in for at least a couple of nights? Will ring you with times later. Can you pick us up?"

"No problems mate, waiting for your call."

CHAPTER 22

7 o'clock that evening saw Dick and Jim sitting in Paul Richards' office at Kent Road Police Station. DS Greg Watts was also present.

"So what do we actually have then, Paul?" Jim asked.

"In this order then, briefly, as we haven't got all the statements yet. We know three cars have been hired, Guy Salmon hired a Jag from Hertz for the Christmas period. The other two were hired by Teal Investments, a Robert Teal hired the Merc, a Joe Andrews hired the BMW, both under Teal Investments, and again for the Christmas period. The mileages on the cars on return were high enough to have travelled to your neck of the woods and back. The Merc, even more."

"Have the cars been checked over yet?" Jim asked.

"We have had a cursory look but couldn't find anything. They are keeping them secure for us for the time being. We actually followed Salmon taking his back with a blonde girl. They went back to his flat then. We called a bit later to speak to him, but he had nipped out. She told us her name was Julie and he had picked her up as she was hitch-hiking down to London. He picked her up just outside of Nottingham. That would be the day after your job I think. She said she had overheard a phone conversation he had with someone called Hannah, who was giving him some earache over her husband, Jerry, not coming home yet. They had been up north and where was he. Evidently she was not a happy bunny. Next thing we get is a hit and run, the victim is a Hannah Bell. Common-law wife of a Jerry Morton. We checked at the address and found this address book, with Salmon's number in it. And a photo of her with this Jerry. He has form for all sorts including firearms and violence. Then Salmon is killed on the motorway in some sort of accident. We got his keys and checked his property. He had Morton's details and also a number for Robert Teal. We tried that but it's unobtainable. He has a lock-up workshop-cum-garage, which we checked out. There was a van in there, with bull bars on the front. We think it might be the one used in Hannah Bell's hit and run. That's being checked by our lads, they found her handbag inside."

"Any sign of the girl at all?" Dick asked.

"Nothing, not even a phone number," Paul replied. "So that's it in a nutshell. Not sure if it's linked to your job or not."

"Has Salmon got any form?" Jim asked.

"One conviction for a safe job at, would you believe, Teal Investments. The other baddy got away, we think it was Jerry," Paul said. "So what do you want us to do for you?"

Jim said, "Well I think the first thing is get the hire cars checked over and fingerprinted. At least they can use them again if they want. But a pint and a bite to eat wouldn't go amiss. We can have a chat, then look at things in the morning."

"Let's go. Greg, lead the way."

CHAPTER 23

Eight Days Later

Paul and Dick had arrived in Spain and had just entered a small bistro bar in Los Boliches, near Fuengirola. They nodded to a couple of men already at the bar, and ordered a beer each. "Thanks Pete," said Paul. "Good to see you again."

"And you Paul. All OK?"

Paul had known the barman for a couple of years. "Fine thanks."

They sat at the bar. "Well mate, cheers," said Paul. "Here's to a good few days. Are you glad you came now?"

"I am," replied Dick. "But I feel a bit guilty really, what with that job at home."

"Yes, I know, Dick, but so far all we've done is sort out the fact that it looks like it was Salmon's van that did the hit and run on Hannah Bell. Why, we don't know."

As Paul turned from the bar, he saw two young women coming through the door. They came to the bar. Paul lifted his glass and said, "Evening ladies, can we get you a drink?"

The blonde one said, "For your cheek, two G and Ts."

"Go and sit down, we'll bring them over."

Dick said, "Do you know them?"

"Not yet, although I've met the blonde somewhere before, sure of that."

They took the drinks across and sat down. "There you

are ladies, drinks as requested. I'm Paul by the way, this is Dick."

The blonde said, "Well, I'm Julie, this is my sister, Alice."

"Have you been here long?" Paul asked.

"A few days. Just after Christmas, we drove over, then down to here from Santander. What about you two?"

"Got here today, it's a decent place to eat." Although it was one of Paul's local bars when he was down there, it was always a good chat-up line, he thought.

Paul said, "I feel I've met you before Julie, I just said that to Dick."

He looked at her, then said, "Now I know where from. I spoke to you at that flat you were stopping at in London. Guy Salmon, the guy with the red Jag."

She said, "So you did, I remember you now, you're that detective. Small world."

"Small world indeed, Dick does the same job in Nottingham. You hitched a lift down with him to London. You know he was killed in a road accident a few days ago, on the motorway?"

"Gosh," said Julie. "I didn't know that."

***

The two men at the bar looked at each other, one was Bob Teal, the other Joe Andrews.

"Well that's a fucking turn up for the books," Bob said. "You know who the blonde is then, she's the one that nicked Guy's cash, the blokes are cops, one from Nottingham, the other must be a Met cop, and by the sounds of it, they are on that enquiry, or linked with it. I think we should move out."

They drank up and left, walking down the road to another bar.

"What do you think, Bob?" asked Joe.

Bob said, "Not really sure to tell you the truth. They may know about Guy, Cat, and Hannah, but nothing ties them to us. All the phones we used are in the Thames, the hire cars we had, we can answer for if we have to. We got rid of all the clothing and stuff at the cottage. What do you reckon?"

Joe said, "Like you, not sure. If we went after that blonde, it could draw attention to this neck of the woods. She's got the money with her no doubt. She's not going to cough to it, but Guy's dead, so she's got no comeback. The cops don't know that and she won't tell 'em."

Bob said, "Let's sit here and see if they come out. We could do with at least knowing where they are all staying. It sounds like the girls are here for some time, the cops for a few days. We can sort something out when they've gone home."

***

Back in the bistro, Paul asked, "Where are you stopping, then?"

Alice said, "Our dad has an apartment just round the corner, he doesn't use it anymore, so he gave it to us. What about you two?"

Paul said, "I have one on top of next door's block. It's a penthouse, my parents had it. Like yours, they don't use it, so I've taken it over. Own rooftop pool and everything."

Julie asked, "When was Guy killed then?"

Paul said, "I think it was the day after I saw you. Look, I know we are on holiday, but can we talk about this?"

She said, "What's to talk about? I was only really there for one night, I left just after I saw you."

"I know that. But you remember telling me he had had a phone call that day, from someone called Hannah, who was asking where her husband was?"

"Yes."

"Well she was found dead the next day as well. She was the victim of a hit and run. Our enquiries lead us to think that Guy may have been responsible for her death. We found a van at his workshop which we believe is the vehicle used."

"Bloody hell," said Alice.

"And you told us Guy and Hannah's husband had been up north on a job together."

"Yes, but I don't know where," Julie replied.

"Well," said Paul. "He picked you up just outside Nottingham. Over that weekend, a security cash handling centre was done over, and about four million in cash was stolen."

"And you think Guy was involved in that?" she said.

"Not sure yet, but apart from the cash being stolen, a police sergeant was shot dead outside the premises."

"God, I didn't know about that at all."

"We don't know who's involved at this stage, but that's one enquiry we are looking into. But I think a million pounds reward money might loosen a few tongues."

"A million pounds, Christ if I knew he'd done it I'd tell you. After all, I won't see him again now anyway."

"One more thing, then I'll drop it. Did he ring anyone else whilst you were with him?" Paul asked.

She replied, "Well, he had a couple of calls, but I don't know who from. After we dropped the car off at Hertz, he had to nip out. I left before he came back, because Alice had rung to say she was home. I did ring to say I was leaving."

"Have you still got that number?"

"I'm not sure." Julie scrolled down her list. "Yes here it is, I think that's it."

Paul jotted the number down. He also swapped numbers with Julie and Alice. “OK folks, let’s get another drink and eat.”

Later that evening, Paul and Dick were sat in the apartment having seen the girls home. They hadn’t noticed they had been followed to both apartment buildings.

They were having a night cap. Paul said, “Well fancy that Dick. What do you reckon now?”

“Not sure. I’ll ring the incident room in the morning, speak to the boss, pass on that phone number and see what’s happening back home.”

Paul said, “Another thing. I know I’ve said it once tonight, but it’s just struck me. Did you see the two men at the bar when we walked in? Well I’ve met one of them somewhere before as well, the one in the blue shirt. I know his face, just trying to put a name to it. If they are in tomorrow I’m going to have a chat, if not I’ll ask Pete, he’ll know.”

***

Back at Bob’s villa, they were having a night cap. “Any more thoughts Bob?” Joe asked.

“Not yet, but I remember that London cop. He met me when Guy and Cat did my office over some years ago. Hopefully he won’t remember me. If he does, well, we’ll cross that bridge when we come to it. I think we should steer clear of that bar, at least till the cops have gone back. We know where they are all living. Let me have a think. See how things pan out.”

CHAPTER 24

Dick was on the phone next morning, relaying to Supt Dee the previous night's meeting with Julie and her sister. He said, "I know we have no proof yet, but there does seem to be some tie-up somewhere. The mileage from the hire cars show they covered enough miles to get to Nottingham and back. You say nothing untoward found in the hire cars?"

"Nothing Dick. There is one thing though. Derbyshire police found a burnt-out Mondeo up on the moors shortly after our job. It was stolen from London the day before our job."

"Look sir, I'm with my mate from the Met, who me and Jim met up with. Do you mind me asking him to see what he can find out? I'll get back to you asap. Have you got the reg number handy?"

"No problems. I thought you were on holiday though?" Supt Dee passed the number over.

"Bit of a working one. Talk later."

"Did you hear all that mate?"

Paul nodded, dialling on his phone, "It's Paul Richards here. Is Greg there?"

"It's me guv. Enjoying your holiday?"

"So far Greg. Do me a couple of favours. Can you visit the car hire firms we did the enquiries for on behalf of Notts police on that shooting job? I want you to get them to check if any of them, the hire cars we are interested in, are fitted with satnavs. If they are, what do they show?

Then see if they have photos of the hirers, the executive ones normally take them. One more thing, a Mondeo, reg number XL 04 XTY was stolen from the London area around that time. Check it out, let me know where it was stolen from, owner and such stuff."

"Am straight on it, guv, ring you as soon as."

Paul finished the call. "He's a good DS, won't take him long."

***

A couple of hours later, Paul and Dick were sat on the rooftop, drinking coffee, when Paul's phone rang. "Hello, Paul Richards."

"It's me guv. Done them enquiries, just in time, they were about to let the Jag go out. I've stopped all hires on all the cars until they hear from us. Not happy but agreed to. Anyway, the satnav on the Jag had an address in Derbyshire programmed into it, the others had been deleted. I've got some photos of the hirers. The Mondeo was stolen from just round the corner from where that Hannah Bell and Jerry Morton lived, the day before the robbery. I've got photos. Everything is being emailed to you as we speak. And I've passed it all on to Notts incident room. I did a quick electoral roll check on the Derby address as well. It's down to Teal Investments. Hope that helps. Anything else you need?"

"No that's great work, thanks Greg. You know that pint you owed me from the other day? Treat yourself to it."

"You are all heart, guv. Your generosity overwhelms me."

"Did you hear all that Dick?"

"Yes, let's look at what he's sent through."

Paul opened it up, and said, "Fuck me, I told you I knew that bloke in the bar, it's Bob Teal, that's him." Pointing at the photos. "I'm thinking the other guy is Joe Andrews and that's Guy Salmon. The Mondeo bit is interesting as well. Wonder what your boss will make of it all, especially when you tell him Teal and Andrews are down here as well. Let's go and talk to Pete at the bar, he'll know where they live if anyone does."

They walked down to the bar. Pete was behind the counter getting a coffee for a customer. "Morning Pete," said Paul. "Do us a couple of bacon rolls and coffees, mate, when you're ready."

"Coming up, Paul."

Pete took the coffee over to the customer, came back and said, "Right lads, two bacon and two coffees, coming up."

"Pete, you know the two guys at the bar last night when we came in? Do you know them at all?"

"Only their first names – Bob and Joe."

"Do you know where they live at all?" Paul asked.

"I don't know the address, but I know where it is. If you go up to the main road, turn left towards Malaga, you come to the crossroad with the big garage on the left. Turn right there, towards Mijas. His house is the big one, fourth on the right, with a big green wire fence all around it. You can't miss it, it's huge."

"Thanks Pete. I've met Bob before and wasn't sure it was him. Don't mention we've been asking about him, will you?"

"Mum's the word. Here you are, two bacon and two coffees."

"Thanks Pete."

They sat eating their rolls. Dick said, "What now then, mate?"

"Not sure, certainly a lot of circumstances, but no hard evidence it's them. I think we ought to hire a car and have a nose round."

Dick said, "Can you contact Greg, see if he can find out when they arrived here, passport control might help?"

"Good idea, if they were here over Christmas, that's them out of it. Whilst I do that, ring the girls, see if they want a ride out."

Paul dropped a quick email to Greg, asking for the checks.

"Any luck with the girls, mate?"

"Yes, picking them up outside their place in an hour."

CHAPTER 25

Paul had used the car hire company before, so his details were on record. He chose a white Honda Jazz, making sure the A/C was working. It also had tinted rear windows.

Dick was driving. "Nice little car this," he said.

They picked the girls up. Julie said, "You could have used ours, you know."

Paul said, "Probably, but we need to check something out and Spanish plates stick out less than English ones. Turn right here Dick, towards Mijas."

As they approached the villa, Dick slowed down. Paul got his phone out and recorded the journey past. "Pete was right, it's huge."

On the drive was a Range Rover and a BMW convertible, both with Spanish plates on. Beyond them was a small silver car they couldn't make out.

"What's that about?" Julie asked.

"Just checking something. If it comes to anything, we'll let you know," Paul said. "OK mate, now to the top."

It was quite a steep drive in places, but well worth it for the views at the top. They drove round the square and parked in a small side street, where it was more shaded.

As they had been driving past, Joe had been looking out of the villa window towards the road and saw the Honda slowly driving past. He recognised the driver as one of the cops from the bar the previous night, the other was alongside him, with his phone pointed towards the villa. "Bob, I think them cops have just driven past. It looked like one had his phone pointing this way. They've gone up towards Mijas."

"Give 'em ten minutes, if they haven't come back past, we'll nip up ourselves. We'll take Santos's car, he's out with his family today."

They got the Ceat out and drove up to Mijas. "What car we looking for, Joe?"

"It's a white Honda Jazz, with tinted windows at the back," Joe replied.

They reached the square, driving round it they couldn't see a white Jazz. "Let's check the side streets."

"There's a white Jazz. Over there," said Joe. "Tinted windows as well."

"Let's see if there are any others."

Mijas wasn't a very big place, so it took them about ten minutes to check. "Looks like that's the only white Jazz up here, Joe."

He said, "Drive up to it. Drop me off."

Bob drove up to the Jazz, Joe had a quick look round, dropped down between the two cars at the front of the Jazz.

After about a minute, he got up, got back in the car, and said, "Let's go."

"What have you done, Joe?" Bob asked.

"There's a small rubber seal on the end of the brake pipes to the front wheels, I've loosened them both off, so with natural braking pressure they will come off altogether, and it's a steep drive back down that hill. The brakes will give out altogether."

"Where did you learn that?" Bob asked.

"Just something I picked up along the way," Joe laughed. "Let's go."

***

Meanwhile, Paul, Dick and the girls were in a tapas bar in the far corner of the square, sat in the shade. As Dick was driving, he was sticking to soft drinks.

"Not very busy today, is it?" Paul said.

"It's always quiet up here at this time of the year," Julie said. "I prefer it like this. In the summer you can't move. I'm actually surprised they are open. How long are you guys stopping over here for?"

"We only have four more days, then it's tea break over, back to work. You know how it is," replied Paul. "What about yourselves?"

"Like I said last night, we are in no hurry to go home. Alice has been made redundant, I'm serving my notice on leave. Our dad gives us a monthly allowance still." Looking at Alice, she continued, "So we can manage, can't we Alice?"

Alice nodded by reply.

"Lucky you two," said Dick. "Will you keep in touch?"

"If we have time," Julie laughed. "Although it would be nice to know how the case is progressing."

Dick was thinking, he would at least like to know they are safe, if things turned out the way they were looking.

"OK, folks, let's have a walk round before we go back down to town, walk them tapas off," Paul suggested.

They walked round for about ten minutes, then made their way back to the car. "At least we had some shade on it. It's like getting in an oven sometimes," Julie said.

Dick started the car and began the drive back down the steep road to the town.

"I think the views are great, overlooking Fuengirola on the way down, it shows the whole coast," said Alice.

The car seemed to speed up a bit. Paul said, "Easy on the throttle, mate."

Dick said, "I don't want to worry you folks, but there's not much on the brakes. In fact, I think they have gone altogether."

Dick was battling to keep the car steady, still stamping on the brakes. He dropped into third gear in an effort to slow down, but all that did was make the engine noisier.

The girls were starting to panic, shouting, "Can't you do something? Turn the engine off, or something!"

"That won't help, I'll have no steering, or power then." Dick was looking for somewhere to run into, but there was nowhere. "Hang on folks."

He pulled the car across the road, toward the grass and gravel at the side of the road, on the upward gradient, hoping it would slow them down. There was a grinding noise as the car met the rock. Dick turned into it a bit more, then the front tyre hit a loose rock, sending the car to the opposite side of the road, towards the road edge and a big drop. The girls were screaming now. Dick pulled the wheel back hard away from the edge, back across the road. He saw a gravel trap about fifty metres down, shouted "Hang on!" and drove straight into it. The car juddered to a stop, buried axle-deep in gravel.

"Fuck me," said Dick. "That made me sweat a bit."

Paul said, "Is that all?"

They all climbed out and steadied themselves. The girls were still in tears.

Hugging each other, Julie said, "What happened?"

Dick said, "No idea, the brakes seemed to go all of a sudden."

"What happens now?" she asked.

Paul said, "I'll ring the hire company and get it recovered. I want it checked over, brakes don't just go like that."

He rang the hire firm, explained what had happened, and asked them to get up there with a recovery truck and a lift back for them. Asap.

They waited an hour before they heard a motor and saw a minibus, followed by a breakdown truck. Paul explained to the minibus driver what had happened and that he wanted to get the car back. He wanted it checking over and pronto. He would be down first thing in the morning and expected some answers.

They left the breakdown truck to it and rode down in the minibus. As they passed the villa, both vehicles were still on the drive.

Paul told the driver to drop them on the corner. Getting out, he said, "Do you want to come up for a freshen-up and have a drink to calm your nerves? My place is on the top floor here."

They got into the private lift, up to the top floor apartment.

On getting out of the lift, Julie said, "Wow, this looks luxurious. A roof top swimming pool as well, poolside lounges, the works."

Paul said, "If you want to freshen up, use the two rooms on the right, off the lounge, both have bathrooms in. G & T girls?"

"Yes please," they chorused. "Large ones."

After they had gone, Paul said, "You did well there, mate, kept your cool. Thanks."

Dick said, "I was looking after me as well, you know."

"Thanks anyway."

When the girls came back, they sat chatting on the pool lounges for about an hour, before Paul suggested they go for an early meal at the bar.

Both girls said they would like to go back to their apartment first, to get changed, and arranged to meet them around 7pm.

***

As Paul and Dick were discussing matters, Paul's phone went.

"Paul Richards."

"Guv, it's Greg. I checked up on the passport details. Check this. They both left on a cross-channel ferry on the Wednesday after Christmas. They told customs they were off to Belgium. They were in a Range Rover Vogue, reg number RK 07 PRA owned by Bob Teal, or his company at least. Not sure where they went after that. But they flew from Belgium later that same day to Spain."

"Any sign of the Range Rover coming back into the UK?"

"Not to date, no."

"OK Greg, cheers."

"Well at least they were in the UK over Christmas," said Paul.

CHAPTER 26

Dick's phone was ringing. It was Supt Dee. "Dick, can you talk?"

"Yes, just a minute, let me put it on speaker so Paul can hear, if that's OK"

"Fine, listen. We got that address from the satnav on the Jag. Derbyshire police have been round and checked it for us, no one in, but they think there has been some activity in the back garden. There's a well at the top of the garden and it appears stuff has been thrown down it. I'm going to organise a better search, with our SOCO and theirs, over the next couple of days. See if it throws anything up. I'm hoping to get a locksmith there to get inside, if Derbyshire agree. I got all the emails from the Met; thanks Paul for all your help. Though not sure where it leads us."

Paul said, "Well, one thing it does do is tie at least three of them to that cottage. I think with that, and the fact that the Mondeo, stolen from near where Jerry Morton lived, he wouldn't have been a million miles away either. We just need hard evidence."

'Which at this time we don't have," Dee said.

Dick said, "You know Teal and Andrews are down here, don't you Boss?"

"I think you might have mentioned it."

"Well we were out today, up in the hills, in Mijas. We drove past his place, it's a huge villa. Anyway, we were with Julie, the lass that stopped at Guy Salmon's place just after our job happened, and her sister. Coming back down, our brakes failed on our hire car. We think they were tampered with, not sure, we are having it checked over tomorrow. Another thing, Paul checked up on when they came here. Evidently they left the UK on the Wednesday after Christmas, in a Range Rover reg number RK 07 PRA. It's owned by Teal's company. They told Customs they were going to Belgium. They flew from Belgium to here later the same day. No record of the Range Rover returning to the UK."

"Right, I've got all that, anything else?"

"Not at the moment, no," said Dick.

"OK, you two, lay low for a bit, let me know about the car. I'll ring when there's something to update you on."

CHAPTER 27

The girls were sat at a table, at the small bar, on the pavement outside their apartment block. They were both drinking gin and tonic before walking down to meet Paul and Dick for a meal at the Bistro bar. "What do you think of Paul?" Julie asked her sister.

"I quite fancy him actually, I know you fancy Dick," Alice said.

"What makes you think that?"

"Oh, the way you look at him sometimes."

"Well he is funny and serious at the same time. I like that in a man," Julie said.

"OK, that's settled then. Paul's mine, Dick's yours," Alice said, clinking glasses. They were running about half an hour late already. "They will wait," Julie said.

A white minibus pulled up at the kerbside, tinted windows at the back. The driver pipped the hooter to attract the girls, a sliding door at the side opened and a man climbed out. As he approached them, he said, "Julie, Alice?"

Alice said, "Who are you?"

The man replied, "Paul sent me to fetch you, after what happened today coming down from Mijas, he asked me to pick you up. Ready?"

They drank up, and walked to the minibus, climbing in the back. The man followed them, pulling the door shut as the minibus pulled away.

Julie said, "You're going the wrong way, town's the other way."

The man said, "We are picking someone else up as well."

Alice whispered to Julie, "I don't like this, ring Paul."

She got her phone out and was about to dial, when the man reached over and snatched the phone from her. "No phones, you," to Alice. "Give me your phone, now."

Alice reacted, "Why should I? Who are you?"

The man said, "Someone you don't want to upset, now pass me the phone."

Alice passed it over.

After a few minutes, the minibus pulled off the road in the driveway of a huge villa. The gate closed behind them and a garage door opened in front of them. They drove into the garage, the door shutting behind them. Another door opened in front of them, they were driven down a ramp, to a lower level, where the bus turned towards a rear wall and stopped.

The rear minibus door was open and they climbed out. The driver now spoke to them. "Get over to those chairs, sit down and stay quiet. No use shouting down here, no one will hear you. And just so you know, phones don't work down here either," passing the phones back to them.

They sat down, the man from the back of the minibus strapped their arms and ankles to the chairs.

"What do you want us for?" asked Julie. "We've got nothing."

"I think you have," said the driver. "About £150,000 of ours."

Julie looked at him, wondering who he was. "I don't know what you are talking about," she said.

"Perhaps if you cast your mind back to the man who gave you a lift to London, just after Christmas. Guy. Does that ring any bells with you?"

Julie didn't reply, just looked at her sister.

"OK. My mate here is going to go back to your apartment and see what he can find. We'll have to wait and see what happens when he gets back."

"Who are you?" Alice asked.

"Let's just say, friends of the man your sister ripped off."

Alice said, "But he's dead, isn't he?"

The other man left with the apartment keys.

Julie said, "So what happens to us now?"

"Depends on what my mate finds. Will he find anything?"

The girls looked at each other but didn't say anything.

"We'll see," he said.

CHAPTER 28

Paul and Dick had been wondering where the girls were, as they were nearly an hour late by now. And as they weren't answering any phones, they had walked up to their apartment block. As they walked round the corner, they saw Joe Andrews coming out of their front door, carrying a sports holdall. He climbed into a small minibus and started to drive off.

"What's he up to?" Paul looked round and saw a taxi dropping some people off. "C'mon mate." Running across to the taxi they jumped in. Paul smacked the driver on the shoulder and pointed to the minibus. "Follow that bus."

The driver was a bit slow on the uptake, so Paul waved a 100 euro note at him.

"Don't catch him, just follow him," Paul told the driver, who was now fully alert.

They followed the minibus onto the main road, then watched as it turned right at the crossroads.

Dick said, "He's going to the villa. OK driver, stop here. Thanks."

As they got out, Paul dropped the 100 euro note in the driver's lap. "Vamoose!"

The taxi turned round and drove back towards town.

They got to the villa; the front gates were shut. "The minibus must be in the garage, both cars are there," Dick said.

"What now, mate?"

"Well I'm climbing over the gate, are you coming?"

"Try and stop me," Paul said.

They both scaled the gate and made their way to the side of the garage. As it was an electric opening door, there was no way in. They crept round the side, nearest the house, and saw that the garage appeared to be built with a lower floor at the back sloping down to garden level. There were a couple of oblong-shaped windows, just above ground level, which were showing a light. Looking through, they could see Julie and her sister tied to separate chairs. Bob Teal stood in front of them with the sports holdall at his feet. It was open and looked to be full of money. Bob was showing it to the girls, but they couldn't hear what was being said.

Inside, Bob was saying, "So now you know what I'm talking about, don't you ladies?"

Julie said, "OK. I took it. Nothing to do with my sister at all. Keep the money, just let us go."

"Can't do that, what about your boyfriend cops out there?"

"Not our boyfriends, didn't even know them till we met them in the bar."

"Well you know them now, don't you? You had a lucky escape today."

Julie said, "You did the brakes on our car today, that's the only way you would know what happened."

Bob said, "Don't know what you are talking about. See, two people can play at not knowing things. Now what are we going to do with you two?"

Julie said, "That money. Was it from that security depot up in Nottingham? You shot that police officer."

Bob said, "Let's say I know about it, and the person who shot the copper has been punished."

"What about Guy, did you get rid of him, because I took his money?"

"Let's say, accidents do happen. Leave it at that, shall we?"

***

Meanwhile, outside, Paul looked at Dick, wondering like he was what the hell was going on. Dick crawled back towards the garage door. He called Paul over. "Mate, the only way we can get in there is to cause some sort of distraction."

Paul said, "Like what?"

Dick said, "I can hot-wire the Range Rover and ram the garage door, then we fight our way down to the girls."

Paul said, "Or we could just set fire to it, they'd have to come out then."

Dick said, "The BMW would be better, it's petrol not diesel. We need some matches."

Paul produced a lighter. "Always carry a lighter with me for emergencies."

Dick said, "Another chat-up line more likely. Do you want a light, love?"

"Got it," said Paul.

Dick went to the rear of the BMW and crawled under the back end. He said, "There's a small rubber pipe to the tank, if I pull that off there should be enough petrol come out to wet my hanky."

He found the pipe, pulled it off and soaked his hanky, wrapping it back around the rubber pipe. "Pass me the lighter. And stand back."

Paul passed his lighter over. Dick moved as far away from the petrol-soaked hanky as he could, then aimed the lighter at it. It caught first time as Dick rolled away. They went to the far side of the garage, as the rear of the car started to blaze. Very quickly, a tyre blew with the heat.

Down below, Bob said, “What’s that?” He could see something flickering through the oblong windows. “Nip up and see what’s going off, Joe.”

Joe went up to the garage level and opened the door to see the BMW on fire. He went to the Range Rover, moving it away to a safer distance. As he did that, Paul and Dick ran into the garage hiding behind what looked like some sailing equipment.

Joe ran back to the open door at the back of the garage, and shouted, “The BMW’s on fire, Bob!”

Bob said, “Looks like your cop friends are around. Have you seen anyone Joe?” he shouted.

“Not a sign of them,” Joe replied. “I can hear sirens, someone must have called the fire brigade.”

“OK,” said Bob. “Leave them down here, they aren’t going anywhere. Better sort the fire brigade out first.”

Both men went out through the garage door, lowering it behind them.

Paul and Dick made their way to the door at the back of the garage and down the ramp to the lower floor. The girls gasped when they saw them. Dick said, “Right girls, let’s get you out of here, quietly does it.”

They freed the girls and started to make their way back up. Julie had picked the sports holdall up as she passed it. “Will explain later,” she said.

Up in the garage, Dick said, “Right when that door opens, and I give the signal, we run like hell to the gate. Meantime, duck down behind this gear.”

They got behind the sailing equipment and waited.

A short time later, the door slid open. Bob and Joe came in and stood watching the fire brigade finishing off. They turned to the back of the garage. As they got to the back door, the garage door started to close.

“Now,” Dick hissed.

They all ran out. "Quick, into the Range Rover. The keys are still in it."

They all piled in, Dick gunned the engine, rammed the stick in drive, and floored it, throwing up a shower of gravel and startling the fire men.

The garage door was opening again. Bob and Joe came running out. "Shut the gate, Joe."

Joe fumbled with the electronic gate opener as the Range Rover raced down the drive. Dick shouted, "Hang on everyone!" The gates were starting to close, but one side slower than the other. Dick raced through with millimetres to spare, tyres screaming as they hit the tarmac.

Paul said, "Back to my place, then I think some explaining needs to be done and phone calls made."

They drove back to Los Boliches and into the secure underground car park beneath Paul's building, locking the Range Rover up next to a lift.

"In here folks, it's my car park lift."

"Two lifts, eh?" grinned Dick.

"Don't worry, once we are upstairs you can lock the lifts from the apartment. No one can get to the apartment without using one of them, unless you've got a 100-foot ladder, or more."

Upstairs Paul got them all a drink. "Now girls, what's gone off?"

Julie looked at her sister, at Dick, then Paul. "Well I started it really I suppose. You know that I got a lift to London with that Guy bloke. Well when we got back after taking the hire car back, he had that phone call from that woman. He had to nip out and see her."

"You mean Hannah."

"Yes, then you called round, Paul. Well he had to nip out again after that and had asked me to pick him up; we were going for a meal. When he rang to tell me to pick him up, he told me the car keys were in the cloakroom. When I went to get them, I stumbled on this sport bag. I saw it was full of money."

"And you took it?" Paul said.

"I couldn't resist it. He had no idea who I was, where I lived. And shortly afterwards he was killed in that accident. Which, after what was said tonight, I don't think was an accident."

"Start at the beginning? What's gone off tonight then?" Dick asked.

Alice said, "We were sat at the small bar on the pavement of our apartment. A white minibus pulled up and a man – that one called Joe – got out, telling us you had sent them to pick us up, because of what had happened to us this afternoon."

"How did they know about that?" Dick asked.

"Well," said Julie, "when we were tied up they almost admitted it was them, they had tampered with the brakes. Then the one called Bob sent Joe off to search our apartment where he found the money. When he came back with it, Bob was asking me about it. I asked him if they had done that security depot in Nottingham and shot the policeman. Bob said he knew about it, and the person who shot the policeman had been dealt with."

"In what way? Did he say?" asked Paul.

"No. I asked him about Guy, he just said, accidents do happen."

"Sounds like this is your team, Dick. You'd better ring it in," said Paul.

Julie said, "Can you keep it quiet about me taking the money? Say Guy gave it to me?"

Dick said, "Not true though, is it?"

"Only a small fib."

Paul said, "You are staying here tonight, take the rooms on the right, one each or share. You will be perfectly safe."

Alice and Julie decided to share for the night and turned in, taking the holdall with them. “Safe keeping,” Julie said.

CHAPTER 29

Back at the villa, Bob and Joe were deciding what to do. Bob said, "Well from a well-planned job to rat shit in a few easy steps. They'll know everything now. That fucker Jerry shooting the cop, Guy's accident. Tampering with the brakes. First time in my life I'm just about stumped. Hang on though, just thought, we could use the boat."

"What boat?" Joe asked.

"It's a sixty-footer, ocean-going. It's moored at Benalmadena marina, just up the road."

"Why didn't you mention it earlier? Let's go."

In half an hour they had got all they needed packed into the minibus. They locked and bolted and set the alarms at the villa. They got to the marina in about half an hour, they loaded their stuff onto the boat, Bob drove the minibus onto a piece of wasteland and left it with the keys in. He suspected it would be gone by morning.

He got back to the boat, around them one or two parties going on, but not near their boat. Bob said, "Unfortunately we can't sail out until 8am, the authorities are very strict on that. No night-time sailings."

Joe said, "What's the earliest we can sail then?"

"Not before 8am at the earliest. We can be ready for then. We might as well get comfortable. I have one or two things to sort out before then. You take the front cabin. I'll nip in to let you know what's what before I turn in. Just in case. Everything you need is in there."

Joe found himself in a spacious fitted cabin. Shower facilities, fully stocked bar with snacks. "You certainly keep it well stocked," he shouted back to Bob.

"I knew it would come in handy one day. Chat soon," Bob shouted back.

CHAPTER 30

Back in town, Paul and Dick had discussed, the day's events.

Dick rang the incident room and asked to speak to Supt Dee.

"Dee here, Dick."

"Listen, Boss."

Dick went on to relate what had happened since they had last spoken.

Dee said, "Right, now you listen. I can't get troops out to you, I'm going to ring Belling. He's got more clout than me. Wait for my phone call."

"One more thing, can you get someone to find out where a boat called *The Heist* is moored, and if poss, who owns it. Maybe round here somewhere?"

"Will try. Ring you asap."

Paul said, "What's all that about a boat?"

"Well when we were in the garage, that stuff we were hiding behind looked like sailing equipment to me. There was a picture of a boat, called *The Heist*. Just my copper's nose quivering."

"Well we can't do much now, may as well try and get some rest before your boss rings back."

***

At 2am, Dick was awoken by his phone ringing. "Dick Jones," he answered.

"Dee here Dick, are you awake?"

"Yes."

"Right, arrangements have been made with the Spanish police to raid the villa at 4am your time. You are to liaise down the road with a Captain Sanchez. He speaks good English. I've text you his contact number. In relation to the boat, it's moored at Benalmadena marina, and would you believe, it's registered to Stephanie Henderson."

Dick said, "I've heard that name before."

Dee said, "Yes, She's the local director we called out at the security depot, and get this, she is Bob Teal's sister."

"It gets more mysterious," Dick said.

"It's down to you and Paul to sort that end out now. All I ask is to be careful."

"Will do our best."

Paul had come into the room. Dick said, "Did you catch that?"

"Not all of it."

"Well, arrangements have been made for the Spanish police to raid the villa at 4am our time. Dee wants us to join them there. A Captain Sanchez will be expecting us. That boat I asked about, *The Heist*, is moored at Benalmadena marina, and is registered in the name of Teal's sister. She is a director of the security firm they raided in Nottingham. It's all coming together."

Julie and Alice then came in. "What's happening?" they jointly asked.

Paul explained what arrangements had been made regarding the raid on the villa.

Alice said, "Can we come?"

Paul replied, "The best place for you two, is here, it's safer. We don't know how things are going to turn out."

Dick got on the phone to Captain Sanchez. Whilst he was making arrangements, the girls busied themselves making coffees and sandwiches for them all.

Paul said, "If they aren't at the villa, me and your mate are off straight down to that marina, Captain Sanchez, and his team can catch us up. We've still got the Range Rover downstairs."

Julie approached Dick, put her arms around him, and said, "You will be careful won't you?" She then gave Paul a hug. Alice did the same.

"Just make sure you get the lift back up to this level after we have gone. We'll ring you when we get back," Paul said.

CHAPTER 31

Paul and Dick joined Captain Sanchez and his team on the main road. They all made their way to the villa; the front gates were shut. The team quickly forced them open, half of the team went round the back, a quick radio message from the Captain, front and back doors were smashed open, the teams stormed in. Paul and Dick waited just inside the front door as instructed.

A few moments later, Captain Sanchez came to them. "The villa is empty. They've gone."

Paul said, "Right Captain, finish off what you have to do here then meet us at Benalmadena marina. They have a boat moored there called *The Heist*. They could be on that."

"Please wait. I will leave two men here, the rest of my team will follow you down there."

They went down in convoy, reaching the marina shortly before 5am.

They quickly identified where the boat was moored, as details had been passed onto them.

The team, led by Paul, made their way down the pontoon. They got to within 20 feet of the boat, when security lights came on, blinding them for a few seconds.

"Shit," said Dick. "Keep your eyes open."

They saw a figure come out onto the stern. It was Bob Teal, he had a pistol at his side. "Whose there?" he shouted.

"It's Det Insp Richards and Det Sgt Jones, Bob. We have the Spanish police with us. Give yourselves up."

Bob shouted back, "There's always a way out."

He raised the pistol and shot towards the sound of Paul's voice, missing him by inches.

They heard Bob shout, "Joe, start this fucking boat up, and get us out of here!"

Joe shouted, "She's still tied up!"

Bob shot again and shouted, "Just do it, trust me."

Bob had planned for this and had loosened the ties earlier, enough to be able to get away as he now wanted.

Dick heard the engines start, just as the police started shooting back at the boat, causing Bob to duck down. Dick sprinted towards the boat, past the stern, and leapt onto the front decking, below the raised cabin, where Joe was starting to pull away from the pontoon. The boat gathered speed and headed toward the marina exit to the sea. Both the police and Bob had stopped shooting.

Paul shouted to Captain Sanchez. "Have you got a police launch in the marina?"

"Over on the next pontoon," he shouted back. "But I have no keys for it."

They ran to the next pontoon where the launch was moored. Paul jumped on board. Looking round he saw a toolbox. Opening it up, he took out a screwdriver and rammed it into the slot where the ignition key went. He hoped it would work, like it did on numerous car thefts he had investigated over the years. He pulled the choke out and twisted the screwdriver. The engine coughed and died. He tried again, this time it caught.

"OK Captain, get the ropes untied."

As soon as they were untied, Paul opened the throttle, and headed to the marina entrance. He had Captain Sanchez and three other men on board.

The launch flew across the marina and was soon following *The Heist*, although a couple of hundred yards behind it.

Although a lot smaller than *The Heist,* the launch was a much faster vessel.

Paul shouted to Captain Sanchez, "Get on the radio, see if we can get any air support – police, coastguard, anything."

Out on the open sea, things were a lot choppier than the marina, but the launch handled well. *The Heist* was running without lights, but Paul was able to see it in the moonlight and follow its wake. They were catching it up when Paul saw a flash from the stern and the left-hand windscreen of the launch shattered.

Captain Sanchez and his men returned fire. Paul switched on the overhead search lights, directing them towards *The Heist*, fully illuminating the stern and Bob.

He shouted down, "Be careful, my mate's on board."

Captain Sanchez had joined Paul at the wheel. He said, "There is an old fort out there, they are heading straight for it. They don't light it at night, because no one is supposed to be out in a boat."

Paul said, "Can you handle this thing, keeping it at full throttle, till I tell you different?"

"Yes, I have driven it many times," he replied as he took control.

Paul looked round the cabin and saw a loud hailer clipped to the cabin wall.

Picking it off, he went to the side of the boat, out of the firing line.

CHAPTER 32

On board *The Heist,* Dick had stayed still. They didn't know he was on board. He quietly made his way round to the stern of the boat and saw Bob, shielding his eyes, illuminated by the searchlights, from the fast-approaching launch shooting at it. Realising it was help, he looked round the deck. There were some ropes and what looked like a canopy with poles lying beside it. He pulled a pole out and went for Bob. At the last minute, Bob swung round. Dick put his full force in the swing, hitting him sideways, pushing him backwards. Dick continued his charge, pushing Bob off his feet. He fell into the small rubber dinghy attached to the boat. Dick grabbed the release lever, causing the dinghy to fall off its holder into the sea.

Knowing that Bob was no longer a threat to him, he made his way to the steps leading up to the cabin where Joe was. He got his head over the top step when Joe turned round and saw him. He left the controls and came at Dick, swinging his foot out to kick him off. Dick saw it coming, moving his head sideways; it was a glancing blow. Joe then went to step on his hands. As he did, Dick grabbed his ankle with his right hand, letting go of the stair rail, and put his left hand round the same ankle. With his full weight pulling him down, Joe was trying to hang onto the handrail and kick out at Dick with his free foot. Dick felt the deck beneath him and threw his whole weight backwards, causing Joe to lose his grip. Dick twisted his body as Joe hit the deck. Dick was on his feet first. He dived at Joe with both knees, crashing into his chest. Winded for a second, Joe automatically punched out, catching Dick in his chest, causing him to go backwards towards the stern. Joe followed up, smashing Dick against the dinghy stanchion. Dick grabbed the stanchion, swinging himself round on it. Bringing both feet up, he kicked Joe fully in the chest, causing him to stagger backwards. He followed up with a full punch to his jaw, sending Joe backwards into the mouth of the cabin.

He heard another noise, and turning round saw that the following launch was nearly alongside them. Paul was shouting through a megaphone, "Dick, jump, jump!"

Dick looked back at him, not quite understanding. Again Paul shouted, "Just jump!"

Dick went to the other side of the deck, hearing Paul still shouting "Jump, jump!" and leaping over the side, the sea smashing his breath away.

As he came to the surface, the launch had slowed right down. He could hear *The Heist* still roaring away. A few moments later there was a terrific explosion and he saw the boat illuminated in a huge fire ball.

"Fucking hell," he muttered.

The launch pulled alongside him. Paul put out his hand to help him aboard. "Enjoy your morning swim then?"

"Yes, I must not do it again sometime soon," he replied. "Did you get Teal?"

"We only just missed hitting his dinghy, but there's nowhere for him to go. Let's see if there's any sign of Joe."

"What did it hit, do you know?"

Captain Sanchez said, "There's an old wartime fort out there. They don't light it up at night, because we don't allow night-time sailing. Big boats are further out."

A coast guard helicopter had been scrambled, and was searching the wreckage area.

"I don't think he will have got out of that," said Dick.

There was plenty of debris, but no sign of Joe.

"OK, let's go back for Teal," said Paul.

Captain Sanchez turned the launch round and headed back. In the glare of the searchlights, they eventually found the dinghy. When they reached it, it was empty.

"Where the fuck's he gone then?" said Dick.

They turned the searchlights out onto the sea.

"He can't have gone far, surely," said Paul. "Captain, ask the chopper if they can see anything."

The Captain relayed the request then turned to Paul and said, "The pilot says it was empty when they flew over it, he didn't see anyone. The tide is on its way in. We'll do a sweep, see if we can spot him."

"OK," said Paul. "Get that dinghy on board. It's getting lighter now, keep your eyes peeled."

Dick went down below and found some dry clothes, not a perfect fit, but dry.

He went back on deck, "Any joy yet, Paul?"

"No, nothing. I think you ought to speak to your tailor though. Shocking fit."

They carried on searching for another hour but could find no trace.

"OK folks," said Paul. "Let's get back. Looks like they've both gone then."

"Hope so," replied Dick.

Getting back to the marina, they thanked Captain Sanchez and his team for their help, and promised to keep him informed of any further developments. Captain Sanchez assured them that he and his team were available if needed.

CHAPTER 33

Paul and Dick got back to the apartment, ringing the girls to send the basement lift down.

Once upstairs, Julie asked, "How did it go?"

"Get us some coffee first. Please," Paul asked.

Alice did toast and coffee, taking it out to the roof top sitting area.

"Right, now tell us what's gone off," Julie said.

Between them, Paul and Dick, told the girls the full story. From the search of the villa, the marina and the boat chase.

Julie said, "So they've both gone then?"

"Looks like it. We couldn't find any trace of either of them," Dick said.

"I'd better ring the incident room and give Dee the update."

Getting through, Dee said, "Good to hear from you. Are you both safe?"

"Yes thanks. A bit of a hectic night though."

Dick related all that had gone off over the last few hours.

When he finished, Dee said, "Sounds like you had some fun out there. Let me tell you where we are up at this end. We have done a full search of the cottage. The SOCO teams found some traces of blood inside. Not sure if it's human or not. They did a search of the garden, and a dog took them to a disused well. We are in the process of trying to excavate it. They think there's something decaying down there by the smell of it. That's still ongoing."

"What about Teal's sister, anything from her?"

"We arrested her before you did the raid on the villa in case Teal contacted her. She will be interviewed later this morning. I've also spoken to the CEO of the security company, and it appears three of their depots have been raided over the years, all undetected, all different MOs. Looks like your girls could be in for the reward money."

By this time, Paul and the two girls had come inside and were listening to Dick's side of the conversation. "Just a minute Boss, let me put you on speaker, so you can tell them." Looking at the girls, he switched the speaker on, then said, "Oh, one other thing, we recovered a holdall from the boot of a Range Rover, it had £100,000 in it."

The girls gasped. "They are here now Boss."

Dee said, "Good morning to you all. I was just telling Dick that you girls are in line for the reward money from the security firm. Congratulations. You did well under pressure."

"Thanks Boss. Can you update us later, on things?"

"Will do. Once again, well done out there."

The girls looked at each other, then at Paul and Dick.

"Wow, is that right? We get the reward money?" Julie asked.

"You heard what the boss said."

CHAPTER 34

A few miles away, in a deserted cove, two dishevelled men sat next to each other.

"That was close," said Bob.

"Too close," said Joe. "Good job you planned things out."

Bob had put scuba tanks and flippers under cover in the dinghy, and put a set just inside the cabin door.

After he had been set adrift in the dinghy, he had waited, knowing the launch would continue the chase on *The Heist*, then put the scuba tanks on and set a point to the shore.

As Joe had been knocked into the cabin, he had grabbed the set there and jumped overboard, seconds before the boat had hit the fort. He had gone deep clutching the tanks to him, fitting the mouthpiece in as he dropped. He had got the set on under water and headed for the same point on the shore.

"Did you know that fort was there?" Joe asked.

"I'd seen it a couple of times," Bob replied.

"Had you planned to crash into it?" Joe asked.

"Joe. You have always got to have a plan B."

Joe looked at him.

Bob said, "Come on Joe, let's get this gear up the beach to the car, it's up there. And anything else we might need is with it."

Joe said, “What about Stephanie? Are you worried about her?”

“Not at all. She doesn’t know anything. Trust me.”

“I do,” Joe said.

EPILOGUE

The conclusion of the enquiry was as follows.

At the cottage in Derbyshire, the well had been fully excavated and human remains found, along with masks, gloves, gas bottles, a couple of shotguns and a pistol.

Forensics had been able to identify the human remains as Jerry Morton, and had established the fact he had been shot whilst in the cottage.

DNA and fingerprints on some of the recovered items were matched to Jerry Morton, Guy Salmon, Bob Teal and Joe Andrews.

DNA and prints from the cottage were matched to DNA and prints from the villa, again to Bob Teal and Joe Andrews.

It was also established that the double-barrelled shotgun was the one that had been used to shoot Sgt Peters. Fingerprints and DNA had put that shotgun to Jerry Morton.

The single-barrelled shotgun had been used to shoot Jerry Morton. Again, fingerprints and DNA had put that one to Bob Teal. There were no identifying marks on them to say where they had originated from.

In relation to the hit and run on Hannah Bell, they were able to establish that it was, in fact, Guy Salmon's van that had been used. Why, they didn't know. There was no evidence in relation to Guy Salmon's accident on the motorway, other than a tyre blow out may have caused it. The blaze had destroyed any potential evidence to prove otherwise.

Teal Investments and his other companies had been wound down over the past year and sold off to other companies. The only property not known to the police was Bob Teal's flat in Park Lane. He had covered his tracks well with that. No address was ever found for Joe Andrews.

CCTV had shown all the vehicles used by the gang were in and around the Nottingham and Derbyshire areas over the Christmas period.

In relation to Stephanie Henderson, Teal's sister, after a thorough investigation into her background and relationship with her brother, there was no evidence to connect her to any wrongdoing. She was totally unaware of the boat in Spain being registered to her. In fact, she informed the police enquiry team that a week before the robbery she had received deeds for full ownership of the villa in Spain, which had been purchased ten years earlier in her name. She had also been sent all the keys and electronic entry keys. She knew nothing about that either. She was allowed to keep it.

Her brother had certainly covered his dealings well.

The security firm had allowed her to leave the company on a redundancy package, without a stain on her character.

There was no evidence found to link this gang with any other offences, nor to any inside help at this stage.

The security firm had agreed to pay the reward money to Julie and Alice for the Nottingham robbery.

No trace of Bob Teal or Joe Andrews had been found.

Dick had been promoted to Detective Inspector, Paul to Detective Chief Inspector.

Both had since married, Julie to Dick, Alice to Paul in a double wedding.

BOOK ONE

HEIST

PART TWO

FIVE YEARS LATER

CHAPTER 1

2013

The phone on newly promoted Detective Chief Inspector Dick Jones' desk rang.

"DCI Jones," he answered.

"Dick, it's Dee here. Can you come up to my office? Someone here I want you to meet."

"On my way, Boss."

Dick made his way up to the next floor at Trent Station. The door to the office was ajar. Dick knocked and walked in.

Dee was sat behind his desk; occupying another two seats was a man and woman. Both looking quite tanned and well dressed.

"Dick," said Dee. "This is Detective Superintendent Michael Broad and Detective Chief Inspector Christine Porter. Both are with Interpol."

Dick shook hands with them both, saying, "Nice to meet you. What brings Interpol, to Nottingham?"

Broad replied, "Take a look at these photos. Tell us if you recognise any of the two men."

He was handed a photo of two men with full facial beards, dressed in boiler suits.

Dick handed the photo back, saying, "Not off hand, why?"

Broad said, "Look at this one. We have digitised this one to show what we think they would look like without their beards."

Again, Dick looked at the photo he was handed.

"No, sorry, can't help with that either. Do you know who they are?" he asked.

Porter said, "We think one is named Bob Teal, the other is named Joe Andrews."

Dick picked the two photos up again.

Shaking his head, he said, "Well if it is them, they both look completely different. What makes you think it's them though? They were presumed dead in Spain, five years ago. We never found any bodies."

Broad said, "That's what everybody thought. These photos are from a CCTV camera, in a jeweller's shop in France."

Pointing to the two men in boiler suits, he said, "About two months ago, it was broken into over one night. The alarms and CCTV were disabled, and the security on the safe was bypassed and opened. Jewellery, to a value of approximately four million euros was stolen. The owners didn't know a thing until they opened the safe the next day for business."

"Wow," said Dick. "How have you linked it to Teal and Andrews, then?"

Broad said, "A car was abandoned about a hundred kilometres away. It had been stolen a week earlier, from the same area as the jeweller's shop. Although they had disarmed the shop CCTV, other CCTV nearby was able to pick up the two men, and at the same time, the car. The local police got a DNA match off the car, which matched to Bob Teal. We are only assuming, very strongly, the other man is Joe Andrews."

Dick looked at Dee, and said, "Well, bugger us Boss. All this time and they have raised their ugly heads again. Wait until I tell my brother-in-law in the Met. He won't believe it."

Porter said, "We have already spoken to Superintendent Richards. We asked him not to speak to you about it until we had spoken to you and Chief Superintendent Dee."

Dick looked at the two Interpol officers and Dee. "So what happens now?"

Dee said, "Well it looks like they altered their features, but you can't alter DNA. I have spoken to the Chief Constable. He has authorised your temporary attachment to the Interpol office, to help out in any way you can. Paul has also been attached from the Met. These two men are involved in the robbery which led to the murder of Sergeant Peters. They need bringing to justice. They are the only two involved who are still alive."

Dick said, "Thank you sir. It will be my pleasure. These two men are the most dangerous men I have ever met. What was Paul's reaction?"

Porter said, "Much the same as yours. He can't wait to get stuck in. We'll all meet at our office, day after tomorrow, to form some plan of action. Mr Dee has all the details. Welcome aboard Dick."

Dee said, "I suggest you get your staff sorted out here, you could be away for a while."

Dick stood up, shaking hands with Broad then Porter. "See you in London, then."

CHAPTER 2

FIVE YEARS EARLIER

Bob and Joe had made their way up off the beach to a blue Fiat estate car. Putting their scuba gear in the back, they changed into some dry clothes. They drove to a small private airstrip where they boarded a light aircraft, flying them to Tunisia. From there, they boarded an international flight to the Cayman Islands, both using false passports.

Once in the Cayman Islands, they settled into the villa Bob owned, and over the next two years they had both undergone extensive cosmetic surgery to their faces, completely altering their features. Once that was done, they had both grown full beards. Their own mothers wouldn't have recognised them. Bob had even flown to the UK to finalise the sale of his flat on Park Lane. He had used a false passport, with a new identity. He had recovered all his papers and documents from the safe, lodging them in a safety deposit box at a London bank, along with some cash and a revolver, before flying back to the Cayman Islands without any problems.

CHAPTER 3

2013

Dick was on the phone talking to Paul when Julie walked in. When he had finished talking and put the phone down, Julie said, "So you are going to London then?"

Dick explained what had happened, and his temporary attachment to Interpol, along with Paul.

"Why don't you come down with me? You can have a few days with Alice while we get sorted out?"

Julie said, "Yes. Don't see why not."

***

Two days later, Paul and Dick were sat in a meeting with Broad and Porter at the Interpol office in London.

Dick said, "So how far have we got then, since we last spoke?"

Broad said, "We have had our facial recognition cameras checking at all French air and seaports. Nothing has been picked up at all. They seem to have got away without going through any of them."

Paul said, "Let's remember though, they have full beards or are digitised. Not easy to pick out, especially if they've shaved them off. Have you tried Spanish airports, seaports, border crossings?"

Porter said, "No, why?"

"That's where they were last seen and obviously escaped from. Teal had a villa down there at Los Boliches. His sister has now got it, just a thought."

"Worth a try," said Broad. "They could have driven down."

Paul said, "We had a contact down there, he was with us when they went missing. Let me speak to Captain Sanchez. See what they can do for us."

Broad said, "OK Paul. That's your first job."

Dick said, "If I remember right, I'm certain that Teal had something to do with the Cayman Islands, an office there or something. It's niggling me."

"OK, Dick. That's your first job then," Broad said. "When you have made your contacts, forward them copies of our photos."

Paul said, "Another thing. When they left England five years ago, they drove to somewhere in Belgium. They flew to Spain from there. Might be worth a check there, as well."

"Christine, get all the details from Paul, see if that throws anything up."

Paul said, "Can I suggest a phone tap on the villa?"

Broad said, "If you can get your Captain Sanchez to sort it, let's go for it. I'll speak to our Interpol office down there and put them in the picture."

Nothing else was thrown into the mix.

Broad said, "OK, let's see what we can get."

CHAPTER 4

In an expensive lakeside restaurant in Geneva, Bob Teal and Joe Andrews were just finishing their meal off when Bob's phone rang.

"Hello," he said.

"Hello. It's me, Petr. I've just got rid of all the jewellery, can we meet?"

"Petr, come to the Boulevard Restaurant, lakeside. We'll meet you there."

"Be about an hour," came the reply.

Joe asked, "He got it all sorted then?"

Bob said, "The best in the business."

Bob had previously arranged a meeting in Switzerland for Petr to get rid of the jewellery stolen in France.

Petr was punctual to the second. The men shook hands.

"Drink Petr?" asked Bob.

"Just a small one. You know what the police are like here for drink driving."

Bob poured him a small glass of red wine.

"You managed to get rid of it all then?"

"No problems. It amounted to two and three quarter million euro. The money is transferred already if you would like to check. I have taken a quarter of a million euro, if that's OK."

Bob said, "Fine. Many thanks."

Petr said, "I have also heard, through a good contact

of mine, that the police have photos of the two men from the jewellery shop. They have also identified one of you."

"How come?" asked Joe, leaning in towards Petr.

"I heard they had found some DNA or something on a stolen car. It showed up to you Bob. Interpol are now looking into it, and have started enquiries with the British police to try and trace you. There is also talk of a large reward."

Bob said, "Well since that job, we've shaved our beards off, so the photos will be no good. I suggest we stay here for a bit longer. When are you leaving Petr?"

"Another couple of days."

"Well stay in touch and stay in touch with that contact. We need to know as much as we can."

When Petr had left, Bob said, "I hate to say this, my friend, but I feel Petr may have to go. What do you think?"

Joe said, "Well, he is your contact, you know more about him than I do. But he is the only person who now knows what we look like."

"He is that, and then talk of a large reward. It only takes a phone call."

Bob sat back, took a drink and said, "I think we ought to invite him out on a short cruise tomorrow."

The next day, Bob rang Petr. "Petr, we are going for a cruise on the lake. Would you join us?"

Petr said, "It's not rough is it, only I can't swim."

"It's a lake, not a sea," Bob replied. "Meet us just at the end of the marina, half an hour."

They picked Petr up as planned. Although sunny, it was still a sweater day, with a slight wind as they got further onto the lake.

Bob got them drinks and sat on the back deck with Petr, whilst Joe steered.

"Any more news Petr?" he asked.

"Not really, I have found out that the British police are called Jones and Richards, the Interpol are called Broad and Porter. That's all I know."

Bob said, "We know the Brit cops. We had dealings with them in Spain. Let's enjoy our day. I thought we would cruise up to Nyon, have a bite to eat on the boat, then cruise across the lake to Evian."

About an hour later, they sat on the back deck eating fresh lobster with a salad. A nice chilled Chablis was doing the rounds.

"More wine, Petr?" Bob asked.

"I'll have to go easy, I'm not really a good sailor."

"It's not rough, the winds picked up a bit, but you'll be OK. When we finish eating, we are going over there, to that point. Where the red-roofed buildings are," Bob said, pointing across the lake.

They finished eating and Joe set a course across the lake towards Evian.

Petr and Bob stood side by side on the deck, Bob had his left arm around his shoulder, pointing out different aspects they could see across the lake. When they were about halfway across, Bob signalled to Joe to slow down slightly.

Bob said, "That's where you are going Petr."

Before he could do anything, Bob put his right hand onto Petr's waistband and hoisted him over the side. There was just time for a muffled scream as he hit the water. He bobbed back up, spitting water out, shouting, "I can't swim, I can't swim!" He went under again. As he came back up, Bob pushed him back under with a long boat hook. As he tried to surface again, he pushed him back under. He didn't come back up.

Bob went to join Joe at the wheel. "Just hang on a bit, see if he comes back up anywhere."

They waited another 15 minutes.

Bob said, "OK, slow cruise back. I think we ought to think about getting out in the next day or two."

***

The following day, they were sat at a lakeside bar near the marina when they saw the police launch coming in and moor up. As they watched, an ambulance pulled up nearby. The officers on the launch stepped aside as the ambulance crew went on board with a stretcher. A few moments later, the ambulance crew came off the launch with a loaded stretcher, loaded it into their vehicle and drove off, for some reason, sirens blaring.

Bob said, "Looks like they found him then."

CHAPTER 5

Back in London, the team were meeting up.

Broad said, "So what updates have we got? Christine, you go first."

Porter said, "I've checked Belgian airports and ports against their facial recognition system. Not picked anything up at all. But whilst I was talking to them, they mentioned that a Belgian national, a Petr Aughty, had been found drowned in the lake in Geneva. He is... was known to them as a money launderer and handler of stolen goods, but never enough evidence to convict."

Broad said, "Christine, get a photo of the drowned man to our office in Switzerland. Get them to put a press appeal out, see if anybody recognises him. Who he was seen with. Get them to flash all the photos about, hotels, restaurants, bars. Get them to do a bit of legwork on our behalf. Paul, get your man Sanchez to call at the villa, see who's there, have they heard anything from Teal. That might stir something up."

CHAPTER 6

Two days later, Bob and Joe sat talking at the lakeside restaurant.

Bob said, "I need to get back to London for a couple of days, empty my safety deposit box out altogether. I think my planning days are over for the time being. Do you want to come with me, or get back to the Cayman Islands?"

"When are you going?"

"Monday, I think. That gives us a couple of more days here, then to London, then back to the Cayman Islands for next weekend."

"OK then, but only for a couple of days, then I'm off back, with or without you. What passports are we using?"

"Not the ones we used to get here, I've a couple of new ones in my room, and some in the deposit box in London. I need to shift some money from here, back to Cayman anyway. It's easier from here than the UK, less questions asked."

As Bob finished talking, he touched Joe's side and indicated to the door of the restaurant where two men had just walked in.

Bob said, "Look like cops to me."

As they watched, the two men approached the manager and began to show him some paperwork. The manager shook his head. They must have said something else to him, as he spread his hands out and said, "Certainly."

The two men split up and began talking to other customers sat at tables.

Eventually one of the men came to Bob and Joe's table and introduced himself as a police officer. In perfect English he said, "Sorry to bother you gentlemen, but could I have a minute of your time please?"

Bob said, "How can we help officer?"

"You are English. I thought you were. Can I ask you to look at these photos and tell me if you have seen these men, or recognise them?"

The first picture was of two bearded men dressed in overalls, from the jeweller's shop.

Bob said, "Not known to me." Passing it to Joe, "Do you know them?"

Joe shook his head, "No."

He then showed them a digitised photo, saying, "This is what we think they look like without their beards." Thankfully it looked nothing like them.

Bob said, "No, sorry officer." Joe shook his head.

The officer then showed them a picture of Petr, obviously taken after his death.

Bob said, "Who is that then, officer?"

He replied, "He was found floating in the lake a couple of days ago. We are trying to identify him."

"Sorry officer, I don't recognise any of them," said Bob.

"Me neither," said Joe.

"Well thank you for your time." He moved away to another table.

Out of earshot, Bob said, "So Petr's informant was spot on. Though they'll struggle with them photos I reckon."

The police officers were still doing the rounds, when the second one approached their table. "Sorry to bother you gentlemen again. I know my colleague has already spoken to you, but a customer I have spoken to says he thought he saw you in here three nights ago, with this gentleman." He showed them the photo of Petr.

Bob said, "I think he's mistaken officer. What night are you talking about?"

"Three nights ago, early evening."

Bob said, "No I think we ate at the hotel that night. In fact, I may have the receipt in my wallet." Bob went into his wallet. "There you are, three nights ago. I keep receipts for expense purposes."

The officer examined the receipt, handing it back to Bob saying, "You are staying at the Grand Metropolitan Hotel, gentlemen?"

Bob said, "Yes."

"So sorry to have bothered you, enjoy your stay."

Out of hearing, Joe said, "Where did that come from?"

Bob replied, "It was on the floor outside my room. Someone must have treated themselves. I now think we should be on our way out of here altogether. I'll do the banking stuff in the morning, first thing, then we fly out. If the cops want us, they'll think we are at the Grand."

Back at their hotel, flights were booked for 11am next morning, to London.

CHAPTER 7

Arriving in London the next day, Bob and Joe caught a taxi to a small boutique hotel, off Bayswater Road, just off Hyde Park. They had adjoining rooms, with an internal door. Once in the rooms, Bob said, "I've arranged to clear my deposit box later this afternoon. Anything you need before we fly back?"

Joe said, "I might have a wander round, do a bit of shopping, that's all."

"OK. I'll ring you when I've done, meet up for a coffee somewhere."

They headed into the City and went their separate ways.

About an hour later, Joe was walking down Oxford Street, doing some window shopping, when he heard a couple of familiar voices behind him. Turning round, he saw Julie and Alice, arm in arm, chattering away as they did so, passing him without a second glance.

He decided to follow them. A few minutes later his phone rang. "Joe, it's Bob. I've finished at the bank. Where are you?"

"Would you believe it. I am on Oxford Street, following them two bitches from Spain."

"Have they seen you?"

"Didn't even give me a second glance when they passed me. Hang on, they've just gone into a coffee shop opposite Oxford Circus underground station."

"Be careful, I'm on my way. Meet me across the road."

Ten minutes later, Bob climbed out of a taxi, clutching his briefcase, joining Joe.

"Are they still inside?" he asked.

"Yes, they went upstairs."

Bob said, "I'd like to cause them some grief, but that might put us in the spotlight. Let's go in, I could do with a coffee."

They found a table at the back, which gave them a good view of the stairs and the front door.

Joe said, "I think we should cut and run, get out of here."

"I agree, but they still deserve some grief."

As they sat talking, they heard the girls talking as they came downstairs, paid their bill and left.

Bob paid their bill, and as they left the coffee shop, saw the girls walking into Oxford Street underground station.

"C'mon, see where they go," Bob said, crossing the road to follow them.

They followed them down the escalators, towards platform one.

Bob said, "Right, when the train comes, as they move closer to it, you shove Alice, I shove Julie. Then we walk calmly away and out. Keep your face down."

They hung back until they heard, then saw the light of the approaching train. Julie and Alice picked their shopping up and began to move towards the edge of the platform. Joe shoved Alice, Bob shoved Julie towards the tracks, then both turned and walked calmly away.

The girls screamed out loud, causing passengers to look to see what was happening. Other passengers began screaming. The next noise was the screaming of the brakes on the train, along with the blare of its horn as the driver struggled to stop it. All hell seemed to have broken loose. The train was getting nearer, people turned away, not wanting to see what was going to happen. Then the noise stopped, as the train stopped feet away from the girls, who were still screaming.

A platform guard was on his radio, yelling to his control room, "Turn the power off on line one, persons on the line!" Jumping down onto the track, he shouted at the girls, "Stay where you are, don't move, just don't move."

Again he shouted into his radio, "Turn the power off on line one. Persons on the line, send help!"

Help quickly arrived, in the form of station staff and the police. The girls were carefully handled back onto the platform, and their shopping bags retrieved from the line. They were taken to the police office, where Inspector Johnson greeted them both with hot sweet tea. Wrapping blankets around them, he asked, "What happened out there?"

Alice said, "I felt I was pushed. Can you contact our husbands please? They are with the Met Police."

Julie said, "I was definitely pushed, no doubt about that."

Inspector Johnson rang the number given. A voice answered, "Supt Paul Richards."

"Hello sir, it's Inspector Johnson from the British Transport Police at Oxford Street underground station. Is Mr Jones with you?"

"DCI Jones is with me, yes. What's wrong?"

"I'll put you wife on sir."

"Paul, can you both come and collect us down here straight away. Someone pushed us onto the line in front of a train. Come and pick us up," Alice begged.

"On our way, stay calm love."

Paul put his phone down, grabbed his coat, shouting at Dick, "Come on mate, someone pushed the girls onto the tracks at Oxford underground, Come on!"

Both men rushed from the office. Broad shouted after them, "We'll join you down there!"

With his siren blaring, Paul quickly got them to Oxford Street underground, where they were met by a uniformed sergeant, who took them to the main police office. Alice and Julie rushed to meet them, clinging on very tightly. Both were in tears.

Broad and Porter had now arrived, introducing themselves to Inspector Johnson. Broad asked, "What happened? Do you know?"

"Well sir, it looks like they were deliberately pushed onto the track in front of an arriving train. Fortunately the driver is quite new and came in slower than normal. He saw the ladies fall and slammed everything on."

"Any witnesses?"

"Plenty of people around. But it happened so quickly, nobody saw them pushed, just heard the screams."

Paul said, "Is that area covered by CCTV, Inspector?"

"It's being checked as we speak, sir. If you would like to follow me, please."

He led them into the office next door where a CCTV operator was running through the incident. He pointed to the screen. "There's the ladies on the platform." It showed Alice and Julie, moving forward as the train came. They then appeared to be pushed forward onto the tracks by two men. The operator pointed the two men out, walking away, back into the station. "Unfortunately, they have their heads down, so not a good image."

Paul, still clutching Alice, looked at Dick and Julie, at Broad and Porter, and said, "Teal and Andrews. It's got to be them. Money on it."

"But they are dead," Alice said.

"We presumed they were. Remember, we never found any bodies?"

Paul turned to the CCTV operator. "Can you try and pick them up in any other part of the station? Coming in or going out?"

The operator scanned the CCTV. "One was carrying a brown briefcase. I think that's him there." He pointed to the screen. "We get our best view of them as they come off the escalator, there look."

Looking at the screen, it showed both men in full face.

Dick said, "They look the same height and build. If it's them, they've altered their looks completely. Can you print copies off please?"

Inspector Johnson said, "Certainly. Do you know them?"

Paul said, "Only if it's who we think it is. Inspector, many thanks to you and your staff for your rapid response. It's much appreciated. Please pass our sincere thanks onto the driver, for his fast reactions. Can I request that you don't publish these pictures until you get our say-so? I realise I can't stop it getting to the media, the way folks use their phones now. But no names please."

"Certainly sir."

They said their goodbyes and left the station.

Outside, Broad said, "Take your wives home. We'll meet at the office tomorrow."

***

Back at Paul and Alice's apartment, having calmed down a bit more, Paul and Dick went through the past few hours, whilst they were out and about, where had they been.

When they had done, and feeling a lot better, Paul said, "I need to speak to Broad."

"Michael, Paul here." He went on to outline what the girls had said. "The last place they went before the tube station was the coffee shop opposite. Remember, they both know Teal and Andrews from Spain. They both feel sure they would have recognised them. This makes us think they have altered their faces, possibly cosmetic surgery somewhere along the line. Can you get CCTV checked in and around the coffee shop area? When that's done, the images, if any, should be put out to airports and ferry ports."

Broad said, "We think along the same lines Paul. How are the girls?"

"Much calmer now, thank you."

Paul stood up, and taking the phone into the hall, said, "Michael, can you ring my boss on my behalf. Tell him what's gone off. I would like it, if possible, to put some covert protection on the apartment for at least a couple of days. The girls will be here on their own, when we come back to the office."

"No problems there, quite understandable. Leave that with me."

"Thanks Michael. We want those bastards now. It's gotten personal."

CHAPTER 8

Back in their hotel, Bob and Joe were eating a takeaway in Joe's room, watching the London news.

The bulletin came on regarding the incident at Oxford Circus underground. The report said that two women had fallen onto the track earlier this afternoon, in the path of an approaching train. British Transport Police praised the quick reaction of the train driver and are investigating the incident. Both women were, shaken, but unhurt.

Bob said, "I'm sure them two fuckers have got nine lives. I'm sure of it."

Joe said, "Personally, I think we should fly out asap."

"I agree. We stop here in the hotel, until our flights back to the Cayman Islands. I'm going to mail some stuff back, rather than risk a customs check."

CHAPTER 9

Next morning, Paul, Dick, Michael and Christine were discussing yesterday's incident.

"How are things this morning?" Porter asked.

"A lot calmer, thank you," replied Dick.

Paul said, "A couple of years ago, as a DCI, I started what we called a hotels' alert scheme. It was to help in the fight against terrorists in the City. We sent photos out of possible suspects to all hotels in the scheme, requesting any sightings. It certainly saved us a lot of footwork, and we got some good results. I got on to Special Branch before I came in here. I've passed them our photos, of the two without beards, and the ones from Oxford Circus yesterday. They have put it down as a priority job. Fingers crossed."

Broad said, "Great idea. Any updates from anybody?"

Porter said, "Our Swiss office reported they questioned a couple of men in a restaurant, after a customer pointed them out, having been shown the photos. The customer told them he thought they were with the dead man, Petr Aught, in the restaurant earlier that week. The men denied all knowledge. On the night they were supposed to have been seen with him, they had eaten at their hotel, The Grand Metropolitan. They produced a receipt showing that. When the officers later visited the hotel, and showed the photos, the manager stated that only non-residents were issued with a receipt. All residents' expenditure, without exception, was added to their final bill. Then a receipt for their stay would be issued, listing expenditure."

Paul said, "Would they be issued with a receipt, as a guest, for checking against their final bill?"

"No. Not a receipt as such. Just a subtotal receipt, as a guest for checking against their final bill. Apart from which, the manager states he knew the majority of staying guests, and the two men did not ring any bells with him, or his staff."

Dick said, "Let's look at the photos again, not the men with the beards, the others."

All were laid out. Comparing them, they all agreed they could not be one hundred per cent matched to each other.

"Just a thought," said Dick.

Broad said, "Well our main concern at this time is identifying those two." He tapped the photos of the two men leaving the underground.

Paul's phone rang. "Paul Richards."

"Special Branch here, guv. On that hotel request. A hotel in Bayswater Road has been on. They reckon the two men are staying there as we speak."

"How certain are they?"

"The manager is one hundred per cent. Adjoining rooms. Been there a couple of days now."

Paul said, "OK. Details and a contact number, please."

He noted the details down, the others watching him.

***

Paul said, "Our photo shot might have worked, I hope. They are in the Grant Hotel, Bayswater Road, near Hyde Park. According to the owner, they are there now."

Broad said, "We need to get a team together."

Dick said, "With respect, we should get straight over there. Get a couple of ARVs to back us up. Get them to meet us there. We move in when they arrive."

That organised, Paul and Dick were in Paul's car, Broad and Porter in their car. Broad put his window down, gave the thumbs up, and shouted, "Two ARVs en route. Will meet us there."

They literally flew out of the car park, getting to the hotel some ten minutes later, as two double-crewed ARVs pulled up. Quickly explaining the situation, they all went into the hotel reception area where they met the owner.

"Where are there rooms?" Dick asked.

The owner replied, "First floor, up the stairs, turn right down the corridor. The last two rooms on the right."

Upstairs, Joe had heard cars pulling up, and doors slamming. Looking out of the window, he saw Paul and Dick with uniformed officers entering the hotel. He went through to Bob's room. "Looks like the police are here. Them two from Spain, and some uniforms."

"Grab your bag, fire escape out back, let's go."

The two men grabbed their packed holdalls, Bob his briefcase. Running out of their doors to the fire escape, which was virtually next door to them. They went through, pulling the door closed behind them. At the bottom of the escape, they ran to the corner of Queensway, flagging a passing taxi down.

Bob said, "Heathrow, quickly, we are running later than we wanted. £200 if you get us there on time."

"On it, guv. Strap in." The taxi pulled away.

Paul and his team had headed up the stairs, the ARV officers leading the way, firearms drawn. Two to a door, they knocked. Getting no reply, they knocked again, shouting, "Management, can you open the door please?"

Again, no reply.

Using the master card key, they opened both doors shouting, "Armed police! Show yourselves!"

Getting no reply again, they cautiously entered the rooms. "Clear here! Clear here!" came the shout from both rooms.

Dick rushed in. "Fuck, missed them."

Looking out of the window, he saw the doors of a taxi closing and pulling away.

He shouted, "Taxi pulling away, could be them. They must have used the fire escape!"

Running back downstairs, passing reception, Paul said to the owner, "No one in those rooms until I say so."

Climbing into Paul's car, they raced round to the junction Dick had seen the taxi at.

Getting onto the radio he said, "Control, I am with Superintendent Richards, Interpol officers and two ARV cars. We are following a white, London-style taxi on to Queensway, off Bayswater Road. It's possibly containing two men wanted for multiple serious crimes. Request backup please."

"Control received. Keep us updated of location."

Dick said, "Contact London taxis. We have lost sight at the moment. See if they can tell us where their white cab is headed."

Paul's phone rang, Dick picked it up. Broad said, "Where are you?"

Dick said, "Queensway, hopefully in the same direction the taxi is going."

Paul shouted, "I think that's them, nearly at the top end."

"Got that," replied Broad, "All behind you."

The taxi was a couple of hundred yards in front of them, nearing the end of Queensway. The driver had just heard his base asking if a white taxi had picked any passengers up in the Bridgwater Road, Queensway area.

Bob heard the message. Leaning forward, he said, "Tell them it's not you." Pressing something cold against the driver's neck he hissed, "Tell them."

"White eight here muscle man. Not me, although in that area," the driver replied.

Unknown to Bob, the term, muscle man meant driver in trouble. At this sign, the taxi firm would activate the tracker on the taxi and inform the police and other taxis.

The taxi firm got back to police control and relayed the message to them. This was in turn, relayed to Paul and the team.

***

In the taxi, Bob said, "Take the next left, driver."

That took them onto Westbourne Grove. "Now next right," Bob said.

The driver did as he was ordered. Pointing to a small car park, Bob said, "In there."

The driver did as he was told. "Stop here," Bob said.

Leaning forward, Bob handed him his £200. As the driver took it, Bob knocked him unconscious.

Leaving the taxi where it was, the two men walked round the corner onto Porchester Road, flagging another taxi down. "Where to mate?" asked the driver.

"Park Lane please," replied Bob. "Bottom end, Queen Elizabeth Gate will be fine, thanks."

Sitting back, Bob said, "Let them sort that out."

A short time later, Paul and his team had found the white taxi and the unconscious driver. Paul got on to his control room, updating them and requesting an ambulance and police presence.

"Dick, get on to taxi control, see if they can find a pickup here in the last few minutes."

Paul, in the meantime, was talking to the team.

Dick joined them. "Not picked up by their control. Could be any one of a number of firms."

"Fuck," said Paul.

He got on to police control and, speaking to the inspector in charge, he explained the situation. Looking at his team at the same time, he asked, "Have you got photos of the two suspects from an incident at Oxford Circus underground station, where two women were pushed onto the tracks? You have, good. I need you to put them straight out to all your media contacts, Facebook, whatever. I only want sighting please. These men are not to be approached. They are dangerous. Can you do that?"

"Will do, straight on it," replied the inspector.

Paul said, "Can't do much more now, until we get something back."

***

The taxi Bob and Joe were in, reached their destination about 15 minutes later, at Queen Elizabeth Gate. They paid the driver off and walked away.

The driver remained parked up waiting for his next fare. Contacting his base telling them he was free, his phoned pinged, telling him he had a message. Checking his phone, it was a Facebook message. He looked at it and realised the two faces he was looking at were the two who had just left his taxi. He contacted his base to report the matter, and was told to stay where he was, they would pass his sighting on. The driver, being an ex-marine, had other ideas. He stuck a notice on the dashboard – 'Taxi broken down'. He put on his big coat and baseball cap and left his taxi to follow the two men. He plugged his phone into his ears and rang 999.

Getting through, he explained to the controller what he was doing. The control room inspector came on. He advised him not to get into any confrontation with the two men.

The driver said, “I’ll be OK. I was in the Marines. I did this sort of thing for a living at times. Just get your troops organised.”

The inspector replied, “We’ll keep this line open. Keep us updated!”

The driver was about 150 yards back from Bob and Joe, relaying the route to the control room.

Paul and his team were linked into the control room conversation.

“Where are they now?” he asked.

Control came back, “Our informant says they have gone onto Constitution Hill, towards Queen Victoria Memorial.”

“Descriptions please, of the two men and our informant?”

“Two white males, both about six foot tall. Very similar build. One man carrying a brown briefcase and a blue holdall. He has a grey three-quarter length coat, dark trousers. The other, a similar coat, but beige colour, brown trousers and carrying a brown holdall. Both still on Constitution Hill. Our informant is wearing a black Puffa jacket, blue jeans and a dark baseball cap. He is about 100 yards behind them now.”

“Thanks,” said Paul. “Did you get that team?”

Confirmation came from the team.

Paul said, “I want one ARV to the Queen Victoria Memorial, the other to follow us from the Arch end. It’s wide open so let’s be careful.”

Control said, “Evidently the informant is an ex-Marine and feels quite safe.”

“Only the best,” said Dick.

CHAPTER 10

The team were now in position, and could see the informant, then the two men, well in front of him. Reaching the informant, they got him into the back of Paul's car.

Paul said, "Thanks mate, we'll take it from here."

Dick turned round, "Well fuck me, it's Dougie Gray, from my old regiment."

"Dicky Jones, good to see you again. Another mess I'm helping sort out for you."

Paul said, "Make love later boys, we have a job to do."

"He's only jealous, Dougie. He'll get over it. Don't worry." They all laughed.

Paul said, "OK team. Move in, but be aware, they are dangerous men."

Bob and Joe had seen the approaching cars, suspecting what was about to happen. Looking round, Bob saw a couple out of their car taking photos. "Come on Joe, that car."

They ran over to it, and before the couple could do anything, they took off in it. Joe was driving. He shouted to Bob, "Hang on mate, this could get tough. Better buckle up."

One ARV car was coming towards them, slowed down, and stopped. The front doors opened, the officers took shelter behind them, firearms at the ready. Joe put his foot down and slammed the front wing of their car, into the open passenger side door of the ARV. The door and the officer behind it slammed back into the ARV, taking the officer out of action. As the car sped away, the other officer opened fire, taking the rear windscreen out, but failing to stop the vehicle. He waved the other cars through, before running round to his partner's side. Fortunately his partner's flak jacket had saved him from any serious injury, although winded him badly. The second ARV was now leading the chase, with Paul, Dick, Broad and Porter following. They raced around Queen Victoria Memorial onto the Mall.

A shot came from the stolen car, shattering the windscreen of the chasing ARV, causing the driver to swerve and collide with railings, putting that one out of the chase.

Paul was now the leading car. Putting his foot down he said, "Dick, we don't want them getting through into the City. See if there's any backup in the area. Admiralty Arch, if anywhere. Tell them both ARVs are out of action."

Control came on. "All traffic cars are linked to the chase."

Paul said, "Well if there's one there, please instruct them to ram the car. Ram it properly."

As the stolen car approached the Arch, a police Range Rover smashed into its front end, causing it to collide with railings and stop. The officers jumped out and ran towards it. Paul screeched to a stop, feet behind it. He and Dick jumped out, followed by Dougie. Bob and Joe were climbing out of the car, Bob raised his arm, pointing a gun at Dick. Dick carried on his run, smashing his left hand into the gun hand, deflecting it away. His right elbow smashed into Bob's face. The gun flew out of his hand onto the pavement. Dick went at the man again, punching him hard between the eyes, knocking him flat. Paul in the meantime was dragging Joe out of the driver's side door, with the two traffic officers. He was struggling violently; Paul didn't hold back. He punched Joe as hard as he could in the stomach. As he came forward, he bought his right knee up, smashing it into his face, knocking him back against the driver's door. He then kicked his legs from under him, pinning him to the ground.

"Get the cuffs on him, quick. You OK round there, Dick?" he shouted.

"Will be in a minute." Bob started to sit up, Dick punched him once more, then shouted, "Any more cuffs over there?"

The second traffic officer came round and cuffed him.

Broad and Porter joined them at the scene with the two damaged ARV cars.

Broad said, "All sorted now I see. Who's who?"

Dick said, "Mine's Bob Teal, the other must be Andrews."

Paul was on the radio. "Uniform assistance please. Two men arrested. Require SOCO and vehicle recovery please."

He turned to the two traffic officers. "Thanks for your help. Much appreciated. Have you got any tape to cordon the scene off until SOCO get here?"

"Leave that with us sir, our Inspector is on his way, he'll sort this lot out."

Dougie came up to Dick. "You had better take this." He handed him the gun Bob had been forced to drop.

Dick said, "Cheers mate, hang around for a bit."

Police had started to arrive from all directions, and the area was soon secured. A Chief Superintendent was at the scene, giving orders. Paul and Broad approached him and identified themselves and quickly appraised him of the situation.

Broad said, "I want them taken to separate, secure stations. Please stress how dangerous they are. Security is of the uppermost importance."

Both men were placed in separate vehicles and taken from the scene.

Broad said, "Well, we still have plenty to do. Forensics and SOCO on all cars involved, both hotel rooms as well. Where's the guy that was following them?"

Dick called Dougie over. "Dougie Gray, Superintendent Broad, Interpol."

Shaking his hand, Broad said, "Well done. Thanks for your help, tremendous work."

Dougie replied, "Only too pleased to help an old colleague out, again."

The team left the scene, the only thing they brought away with them was Bob's briefcase.

Dropping Dougie back at his taxi, Dick said, "Can you go to Tottenham Court Road Police Station? They need to SOCO your taxi and take a statement off you. Well done, mate. Marines two, baddies none. Catch up later."

Paul said, "I must say, you marines stick together."

Dick replied, "Another boys' club mate, another boys' club."

CHAPTER 11

Back in the team office, they had opened the brown briefcase. It was a minefield. It contained a number of false passports, in both men's names. It was apparent, looking at the photos on them, the two men had altered their appearances with cosmetic surgery since their time in Spain. Bank account details in the UK, Switzerland and the Cayman Islands, again in names matching some of the passports.

Plans were found for the Midland Express Security office in Nottingham, and the jeweller's shop in France. Both with various markings on, outlining cameras, electrical facts, times and dates. An address book, among which Petr Aught's name was found, along with contact numbers.

Broad said, "All this needs is topping and tailing. Christine, you sort the Swiss side out, and do the same. Do the UK banks through your Fraud Squad here."

He handed them a contact high up in the Fraud Squad. "They are aware and expecting your call, when you are ready. Paul and myself will do the interviews. Any problems, let us know."

EPILOGUE

2013

Bob Teal and Joe Andrews were interviewed at length, but refused to answer any questions put to them about anything.

Through enquiries done by the team, they were able to establish that the two men had been involved in the robbery in Nottingham where Sergeant Peters had been shot and killed. They were jointly charged with both offences.

They were also able to establish that they had been responsible for the jeweller's shop theft in France. They were jointly charged with that offence.

They were able to link them to Petr Aught, but not prove they were responsible for his death. Swiss police were still investigating.

Bob Teal was charged with the murder of Jerry Morton.

Both men were jointly charged with the attempted murder of Julie Jones and Alice Richards at Oxford Circus underground.

Both men were jointly charged with the attempted murder of the three of the ARV officers and the assault on the taxi driver.

Their assets traced in the UK, Switzerland and the Cayman Islands were seized under the Police Financial

Seizure Act. From that, money was paid out to the security firm's insurers and the jeweller's insurers. All other money was seized, pending an appeal by them. Neither man appealed.

At their subsequent trial at the Old Bailey, both men pleaded guilty to all charges. The judge sentenced them both to full life terms, meaning they should never be released. No appeal was made.

At a celebration meal afterwards, all the team was present, as was Julie and Alice. Dougie had also been invited.

Paul asked, "Where are your partners, Michael?"

"Didn't you know? We are partners. Chris and I have been married five years."

Paul said, "Well you certainly kept that quiet."

Broad said, "I raise a glass to you all for your hard work and diligence. Excellent work."

Paul said to Alice, "Shall we tell them our news?"

Julie said, "You're pregnant?"

Julie hugged her sister. "Wonderful news."

Alice said, "Yes. That's my news. Paul's got some as well."

Dick said, "C'mon mate, out with it."

Paul said, "We are moving to Nottingham, your boss Dee is retiring. I've been promoted on transfer to his job."

Dick looked at him. "Bugger me, mate, brother-in-law, now boss."

Paul said, "And Dougie has accepted a job on the Surveillance Unit as an instructor and operator, to work with the Nottingham teams."

Broad raised his glass. "Good luck to all of you."

BOOK TWO

GOOD COP, BAD COP

CHAPTER 1

2015

The mobile banking unit pulled on to the square in the centre of Bingham, a village east of Nottingham. As well as mobile banking day, it was also coming to the end of market day. Market traders and other retailers were happy to use the banking system.

Unknown to the staff on board, their vehicle had been followed since their last two stops.

A white Transit van was parked on the perimeter of the square, two men in the front seat.

The driver, who was a local criminal, said to his passenger, "When he leaves, around 3pm, they drive from the square, out of Bingham, then turn right to over the level crossing, towards the A46. We hit it after the crossing, before it reaches there."

An hour later, the mobile unit moved off the square. They drove down to the level crossing and as they were about to pass over it, the warning lights flashed for an oncoming train. The Transit followed them across, whilst the vehicle behind stopped, holding traffic back.

They followed the bank vehicle until it came to a sharp left-hand bend in the road, where a broken-down car was sat, with hazard lights flashing. As the bank vehicle slowed, the Transit pulled alongside it and a man appeared from the broken-down car, brandishing a sawn-off shotgun. He aimed it at the top of the windscreen and pulled the trigger, shattering the glass on the driver and passengers. The two men from the Transit appeared alongside, yelling, "Get them doors open now, now!"

The driver climbed from his seat, through to the rear doors and opened them. The two gunmen climbed in and ordered them to open the safe. When the driver hesitated, one man put his gun up, and said, "The next one's yours."

The cashier came through and opened the safe. The two men emptied it completely within less than a minute. All three staff were then tied with plastic cuffs and left in the back of the bank vehicle.

The broken-down car and Transit van drove away towards the A46, before any other vehicle came through.

The first driver on the scene saw the bank vehicle with its rear doors open and staff apparently in some form of distress inside. He stopped his car. As he approached it, he saw that the three occupants were tied up.

He reached for his phone, dialling 999. As he dialled he asked if anyone was hurt.

When the police answered, he told them where he was and what he believed had happened, and that all the occupants were tied up, but uninjured. He was asked to remain there, but not enter the vehicle.

A police car arrived within minutes, the officers releasing the three bank staff, and sitting them in a couple of police vehicles. They were badly shaken, but not hurt.

The only witness was the driver reporting the incident. He stated he had seen the mobile bank unit leaving Bingham, and saw it cross the level crossing as the lights started flashing. A white Transit van had crossed behind it, but the next vehicle stopped, so he was unable to cross. He had lost sight of the vehicles. When the lights changed, and the barriers lifted, he followed the car in front, which turned left into a supermarket car park. He was first on the scene. He said everything appeared normal.

The CID officers at the scene were DS Bob Flowers and DC Chris Sansom.

On speaking to the driver, they established that the vehicle had dashcams front and rear.

They showed the broken-down car to be a blue Ford Mondeo, but as the boot lid was up, it showed no number plate. The man with the shotgun was wearing a full facial mask. When it eventually drove away, a rag was covering the rear number plate.

The rear dashcam showed the Transit following the Mondeo but its number plates at the front had been taped over. When it drove round to leave the scene, the rear number plate had also been taped over.

DS Flowers said, "Well that's fuck all to go on. Get SOCO out here to do the van, the rest of us back to the station for statements. Chris, on your way back call at the level crossing, see what their cameras show." He organised a couple of uniformed traffic officers to stay with the bank vehicle, until SOCO finished, then to bring it into Trent Station.

Back at the station, DS Flowers met up with Dc Sansom. "Any joy at the level crossing, Chris?" he asked.

"All it shows are the two vehicles crossing, like the dashcams show, no clear shots of number plates."

"None of it?"

"No. I've got photos printed off, but nothing."

He handed copies to Bob Flowers, who looked at them and agreed. "And no ANPR cameras on the A46. Could have gone anywhere. Chris, check the cameras on the Gunthorpe Road, see if that shows anything."

On completion of statements, it was ascertained that just over £30,000 had been stolen, no one hurt, and no leads.

CHAPTER 2

The gunshop had only just opened when two men walked in.

The manager asked, "Can I help you guys?"

They had walked over to the air rifles. One asked, "Can we speak about air rifles, please?"

The manager said, "Certainly sir." Walking over from behind the counter, he asked, "Which ones are you interested in?"

The man said, "None." Turning round he produced a small handgun, and pointing it at the manager he said, "We want you away from the counter and the alarm. Give me your keys for the security chains on them and your rifles."

The manager then noticed they had stocking masks on and surgical gloves.

He passed them his keys. One man went over to the shotgun and rifle display, quickly unlocking the security chain. He placed five shotguns and five rifles on the counter. Going to another cabinet, he unlocked it and took out eight pistols.

Calling the manager over, he said, "Show me the ammunition for them all, keep your hands where I can see them."

The manager pointed out different boxes of ammunition. The two men loaded all the weapons into two large holdalls.

"OK," the gunman said. "Move back into your office and sit away from your desk."

The manager complied, sitting in a spare chair. The phone was ripped from the wall, the flex was used to tie the manager to the chair. One of the men took the DVD cassette from the security camera system, throwing it in the bag.

Leaving the shop, they locked the door behind them, then put the keys back through the letter box.

The shop was situated on one of Nottingham's main roads into and out of the city. The premises next door was a coffee shop/bar. The owner was cleaning his front window from the inside when he noticed the two men leaving with large holdalls. Noticing that one of the men was pushing the keys back through the letter box, he watched them walk up to a blue Range Rover parked between two other vehicles and put the bags in the boot. As he watched it pull away, he was only able to notice the numbers PPT in the number plate.

He went round to the gunshop. Looking through the shop door, he could see the manager apparently tied up.

He opened the letter box and shouted through, "Jonny, you OK? Are you hurt?"

Jonny shouted back, "Call the police, I've been robbed."

Mick rang the police on his mobile, telling them what had happened, and that the keys were inside the locked front door. The police quickly arrived, and realising they couldn't reach the keys, asked Mick for a wire coat hanger. One officer fashioned it into a hook and was able to fish the keys back through the letter box and gain entry.

The officer said, "Stay outside please sir."

They released the manager and called for CID backup, who replied they were about twenty seconds away.

DS Nathan Kite and DC Ron Staples arrived and introduced themselves.

The manager, Jonny Gilflow, spoke to DS Kite, explaining what had happened, whilst DC Staples spoke to the coffee shop owner next door.

Meanwhile, on the other side of town, in West Bridgford, a man wearing full motorcycle gear walked into Stephens Bank. When he got to the front of the queue, he put his briefcase on the counter and opened it with the inside showing to the teller.

He said, "You see I have a sawn-off shotgun in here?" and put his left hand on it.

"No alarms or anything, just put all your used notes, and your colleagues', into a bag, nice and gently, no one gets hurt."

The tellers looked at each other. The man said, "Now."

Both cashiers obeyed, the one furthest away had pressed her silent alarm, which alerted staff in the adjoining office. The teller in there looked up as the money bags were passed over to the man, whilst another staff member rang the police.

The man closed the briefcase and walked calmly out of the bank, turning left to a small car park. A quick-thinking member of staff went out of the back door, walking round to where he thought the motorcycle-gear-clad figure would be. There was no sight of him, nor any sound of a motorbike.

The police were quickly on the scene, and descriptions, as they were, were passed out.

DCI Dick Jones was at his desk, he had heard all the calls. He rang down to the CID office, speaking to DI Nugent. "Dave, it's Dick Jones upstairs. Just heard the calls about the gunshop job, and the two bank jobs. Find out what you can, and get me updates please?"

"No probs, Dick."

CHAPTER 3

About an hour later, DI Nugent, DS Mick Kite and DS Malc Piggott were seated in Dick's office.

"OK, yesterday, we had a mobile banking unit attacked on the outskirts of Bingham, what's the update on that, Dave?"

DI Nugent replied, "It was ambushed as it left Bingham. A van had followed it across the level crossings as the barriers came down. It was attacked at gunpoint further down the road. Shots were fired, but no one was injured. The staff were left tied up in the back. DS Bob Flowers is dealing with that, he's still out on enquiries last I heard. They got away with around £30,000. No witnesses. Dashcam footage and level crossing cameras don't show reg numbers, well they do, but they were covered up."

"Right, Mick. What have we got at the gunshop robbery?" Dick asked.

DS Kite replied, "Two men went in, just after it opened. They asked the manager about air weapons. When he came from behind the counter, they pulled a gun on him and asked for the keys to the security chains on the shotguns and rifles. They picked five shotguns, five rifles. Then they opened the pistol cabinet and took eight pistols. They got him to pick out the ammo for them as well."

"Were they masked up?"

"When he got to them he realised they had some sort of mask on, which he hadn't noticed earlier, and they were wearing flesh-coloured surgical gloves. They tied him up and left him in the back office. They locked the door and put the keys back through the letter box."

"Any CCTV in the shop?"

"There is, but they took the disc with them. The coffee shop owner next door called it in, he saw the men leaving with the holdalls. They got into a blue Range Rover, all he got was partial number plate PTP. That's been passed out to all units."

Dick asked, "How's the manager now?"

"He's shaken but making a statement. He actually was quite astute though."

"Why's that?" Dick asked.

"When they asked him for the ammo, he pointed out the wrong stuff, so they have ammo, but it's not suitable for any of the guns they took."

"Meaning they could misfire, or even blow the gun up. That could cause some damage to someone, with a bit of luck, the baddie," replied Dick. "Give him a pat on the back for his quick thinking."

"Right, Malc. What about the bank job at West Bridgford?"

"Well sir, appears a man went in dressed in motorcycle gear. When he got to the counter he put a briefcase on it, opened it up, and showed the two cashiers he had a shotgun in it. He had the lid to the back so folks behind couldn't see in. He told the two cashiers to put all the used notes together in a bag and pass it over. Which they did, then he walked out. One of them had managed to press the silent alarm and alert the back office. They rang the police. A member of staff went out the back door to see if he could see anything, but had no luck. He didn't even hear a motorbike."

"Any other vehicles seen?"

"It's quite a busy area, so all he was looking for was a

motorbike."

"OK, thanks for that. Dave, set a small team up on each job, Mick, Malc you will be attached to your teams. Keep Bob Flowers on the mobile job. I want all CCTV in the areas checking. I want PNC on that part number plate, running off. I want full details of all the firearms circulating, as well as the ammo. When you get CCTV, check all vehicle registrations shown, ten minutes either side of the jobs. Most of all, I want you to all report to Dave on updates, we might have some links, you never know. Anything else you guys can think of?"

DS Kite replied, "We have arranged for the gunshop and coffee shop manager to do a photo viewing."

"Good. When's that being done?"

Just then the phone on Dick's desk rang. He picked it up and his secretary said, "Call for DI Nugent sir."

Passing the phone over, Dave said, "DI Nugent."

"Whereabouts?" he asked. "OK. Get SOCO straight on to it, we'll be out to you asap."

Handing the phone back to Dick he said, "They've found a blue Range Rover out near Calverton, it's on fire as we speak, fire brigade are there."

"Right, get out there with Mick, take another couple of DCs with you. Do some door-knocking. Back here at 4pm for updates please. Dave, check with the banks, see if they are putting any reward money up at all. If they are, get it to the press officer."

CHAPTER 4

Just outside a village called Ravenshead, two men were unloading their car inside the garage of a large, detached house. They were brothers, John and Derek Biston, John was the elder of the two. The house had been their home and passed onto them on the deaths of their parents.

They carried the bags through to the kitchen and started unloading the rifles, shotguns and pistols on to the kitchen table.

"Looks like we're in for a few quid for this lot bro," John said.

"Let's hope so. How much do you reckon?" Derek asked.

"I'd like to think at least three to four grand, and the ammo. I've got Parr lined up for most of them. He'll want some to replace them he used yesterday."

John picked the phone up. Dialling, he said, "Ay up mate, it's me. Got some new stuff for you if you're interested. All brand new, rifles, shotguns, pistols and some ammo. Any good to you? That's great, see you later." Putting the phone down, he said, "Pat Parr's having them. He's coming round later."

***

Across the other side of town, the motorcycle-dressed robber was sat in his living room in Wilford with another man. They had just counted the cash out, twice, and got it to £6,240.

The man in the motorcycle gear was called William Lowe, Billy to his friends. The other man was Les Smythe.

"Not bad," said Billy, "Great getaway as well"

Just then the local news came on the radio. The first announcement was regarding the gunshop robbery. The announcer stated that the suspects' getaway vehicle had been found on fire at Calverton. Police and fire were investigating. Police are also investigating an armed robbery at a bank in West Bridgford, where cash was stolen. It's believed the offender escaped on a motorcycle. The bank has put up a reward of £10,000 for any information leading to the arrest and conviction of persons responsible.

Police are also continuing their enquiries in to the armed raid on a mobile banking unit on the outskirts of Bingham yesterday afternoon. Again, a £10,000 reward has been offered for information leading to the arrest and convictions. At this stage, police are not linking the raids together.

"Fuck me," said Billy. "The reward money is more than we nicked."

"No problems," said Les. "Sounds like the police have had a busy couple of days and are still clueless."

CHAPTER 5

The detectives were gathered in Dick Jones' office. Also present was Det Chief Superintendent Paul Richard, Dick's brother-in-law and boss.

"Right, updates please. Mick, can you start please?" Paul asked.

DS Mick Kite said, "We have taken statements from the gunshop manager, and coffee shop owner, we thought he was the manager at first. Anyway, great descriptions of the two men, In fact, the coffee shop guy said he thought they looked like brothers, they were that much alike. We have a DVD from across the road from the gunshop we are looking at. The Range Rover they were using was found burnt out at Calverton. Nothing useful from the vehicle, too badly damaged. We did some door to door there, and found another camera from a house nearby had picked the two men up, coming away from it." He handed copies over and said, "To me, they look like the same two men."

"Where was the Range Rover reported stolen from?" asked Paul.

"Funnily enough, from Calverton, a Mr Patrick Parr, is the owner. And he is also a bit of a Mr Big. He has form for firearms, and strongly suspected of being involved in a couple of armed robberies, but never enough evidence. He is also suspected of supplying firearms."

"He needs looking at further then, see if there's any connections to the gunshop robbers," said Paul. "Anything else to add on that job anyone?" No reply came. "OK, Malc, your update please?"

DS Malcolm Piggot replied, "Nothing much than we already know, really sir. The amount stolen was just over £6,000, the bank has put a reward of £10,000. The strange thing is though, no motorbike was heard or seen leaving the area. We are obviously checking CCTV and ANPR. But nothing so far."

"Bob, what about the mobile bank unit. Anything there?" Paul asked.

DS Bob Flowers replied, "Nothing more than was reported earlier sir. CCTV on the Gunthorpe Road is not working at the moment, and as you know, there aren't any on the A46. The dashcams from the van are still being checked over, but nothing of any value yet. We did get a make on the car that stopped behind at the crossing, that's registered to a Leslie Smythe, one of our lot.

"Right," said Paul. "Get press appeals out on all three jobs, Any CCTV shots as well. Plus get the rewards pushed out. Someone must have seen something. Bob, speak to this Smythe, see what he saw. DI Nugent, is the joint liaison officer between you all, so pass everything back to him. As I said earlier, there may be connections. Get your snouts active. Big rewards here."

CHAPTER 6

The press appeals and photos at hand went out on the early evening news bulletin on local television at 6.30pm, outlining all three robberies. A phone number was given out for any information to be passed on, anonymously if preferred.

Within minutes, the phones were ringing, with a number of calls identifying John and Derek Biston as the gunshop robbers. A couple of callers even gave their address at Ravenshead.

DS Kite checked their names in the system. Both men were known to police and had convictions for theft, varying offences. Intelligence said they were known to have been involved with firearms, but no convictions involving them.

He rang the details through to Dick Jones. "We have a couple of names for the gunshop job, some callers giving the same names."

"Leave that with me, Mick, I'll get back to you in a few minutes."

Dick rang through to Dougie at the surveillance unit. "Dougie, we have a couple of names for the gunshop robbery. Any chance of a surveillance on them? Just thinking they may still have the guns at the address."

Dougie said, "We are about to go out on a practice job, so a live one can take its place. Send me photos and detail by email, I'll get the team sorted."

Within ten minutes, Dougie was briefing his team of 14 officers, including himself and a motorcyclist. As they were at HQ, Ravenshead was only a few minute's drive away, and were quickly plotted up on the address.

Dougie had a view of the front of the house, another crew had a reasonable view of the rear.

After about an hour, Dougie got on the radio to the team. "Stand by team, blue Jaguar just pulled onto driveway, backing up to garage doors. One occupant, white male, mid-thirties, stocky build, black top, black trousers. reg number XK 18 XXX. Driver out and into open garage, door now closing. Have you got all that log?"

"Affirmative, just checking vehicle."

"Log to Dougie, can you talk?"

"Go ahead."

Jag is registered to a Patrick Parr at Calverton, funnily enough, he was the owner of the burnt-out Range Rover involved in the gun theft. Form for armed robbery ten years ago. Been out a couple of years. Intel says he is a bit of a Mr Big in the criminal world."

Meanwhile inside the house, Parr was examining the guns. John said, "All brand new, Pat."

Parr said, "Very nice. Can I have the lot, give you four grand for the lot."

John said, "We want to keep a couple of pistols, but the rest are yours, still four grand with all the ammo."

They shook hands. "Deal."

Dougie came back on the radio. "Standby team, garage door opening, Jag driver and two white males, our suspects, are at the rear of the vehicle, and boot lid is open. Appear to be loading something into it. Boot lid down, all shaking hands. Driver back in, Jag moving off. Cars one and two, stay on this address, others follow Jag. Who has eyeball?"

"Car 4 has the eyeball. Onto Longdale Lane, towards Calverton, two car cover, at roundabout A614, straight across onto Whinbush Lane, still towards Calverton."

Dougie rang Dick to update him.

"Dougie, follow the Jag, to wherever. Any of your team armed?"

Dougie replied, "No, still in the direction of Calverton."

Dick said, "I'll get a couple of ARV to you. We don't want them guns on the streets."

Dougie relayed this to his team. Car 4 came in. "Still heading to Calverton, over the traffic lights on Oxton Road. Now turning into the community rubbish centre, foot man out."

The foot man came on. "He's gone round the back, looks like he's dumping old paint tins. Can't fully see the back of his car. Car moving off and exiting rubbish centre."

"Car 3 now has eyeball, vehicle onto Flatts Lane, now turning into Hoyle Road, and into first driveway, electric garage door opening, Jag in, door closing."

Dougie said, "Stay on it eyeball. Are you safe?"

"Yes."

Dougie ran the control room, informed them what they were doing, and asked for two ARV cars to meet him in the lay-by on the Oxton Road asap. "Put them onto channel 7 please."

"Control, two cars en route, ETA five minutes, just leaving HQ."

Dougie relayed to his team, "Hold positions, I'm meeting two ARV crews on Oxton Road."

The cars met him in the lay-by. He briefed them that his team would smash the door down, then the ARV crew would go in behind shields. "Have your firearms ready. No time for an appraisal I'm afraid."

The crew got themselves ready and made their way to the address. As the cars pulled up, the two ARV crews ran to the front door. As Dougie's team smashed the door in, the armed officers ran in behind shields, shouting, "Armed police, show yourself!"

A man came out of the kitchen with a cocked shotgun in his hand. "Drop the weapon now. Put your hands where we can see them. Do it!"

The man dropped the weapon and raised his hands. "Keep them where we can see them."

The man obliged and was quickly secured. He was identified as Patrick Parr.

On the kitchen table was one shotgun, one rifle and a pistol, plus some ammunition. The ARV crews made them safe.

DS Kite was at the scene now, and said, "Patrick Parr, I am arresting you on suspicion of handling stolen property, and possession of part one firearms and ammunition." He cautioned him.

Dougie said, "Mick, we are going back to Ravenshead, two of my team can take Parr to the nick. If you want to come with us, you can nick the other two."

"Great, thanks."

En route back to Ravenshead, with the ARV crews, Dougie established the brothers were still in the address. He radioed through to his team and the ARV crews. "Same plan here, as we have just done, OK?"

All came back affirmative.

On arrival, Dick drove his car up to the front of the house, followed by the two ARV cars.

The front door was smashed open, the ARV crews went in behind shields, shouting, "Armed police, show yourselves! Armed police!"

A door opened and Derek Biston came out with a pistol aimed at the officers.

"Drop the weapon now."

Still aiming at the officers, he pulled the trigger. The gun exploded in his hand, as the officers opened fire, killing him instantly.

The other man came from the same room, hand raised above his head. “Keep your hands where we can see them.”

DS Kite moved forward and handcuffed the man, now identified as John Biston. He was arrested for the robbery at the gunshop, and possession of part one firearms and ammunition.

A second pistol was found in the kitchen, with some ammunition and a large amount of cash, counted out at £20,000.

Dougie called the control room to organise SOCO at both addresses. He was told to keep all officers there until the arrival of a senior officer, and to seal both of the scenes off.

CHAPTER 7

Det Ch Supt Paul Richards, DCI Dick Jones and Det Insp Dave Nugent arrived at the scene of the fatal shooting at Ravenshead. The immediate area had been cordoned off. SOCO and forensic officers were already inside. They could see the body of Derek Biston, lying in the kitchen doorway.

Dougie came up to them. Paul said, "Briefly Dougie, what went off?"

Dougie replied, "We smashed the door in, the ARV boys went in. I heard what I can only describe as a muffled explosion then shots fired. The ARV detained a second man, he's gone to the nick with DS Kite."

Dick came up to them. "I've just been inside, talking to SOCO. Looks like the dead man had a gun in his hand, aimed at the officers. When he pulled the trigger, it blew to bits. He has obviously loaded it with the ammo stolen from the gunshop."

Paul said, "There will be a full enquiry into the shooting. I understand Northants police will be doing that."

It was standard procedure for a foreign force to take this sort of enquiry on, without any bias.

"OK Dougie. Get your team back to HQ and get their reports written up before they go off duty," said Paul. "Where are the ARV officers?"

Dougie replied, "Already gone back to HQ, their inspector called them back."

Paul said, "Dave, can you go and liaise with them. I'm

sure they will do the things right, but their weapons need seizing and swabs taken. Get a SOCO to meet you there."

"On my way, sir," replied DI Nugent.

Dick said, "Nasty end to a great job. Speak to you and Dougie later. I think we are done here, Paul."

"Back to base then, let's see what the arrested men have to say. I'll update the Chief."

On arriving back to his office, Paul rang the Chief Constable. He already knew that Northants police were doing the shooting enquiry, they were travelling up as they were speaking. All staff were to remain on duty until they had sorted out who they needed to speak to.

Paul informed him he had compiled a list of officers he thought needed speaking to. All officers on the periphery were to make a full report before going off duty, the others were making them and remaining on duty until Northants police arrived.

"Paul, if any officers need counselling, can you sort that?"

"Will do, have already started that ball rolling sir, and updated the Police Federation office."

"Thanks Paul. Any problems, get back in touch."

***

In the cell block, DS Kite and DC Staples had sat down to do an interview with John Biston and his solicitor, Jim Barnes.

After the introductions were recorded on tape, Barnes handed a written statement to DS Kite.

"My client is not prepared to answer any of your questions until the matter of the shooting of his brother is sorted out. As he was shot in cold blood."

DS Kite read the statement and said, "Can we say how sorry we are about your brother's death. That matter is being investigated by another force. That is standard practice. I know you have made this statement, but I still need to ask you some questions in relation to the robbery at the gunshop earlier today on Mansfield Road."

Barnes said, "I have already told you, he is not answering your questions."

DS Kite put his hand up. "Let me stop you there Mr Barnes. Just because you and your client have stated you won't answer any questions, does not mean we can't ask some. You know that."

Barnes said, "Tell us what evidence you have that puts my client there?"

DS Kite said, "You have already been told, that is the point of this interview. If you stop interrupting, we can get on. By the way Mr Barnes, are you a qualified solicitor or a legal representative of the firm?"

Barnes glared at him. "How dare you. I'm here to represent my client."

DS Kite said, "As what, solicitor or legal rep? You haven't answered my question. You see John, you may think you have a qualified solicitor representing you, when he may not be. You ask him?"

Before Barnes could answer, Biston asked him, "Are you a solicitor or not, Mr Barnes?"

Barnes was furious, but answered, "I am a legal rep, representing the solicitors."

DS Kite said, "But not a qualified solicitor?"

Barnes replied, "No."

Biston asked, "What difference does it make then?"

"It means, Mr Barnes is representing a firm of solicitors, and they are instructed to tell their clients to make no comment in reply to police questioning. This is basically to find out what evidence the police may have. Of course, if you want to answer our questions, that is up to you entirely, because at the end of the day it's you that will be facing the court and being prosecuted, not them. At some stage you will be asked to give some explanation regarding your actions, one way or another. Or of course you can still go no comment. But we will be asking questions; whether you answer them or not, is your choice."

Barnes said, "This is outrageous. You are challenging my legal standing. I'm going to make a full complaint regarding your conduct."

DS Kite replied, "That is up to you Mr Barnes, but at the moment I want to ask John some questions. What can you tell us about the robbery at the gunshop on Mansfield Road earlier today?"

Biston looked at Mr Barnes, who was shaking his head, and replied, "I want to tell you."

"In your own words then John. What happened?"

He replied, "Well, me and Derek had looked at it a couple of times and decided to do it today. We used a Range Rover from a mate of ours."

DC Staples said, "Is that Patrick Parr, from Calverton?"

"Yes. He said when you've done with it, torch it. He would report it as stolen."

DC Staples said, "So talk us through the day."

"We picked the Range Rover up and left our car nearby. We drove to Mansfield Road. There was no one else in the shop. We looked at the air rifle display, then called the manager over, really to get him away from the counter and the alarm."

DS Kite asked, "Did you have any weapon with you?"

"Derek had a small handgun, but it wasn't loaded. He told the bloke to unlock the security chains on the shotguns and rifles and not to touch any alarms."

"Were you wearing masks at all?"

"We had, like, stocking masks tucked under our caps when we went in. We pulled them down when we called him over. We had some flesh-coloured surgical gloves on as well."

"What happened then?"

"When the chain was off, Derek got six shotguns, six rifles and eight pistols. He made the bloke get some ammo as well. We loaded it all into our holdalls and cleared off."

"Who tied the manager up?"

"That was Derek, he used the phone cable in the back office. We took the disk from the security system as well. When we left the shop, we locked it up and posted the keys back through the letter box."

DS Kite showed him a picture of two men in the shop. "Is that you and Derek?"

"Yes, that's me on the left."

"There were two security cameras in the shop. What happened to the disk you took?"

"That was left in the Range Rover, so burnt out I would think. We left our gloves and face masks in it as well."

"So you set fire to the Range Rover. What then?"

"We went and picked our car up first, loaded the stuff in, then set it on fire, and drove home. I knew Parr needed some guns, so rang him. He came and picked them up a bit later."

DC Staples, "What did he take from you?"

"He had them all, apart from a couple of pistols and most of the ammo."

"What did he pay you?"

"About four grand."

"Why did you need to keep a couple of them?"

"Derek wanted to. He loaded one for some reason. I think he wanted a gun around."

"You know Derek was shot because he pointed his gun at armed police and fired, don't you?"

"Yes, I do now."

"Did you hear the police shouting they were armed?"

"Yes."

DS Kite said, "Unfortunately, all the ammo you took today was not suitable for any of the guns you took. That's why Derek's gun misfired and blew up. Basically he had the wrong ammo in it. You said earlier, you knew Parr needed some guns. How did you know that?"

"Well that's another story."

DC Staples said, "Do you want to tell us about it?"

"I will, but can we have a break first please?"

DS Kite said, "No problem. Mr Barnes, we are taking a break. Anything you would like to say before we turn the recording off?"

Barnes said, "A lot actually. You bullied me and harassed me. You made my client answer your questions when I had advised him not to. A big complaint is coming your way, Detective Sergeant Kite, rest assured."

John Biston said, "Mr Barnes. Shut the fuck up. It was my choice. I wanted to tell them from the beginning. If you want to complain, go ahead. I'm sacking you anyway. Now fuck off."

The interview was terminated. Barnes raced out of the interview room, reporting the matter to the custody inspector. When he had left, DS Kite, DC Staples and John Biston went to the counter.

The Inspector asked John if he was alright and did he have any complaints.

"Fine thank you. No complaints. I have told the officers my side, the solicitor or whatever he was didn't like it, but it was my decision. I've sacked him anyway."

DS Kite said, "He has admitted his part in the offence, we're taking a break, then we need to do another interview. *If* you want some legal representation John, please sort it with this officer."

"No, I'll do it on my own next time."

On the way back up to their office, DS Kite said, "I think before we speak to him again, we ought to talk to the team who have interviewed Parr. You OK with that Ron?"

"Fine."

"Depending on what they say, whether we interview him tonight or again tomorrow, I'll let the custody inspector know."

CHAPTER 8

Back in the CID office, they spoke to the officers who had interviewed Parr. They told DS Kite that Parr had refused to answer any questions and had completely ignored them.

"Righto then, we interview Biston again in half an hour."

Back in the interview room with John Biston, DS Kite asked if he wanted any legal representation. If he did, he would ensure it would be a qualified solicitor.

Biston said, "No, I'm willing to talk without one."

DS Kite said, "If at any time you want one, just let us know. Right John, at the end of our last interview, you were asked why Parr needed the guns. Are you prepared to tell us?"

"Well yesterday they did a mobile banking vehicle over."

DS Kite said, "The one near Bingham?"

"Yes. I wasn't on it, but Derek and Parr were. I don't know the other man with them at all."

"Not you then?"

"No. If it was I'd tell you. When they had done it they drove back over Gunthorpe Bridge. Parr has this thing about not keeping guns. He dumps them after each job. Derek parked just over the bridge on the left, walked back and dropped them into the Trent. That's why he wanted the ones we took today. One snippet I did pick up though, I think I heard right. A cop was involved somewhere along the line."

DC Staples said, "Any name to this cop, John?"

"No, I just heard it mentioned somewhere. I know you didn't get all the guns back we took, because Parr was passing some on to someone on his way back home. Who, I don't know. All he said to us was he had a buyer for most of them already, they would be gone before he got home."

"What was Derek's role in that job?"

"He was supposed to have broken down, that's what stopped the van."

"So some of that cash at your house was from the sale of the guns and Derek's share of that job then?"

"Yes."

"Anything else you want to tell us about John?"

"No, that's it. You've been very fair with me, thank you. What's happening about Derek now?"

DS Kite said, "Northants police are doing the enquiry into the shooting of your brother. There will be a post-mortem, and a coroners hearing. Once that's done, Derek can be released for a funeral."

"Will I be able to attend that?"

"I feel sure you would, one way or another. If that's all for now, we'll let you get some rest."

***

Back in the CID office, DS Kite spoke to DI Nugent. "Dave, just had our second interview with John Biston. He's fingered his brother Derek and Patrick Parr for that mobile banking job near Bingham. He said the firearms used on it have been dumped in the Trent afterwards, that's why they did the gunshop job. Parr needed some new weapons. He also said Parr had got rid of them on his way home somewhere along the line. He already had a buyer lined up. One more thing, he reckons there's a cop involved somewhere amongst all this."

DI Nugent said, "There was mention of a cop at the front of the queue at the level crossing, might be him. Any name given?"

"No, he doesn't know any name. We think if he did, he would tell us."

"Right, I'll pass that info on to the Boss. Have you spoken to Bob Flowers about this?"

"No, Dave, came straight to you."

"Leave it with me, cheers. Good job."

DI Nugent went upstairs. Dick Jones was in his office.

"Dick, just had Mick Kite in. They have spoken to John Biston. He has admitted the gunshop job with his brother. He said the guns were for Patrick Parr, to replace ones they used on the mobile banking robbery."

"Was he on that then?"

"No his brother, Parr and another man he doesn't know. Evidently whenever Parr does a firearms job, he dumps them afterwards. These were dumped in the Trent at Gunthorpe. That's why he needed new ones. He also said Parr had got rid of them on his way home somewhere, he had a buyer lined up. The best part, he said he thinks a cop is involved somewhere along the line. No name known though."

"What makes him think that?"

"He's heard it mentioned. The only cop near the scene that day was a Les Smythe, he was behind the van when it crossed over. He was first in the queue at the level crossing."

"Do you know this Les Smythe, Dave?"

"I know he works here, but not personally. I've checked up, he's on leave at the moment. Back next week."

"OK, leave that with me, I'll get his file sent over. Tell Mick and Ron, well done. Get Bob Flowers to have another go at Parr, you never know, it might shake him up a bit. See if you can get Dougie to send him a copy of the log, where they followed him home. If he dropped them off, it should be on the log. And can we organise a dive team? See if the dumped guns can be recovered?"

"Will do."

CHAPTER 9

The motorcycle-gear-clad customer stood in Stevens Bank at Sherwood, behind one other person. When their turn came, they moved forward, putting a briefcase on the counter, opened it and said to the cashier, “Do not press the alarm or your mate. Put all the notes in a bag and pass it to me. Do it now.”

The man tilted the case forward. The cashiers, seeing the gun, did as they were instructed. Both emptied the cash drawers of notes and passed the bag over to the man. He put them in his case, closed it and calmly walked out. As he did so, one of the cashiers hit the alarm buttons, one silent, one noisy. As the man got out of the door, he ran left. A customer coming the opposite way heard the alarm, saw the man running and made to follow. As he got to the side of the bank, there was no sign of the motorcyclist or a motorcycle anywhere.

The customer made his way into the bank, being informed they had just been robbed. When the police arrived a short time later, he told them that he had seen a man dressed in motorcycle gear run from the bank as the alarm sounded. He followed him to the corner. When he got there, there was no sign of him or any motorcycle, nor had he heard one at all.

DS Malc Piggott arrived at the bank, accompanied by DC Jill March. On hearing what had happened, he shook his head and said, “Another disappearing motorcyclist.

Let's see what CCTV can throw up in the area, Jill. I'll see you back at the office, but get a quick statement whilst it's fresh, we can get a fuller one later."

***

Back in his office, DS Piggott began to mark a map of the area where the banks were, Stevens at West Bridgford and Stevens at Sherwood. A motorcycle-gear-clad person at both banks, but no bike seen or heard in the areas.

"Jill, have you got the CCTV sorted out from Sherwood?"

"Nothing covering the way he left, Malc."

"Do you know how much he got on this job?"

She said, "About £7,000."

"So that's around £13,000, from the two banks. And both Stevens Banks. Come on, let's go and see Dave Nugent, he's the liaison officer on these jobs."

In DI Nugent's office, DS Piggott said, "Dave, we've just had another Stevens Bank done, at Sherwood. Same MO as the last one."

"Any leads, Malc?"

"No. Again no motorbike seen or heard. A week between each job. I'm thinking is there any chance of you speaking to the gaffers, see if we can get a surveillance car on the banks next week? There's only ten in the city area. What do you think?"

"That could be a big ask, let me see what I can do."

DC March said, "I'm sure we could get a couple of CID to help out in their own cars."

DS Piggott said, "Because we have nothing else to go on."

DI Nugent said, "What about if they are not using a motorbike to get away on, they could have driven off in a car?"

"Could have I suppose," replied DS Piggott. "Come on Jill, let's look at CCTV for cars in the area. If he's wearing motorcycle gear in a car, that should show up. Thanks Dave."

"I'll let you know what the gaffer says about next week."

CHAPTER 10

The following week, all ten branches of Stevens Banks throughout the city centre area were covered by a car from the surveillance team, or crewed by a pair of CID officers in a plain car.

Dougie was teamed up with DI Dave Nugent. He asked Dougie how he knew Dick Jones.

"We served in the Marines together in the 90s. He left about 1998 I think, then I left three years later. He was a Troop Sergeant on one squad, I was on another. We served in Iraq together. Great soldier, got stuck in, not frightened. We lost touch, then met up a couple of years back in London."

"Was that the security depot job?"

"Yes. The two men he was after had been in my cab, on the run from Dick and Paul. When I found out, I followed them. Dick and Paul got stuck in at the arrests. I'll tell you another thing, Dick is very shrewd and doesn't miss much, and he doesn't like slackers, nor does he suffer fools."

Dave said, "I've realised that. I find him a great boss, and very approachable."

Then the radio came to life. "To DI Nugent and surveillance team. A robbery has just occurred at Smiths Bank at West Bridgford. Man in motorcycle gear again. Any team nearby?"

"Car 5, we are at London Road. We'll attend."

"DI Nugent to Car 5. Leave the bank to the CID, have

a scout round on surrounding roads, if he's in a car with motorcycle gear on, should be easy to spot."

At the later debrief attended by Dick Jones, the team learned that the man dressed in motorcycle gear had got away with £7,500, and again no motorcycle seen or heard.

Dick said, "Makes you wonder how we missed him, why he picked an out-of-town bank. Dave, Dougie, can I see you in my office after the briefing please?"

Briefing completed, they sat in Dick's office. He said, "Don't like this guys. It's as though someone knows what we are doing, and where."

Dougie said, "You mean a cop?"

"Cop, or someone in our group who knows what we are doing. Next week I want a surveillance done on banks of your choice. Keep it in house, on a need-to-know basis. Brief the teams separately so only that team knows where they are going."

Dougie said, "Sorry Dick, can't do that. My team work as a unit and need to back each other up in case anything happens. I can't not let them know where backup is if they need it. Sorry mate. The best I can do, is brief on the day, last minute sort of thing."

"OK, I can go with that. Dave, you ride with Dougie again. Keep the CID on standby in the office. You two sort the banks out to be watched."

***

A week later, the teams were plotted up on various banks around the city centre.

"Car 4. We are at Smiths Bank, Sneinton. Motorcyclist just entered the bank."

DI Nugent replied, "Stay in situ teams, we are joining Car 4. Car 4, can you see into the bank from your location?"

"Car 4, my footman is out and taking a walk by, he's

telling me the man has taken his helmet off and talking to the cashiers. All seems to be in order, nobody panicking. The man is leaving the bank and putting his helmet back on. My footman will check to make sure bank staff are OK."

"Car 4. Any motorcycle seen at all?"

"Not by me, no."

"Car 4, all in order, customer paying in."

"Dougie, to all teams, stay alert."

Dave said, "Do you think someone's taking the piss?"

"Might, be. You never know."

An hour later, a call came through that a bank at Stapleford had been robbed by a man in motorcycle gear. With no cars in that area, DI Nugent rang and asked for an update from control.

They informed him a man done the bank in the same manner as the others, but a customer had seen the man walk round from the bank, climb into the boot of a waiting Blue BMW, closing the boot lid, and being driven away. He hadn't got the car number.

Ringing off, he said, "That's how they do it. He dresses as a motorcyclist, walks round the corner and gets in the boot of a waiting car. Crafty fucker."

"From Dougie, stand down. Back to base for debrief."

At the debrief, it had been decided not to include the fact the man had been seen climbing into a car boot, but a Blue BMW was suspected to be the getaway vehicle. This info was to be kept in-house.

Meanwhile, in Wilford, the driver of the BMW and the motorcycle-clad man were counting their proceeds from their last robbery.

The driver said, "Eight grand, getting better. Good idea to move out of town a bit, you thought they might be watching some banks."

"They are, and keeping it tight. I reckon, one more next week, then call it a day for a while."

The driver said, "Which one next week?"

"Not sure yet. It looks like the two banks have rewards of £20,000 now between them."

CHAPTER 11

Dick Jones answered his phone. "Control room here, sir. We have a possible murder. Body found behind the pavilion on the Forest Recreation Ground. Looks like he's taken a beating."

Dick asked who the Senior Investigating Officer was.

"DI Girling sir, he's at the scene now."

"Thanks."

Dick rang DI Girling. "Bill, Dick Jones. What's the situation there?"

"Male, white, mid-thirties, medium build. SOCO are here. Looks like he's been here for a few hours. No ID on the body. SOCO are printing him as we speak."

"Keep me updated, Bill. If you need any more troops, let me know."

Dick walked round to the Chief Super's office. Paul said, "Come in mate, what's up?"

"They've just found a body on the Forest, white male, looks like he's had a beating. SOCO are printing him now. Bill Girling's SIO, he's a sound officer."

"Keep me updated on that. How's things going on the bank jobs?"

"Well, we know he doesn't use a bike to get away on. He climbs into the boot of a waiting car. We haven't made that known to all and sundry. Dougie's team don't even know that."

"Why's that?"

Dick said, "Just a feeling. Partly because if we see someone leaving a bank in motorcycle gear we get the one getting into a car boot, and not on a bike. We're running it again next week, but the cars will rotate between two or three banks each. They will overlap at times, to make spotting them a bit more difficult. As one car pulls up, the other car moves to his next bank, as he pulls up the other car moves to his next bank, and so on."

"Sounds a good plan, let's hope it works. Are we still on for tonight, at your place? Babysitter arranged."

"Yes, see you later."

Dick walked back to his office, seeing DI Girling on the way back. "Hello Bill. How's the murder going? Any identity yet?"

"Yes, he's a local man. He runs a coffee shop on Mansfield Road."

"The one next to the gunshop?"

"That's the one."

"Well he pointed out the two blokes who robbed it. He saw them leaving. Do you think it might be a revenge attack?"

"Too early to say. But that jobs virtually done and dusted, two men charged, one man dead. We'll certainly look at that angle as part of the enquiry."

"Keep me updated, good luck."

***

The following week, the bank surveillance operation was in full swing. Around 11am a call came in. "Car 7, outside Stevens Bank, Radford Boulevard. Man in motorcycle gear just entered the bank, carrying a briefcase."

Dougie replied, "DI Nugent and myself travelling in Car 1, any others nearby?"

"Car 5, we are just down the road, travelling."

"Car 1 to Car 5, make your way to the rear of the bank, be on lookout for a blue BMW parked up."

"Car 5, Will do."

Moments later, "Car 5, Blue BMW, Reg number X333 RJR parked on Denman Street to the rear of the bank. One man in the driver's seat, engine running."

"Car 1, Keep obs on it. Rest of the team, move in and await instructions. Do not approach the vehicle."

"Car 4, PNC check on vehicle please?"

"Car 7, man out of bank, still full motorcycle gear on and carrying briefcase. Moved round onto Denman Street. Have you got him Car 5?"

"Car 5, affirmative, he's just climbed into the boot of that BMW, car now moving off. Car 5 has the eyeball. Driving up Denman Street, now left onto Ilkeston Road, towards Canning Circus."

"Car 1. All cars close up, we are now live."

"Car 4, quickly, BMW registered to Richard Rogers, lives Ruddington Lane, Wilford."

The driver of the BMW shouted to the man in the boot, "Looks like we're being followed."

The man in the boot opened it slightly and saw the car about fifty yards back. Shouting to the driver he said, "Put your foot down and lose them."

The car leapt forward, running through red traffic lights at Canning Circus, diving in and out of traffic, cutting across a bus the wrong way and onto Derby Road, across again into Park Terrace and into the Park area of Nottingham.

"Car 5, been baulked by a bus. Temporary loss, Canning Circus area. Now total loss. Total loss team."

"Car 1. OK team. Cars 4 and 6 to driver's home address, rest of us spread out for search pattern. If no sightings in ten, we all move to Ruddington Lane area. All confirm please?"

All drivers acknowledged.

The BMW driver drove down through the Park, onto Castle Boulevard and through the large retail park, out onto Wilford Road, turning right towards Clifton Bridge. Reaching the address at Ruddington Lane, he pressed the electric garage door opener and drove in, closing behind him. Going to the rear of his car, he opened the boot and let the other man out. "Fuck me that was close." The two men hugged and went indoors.

In the meantime, Dougie and his team had arrived at the registered keeper's address. "Car 1, looks like our Blue BMW is on false plates. This car here hasn't moved in ages. It's got condensation all over it and it's stone cold. On checking with the occupant, it was obvious he was not the man they had been chasing.'

"Car 1, all teams back for debrief please. Acknowledge?"

CHAPTER 12

Dick Jones had Dougie, DI Nugent, and DS Piggott in his office with him.

Dick said, "So we know the bank robbers are not using a bike for sure. The car has cloned plates on it. How did you lose them, Dougie?"

"I reckon they must have clocked us. The driver suddenly put his foot down, made some absolutely crazy manoeuvres, our lads got baulked by a couple of buses, and they got away. Just unlucky. We did a search pattern, and went to the registered keeper's address, but as you know it's on cloned plates."

"Nothing from the reward side yet, then?"

"Not yet sir, no," replied Dave Nugent.

"So what's next?"

Dougie said, "We can't keep the surveillance running on a permanent basis, as we have other work on. We can try it, but others need us as well."

"I understand that, but these two need catching. I still think we are missing something."

"Like what?" asked Dougie.

"Not sure, Dougie. Just a gut feeling I have. Dave, moving on, how's the murder enquiry coming on? Do you know?"

"Well we know his name is Michael Belking. He owns that coffee bar on Mansfield Road. We think it's a domestic gone wrong. Belking was gay and into the gay scene in a big way. We think he fell out with whoever, whilst having sex or meeting for sex. We're checking his phone records, we know his number, but not got his phone back yet."

"Is it anything to do with the gunshop job then?" asked Dick.

"We don't think so, but haven't fully discounted it."

DS Piggott's mobile rang. "Excuse me, Malc Piggott."

He walked out of the room. As he walked out, they heard him say, "Are you sure? OK, I just want to make a note."

He walked back into the room with his fingers to his lips. Switching the speaker on, he said, "Go on."

The voice on the other end said, "Are you alone?"

He replied, "I am now."

The voice said, "A couple of things. If what I tell you is right, can I claim the rewards from the banks?"

"If it's right, yes."

The voice said, "The two men you want for the bank jobs are Billy Lowe and Les Smythe. Smythe is a cop at Trent Station, Billy is a mechanic in the police garage. They're both on the gay scene. Billy has been having some sort of relationship with Mick Belking, the man found dead on the Forest. They had an argument when Mick found out they were robbing banks, and because Billy and Les wouldn't give him a share, he threatened to grass them up."

"What cars do this Billy and Les drive, do you know?"

"Billy has a blue BMW, he puts false plates on when they do a job. He told me he got chased the other day after a job but got away. Smythe was in the boot. I think Smythe has a new Honda Civic, grey or silver colour."

"How well do you know these two then?"

"I've met them a few times, big-headed bastards, don't like either of them. I know Billy lives at Wilford, don't know where Smythe lives, although he does spend a lot of time at Billy's."

"Are you willing to make a statement about what you are telling me?"

"Only when they are off the streets."

"One last thing, I have to ask. Are you involved in any of these jobs at all?"

"Honestly, no."

"Leave that with me, I'll get back to you. You've earned that reward. Can I get back to you on this number?"

"You can, but if anyone apart from me answers, say wrong number. Cheers."

Dick said, "Who was that, Malc?"

"A guy I've known for a few years. He's never let me down yet."

"Well, if what he says is right, we have a bent cop in our midst, and I don't like bent cops, and especially ones who rob banks with firearms. Do any of you know him?"

Dave Nugent said, "I know him, but only in passing. I don't think I've ever spoken to him."

"Dougie, he is your team's next target. Any of your team know him, stand them down. Tell your team, under no circumstances are they to have any contact with him, or officers on his shift."

Dougie replied, "Understood."

"Malc, I want you to check his duty rotas over these bank jobs. I knew there was something we were missing. If he was at that level crossing, after the mobile bank unit went over, why didn't he come forward? There's been no shortage of news about it. I'm beginning to think him and his mate were in on it somewhere. Probably this Billy was the third man, John Biston didn't know. Dave, check up on this Billy Lowe. His work record at the garage, see how they match up to Smyths rotas. And phone records for them both. Meet back here in a couple of hours. Dougie, can you plot up on this Billy Lowe's address, till I give you further instructions? Anybody gets any problems, get straight back to me."

Dick went along the corridor to Paul Richards' office. He sat down and explained what had just taken place, and what was being done.

When he finished, Paul said, "Hang on whilst I ring the Chief."

When he got through, he began to explain, when the Chief said, "Hang on Paul, I've got the ACC Crime with me. OK you are on speaker now."

When Paul had finished, the Chief said, "Is Dick Jones with you?"

"Yes sir, he's listening on the speaker."

"DCI Jones, I like what you have organised. Well done. Is Bill Girling aware of this?"

Dick said, "He's on his way in sir."

"Fine, keep us updated Paul, well done."

"Well you're in the good books with the Chief and ACC, mate," said Paul.

"Let's hope it stays that way," Dick replied.

Bill Girling walked into the office. Paul said, "Sit down Bill, Dick will update you."

When Dick had finished, he said, "I know that PC Smythe, he was on my section for a short while till I transferred to CID. To be honest, I always had him down as suspect, but couldn't quite bottom him. If you excuse the pun. He was always trying to please, sticking his nose in on all sorts of jobs, but not his own. A bit flash I thought."

Dick said, "Well he's on duty at six tonight. Hopefully Dougie and his team will have him under surveillance, watching him until he comes on duty. What do you want to do, Paul?"

"I would like him to come to my office on arrival at the station. That's if he turns up. Get his section sergeant to ask him to come to my office for an appraisal if you like. I would like Dave Nugent to arrest him, then you team up with him for interviews. Is that OK with you Bill?"

"Yes, sir. That's fine."

Dick said, "Let me check with Dougie, see what the situation is." He rang through to Dougie and was informed that the team had picked him up at his home address, and followed him to an address at Wilford. He was still there. The address at Wilford was Billy Lowe's.

Dick informed Dougie that Smythe was on duty at six this evening. When he left the house, they were to follow him to the station, hopefully. Once at the station, and inside, arrangements had been made regarding him. Then to return to Wilford and detain Lowe, leave a car on him if they had to. Do a quick search, then leave the place secure for SOCO.

Dougie replied, "Got that."

"All being well, six o'clock is our strike time," said Dick.

CHAPTER 13

About half past five, Paul, Dick, Dave Nugent and Bill Girling got the message that Smythe had left the address at Wilford and was heading for Trent Station. Getting the news that he had arrived, locked his car up and was now inside the police station.

Smythe was at his locker getting his equipment ready for duty. His sergeant came in and said, "Les, Chief Super wants you upstairs. Appraisal time."

PC Smythe went up to Paul's office, knocking he was told to come in.

On entering he saw Paul and DI Nugent.

DI Nugent stood up. "PC Smythe, I am arresting you on suspicion of armed robberies at Stevens Banks and Smiths Banks. And suspicion of murder. Do you understand?" Whilst he was cautioning him, he turned around as though to run out of the door. Dick was leaning on the door. "Try it if you want."

Instead, he ran full pelt at the window, crashing into it and back into the room.

Paul looked at him and said, "Toughened glass son, if you look in the top right-hand corner, you'll see the kitemark. Get him out of here."

He was handcuffed and taken to the Custody Office, where he was booked in.

Dick said to the custody sergeant, "No phone calls yet, and an officer to sit outside his cell."

"Cell 15 will do."

Smythe was placed in cell 15, with the door not fully shut; a detention officer sat outside.

Dick said, "OK Dave, let's do his locker first."

He and DI Nugent, accompanied by a SOCO, used Smythe's keys to open his locker. Inside a box at the bottom of his locker, under a rucksack, they found £3,000 in notes, some with Smiths and some with Stephens, bank wrappers round them. Inside the rucksack were motorcycle leathers and gloves.

Dick said, "Nothing like rubbing our noses in it is there? Keeping it on police property."

All the items were bagged, tagged and sealed up.

"Now his car," Dick said.

They went out to the car park and found his car. "Nice car for a young PC," DI Nugent said.

In the boot they found a crash helmet in a cloth bag, and a briefcase, with a combination lock on. Dick forced it open. Inside was a sawn-off double-barrel shotgun. The shotgun was fully loaded. Dick knew his weapons and carefully checked it to make it safe.

They bagged, tagged and sealed all the items up.

Dick said, "Now I want a search team at his home address. This lad's got some serious jail time coming to him."

All the secured items were left with the SOCO. He had also photographed the items in situ, during the searches.

Dick informed Paul about the property they had recovered and said, "I reckon Dougie and his crew can do their arrest now."

***

Over in Wilford, DI Girling, Dougie and another officer knocked on the door.

DI Girling identified themselves and said, "Are you Billy Lowe?"

The man replied, "Yes."

DI Girling said, "You are under arrest on suspicion of armed robberies at Smiths Banks and Stephens Banks, and also on suspicion of the murder of Michael Belking." He was cautioned and asked if he understood.

Lowe replied, "I understand, but I don't know what you are talking about."

He was handcuffed and taken into the lounge. On the table was a large pile of bank notes.

DI Girling said, "What's this then?"

Lowe said, "I sold a car for cash."

"Dougie, get the SOCO man in. I want this lot photographed. Any other money in the house, Billy?" he asked.

"No, only this."

They had a quick look round, and in the kitchen, stashed at the back of a unit, they found another £10,000, again some were in Smiths Bank and Stephens Bank wrappers.

DI Girling said, "Sold another car then, Billy?"

Lowe made no reply.

"OK. Photo what we have here. I want the place secured until we get a search team here. Dougie, one of your lads can drive the BMW back to the station, we can let SOCO sort it there."

Lowe was taken to the police station where he was also booked in. Again, no phone calls allowed.

CHAPTER 14

DI Nugent and DS Piggott sat down in an interview room with Les Smythe. He had refused any legal representation or a Federation rep to support him. When asked why, he replied, "I don't want one. Full stop."

DI Nugent said, "If at any time you change your mind, let us know and we will halt the interview."

"I understand sir."

"Right, you have been arrested today on suspicion of bank robberies and murder. What have you got to say in relation to the robberies?"

"I was involved in them, but only as the driver, it was Billy's idea."

"Why have you got all the motorcycle gear with you, if you were only the driver?"

"It was something we agreed on. I could keep it safe at the nick."

"And the shotgun as well?"

"Yes."

DS Piggott said, "Right, let's start at the beginning. Who is the other guy running with you?"

"His name's Billy Lowe, he works in the police garage, I know that now."

"Is that where you first met him then?"

Smythe looked at both officers and said, "I'm gay. We met in a gay bar in town last year. We got talking, and that was it."

"So when did you decide to rob banks?"

"We just sat talking about crime one night and came up with the idea. One man kitted out in full motorcycle gear, the other doing the driving. When the bank job was done, whoever was in motorcycle gear would get in the boot. Cops would be looking for a motorcycle as a getaway vehicle. I was able, to a point, to keep up on the enquiries into them through work."

"So that's how you knew which areas to work them?"

"Yes. We just picked them at random. They had to have a place to park round the corner."

DI Nugent asked, "Why did you do it?"

"Not sure really. The thrill, the inside knowledge and money really. Easy money."

"Where did the shotgun come from?"

"Billy got that. We sawed it off at his house, to fit the briefcase."

"You, or whoever did the bank, indicated to bank staff that you had a shotgun. Would you have used it?"

"I wouldn't, I don't think Billy would either."

"So why was it loaded?"

Smythe made no reply.

"Recovered from your locker was some cash and motorcycle gear. Is that from the banks and the gear you dressed up in?"

"Yes."

"So you admit doing the banks at West Bridgford, Sherwood, Stapleford and Lenton?"

"Yes."

"All in company with Billy Lowe?"

"Yes."

DI Nugent said, "What about Michael Belking, the man found dead on the Forest. What happened there?"

"That was down to Billy. We met him at a gay bar and formed a threesome. He called round one day as we had just got back from a bank job. He walked in and saw the money on the table, so Billy told him about us."

"What did he say to that?"

"He thought it was great. He wanted to join in. When we told him no, he said if we didn't give him a share he might make a phone call and claim the reward."

"So what did you do?"

"We let him dress up in the gear, to go to his own bank at Sneinton. But to take the helmet off inside. We drove him down there, that's when I realised some banks were being watched."

"So what happened to him?"

"He got in touch after the Stapleford job, and again asked for some money. So Billy arranged to meet him on the Forest."

"Did you go?"

"No. Billy went on his own."

"Did you know what was going to happen?"

"I had no idea. That was nothing to do with me."

"What about when you found out? What did you do?"

"Nothing. I couldn't split on him, could I? We are... were lovers. But we decided no more jobs for a bit. Let the heat die down."

"Did you have any relationship with Belking that Billy didn't know about?"

"A couple of times, at the coffee bar, in the back office."

"Right. We'll call this interview to a halt now. Anything else you want to say?"

"Sorry, that's all. I've let the force down."

"No son. You have let yourself and your family down. Think on that."

The interview was terminated

Whilst that interview was taking place, DI Girling and DS Flowers were interviewing Billy Lowe.

He had elected to have a solicitor present.

DI Girling said, "You have been arrested on suspicion of armed robbery at banks in and around the city centre, and also suspicion of the murder of Michael Belking. Do you understand?"

"My solicitor has told me to make no comment."

"That is your right. But I still intend asking you some questions. Tell me first, how do you know Les Smythe?"

Lowe looked at his solicitor, burst into tears, and said, "We are lovers."

"As in a homosexual relationship?"

Sniffing he replied, "Yes."

His solicitor said, "Billy, you don't have to say anything."

"I want to. We have been lovers for about a year now."

"Did you know he was a serving police officer?"

"Not at first no, but I saw him in town in his uniform one day."

"Knowing he was a police officer, what made you turn to crime together?"

"Well, I found out one day they had been using my car and done a bank job."

DS Flowers said, "Who had done a bank job?"

"Les and Michael."

"Tell us about it."

"Les asked if he could use my car one day for something. Then I found out they had done the bank job at West Bridgford. I was livid. Then we sat down and talked about it after Michael had left. We decided we would do a couple ourselves."

"How did you find out?"

"I came back when they were counting it out at my house."

"How did you meet Michael?"

"At a gay club in town. We all hit it off and made a threesome up. I think Les was seeing him on his own as well."

"Getting back to the bank jobs. Who decided to leave Michael out?"

"We did. I got some plates made up. There's an old guy down the road with a nearly identical car, so I got some plates made up."

"Who went in the bank?"

"We took it in turns, me and Les."

"Where was the shotgun from?"

"It was my dad's old one. I sawed it off to fit the briefcase."

"Who loaded it?"

"I did, don't ask me why. I don't know. It was really only for show."

"You moved round a bit doing the banks. Why was that?"

Les said, "He thought some were being watched."

"What about Michael in this set up?"

"He found out we were doing them without him, and said he wanted a share or he would go to the police."

"So what did you do about that?"

"I arranged to meet him on the Forest, to talk about things. We ended up arguing and throwing punches. He fell and banged his head. He didn't move. I kicked him to wake him up, but I think he was dead."

"Were you on your own."

"Yes."

"What clothing were you wearing at that time?"

"Blue jeans, black sweater. They are all in a bin liner in my car boot, ready to dump or burn."

DI Girling said, "So you admit the bank robberies, and also being responsible for Michael Belking's death?"

"Yes. But I didn't mean to kill him."

"Right, that's all for now. Anything further you want to say?"

"No."

The interview was terminated.

Half an hour later, DIs Nugent and Girling were sat in Paul Richards' office. Also present was Dick Jones.

Both DIs had outlined the interviews they had had with Smythe and Lowe.

Paul said, "Well, it makes a change to get full admissions, of sorts. What's left now?"

DI Nugent said, "Really, just topping and tailing certain things. We want to ask them about the Bingham job. And also what comes back from the house searches."

Paul said, "What a stupid pair they are. What time are the next interviews set for?"

"Both set for around 11.30am tomorrow."

"Right guys," said Paul. "Quick pint across the road, on me."

CHAPTER 15

The following day, DI Nugent and DS Piggott again interviewed Smythe. Again he refused the use of a solicitor, but accepted a Federation representative being present.

After the introductions and caution, DI Nugent said, "Do you know a Patrick Parr?"

Smythe replied, "Yes."

"How do you know him?"

"I met him a couple of times. We were out in Calverton having a drink, he lives out there I think. He's a mate of John and Derek Biston."

The two officers looked at each other. DS Piggott asked, "How do you know them?"

"Oh just from being out and about."

"What do you know about them, Parr and the Biston brothers?"

"Not much really. I think they are a bit involved in crime, but not sure."

DI Nugent said, "Considering you are, or were, a member of this police force, you certainly mix with some unsavoury characters. Did you ever consider reporting your relationship with these people?"

"No. Look, I know in your eyes I'm a bad cop, but these people were mates."

"Mates? These people are villains and you are running with them. What does that make you?"

"If I tell you something about them, can you help me?"

"In what way?"

"A lighter sentence, a safer prison. I know I'm going down."

"I can't make that decision, but I will pass it on. What do you want to tell us?"

"I know Derek Biston and Patrick Parr did a mobile bank just outside Bingham a couple of weeks back. They got about thirty grand out of it. Derek shot at the windscreen. I know the guns were dumped off Gunthorpe Bridge, into the Trent afterwards. I know they always dump the guns after each job."

"Who else was on that job?"

Smythe looked at the officers. "You know, don't you?"

"You tell us. You were involved, weren't you?"

"Yes. I stopped at the level crossing after the bank van and the Transit went over, so traffic couldn't follow. The time the barriers were up, they'd done it."

"And I suspect your mate, Billy, was with them as well. Wasn't he?"

"Yes."

"Where did you go when the barriers went up?"

"I crossed the crossing and went into the supermarket car park, turned round and drove back to Calverton the long way round."

"What did you get out of it?"

"We got a couple of grand each, and a shotgun from the Mansfield Road gunshop job. Derek gave me that."

"What did you do with it?"

"Sold it on, got a hundred quid for it."

"Who to?"

"I don't know his name, he was a friend of Mick Belking."

DI Nugent said, "You know, for a police officer, you have got mixed up in some bad jobs, with bad people. If only you had used your brain and informed a senior officer, you would be a top cop, instead of a bent one looking at a long prison sentence."

"I know. What happens now?"

"You know we have to put the facts to the Crown Prosecution Service and decide what charges you will face, which quite honestly are serious ones. The only good thing you have done, is admitted your part in these offences. Can I ask you why you went bent, if you'll excuse the pun?"

"I just got dragged in really. Once I was in, I couldn't get out. I didn't want my mates to know I was gay."

"Well you won't be the first gay cop, or the last one. Can we just clarify, all monies recovered from your locker are from crime?"

"Yes, and any from my home."

"You will be detained pending charging, and then to court. Bail will be opposed."

"Why is that?"

"Likelihood of interfering with witnesses, seriousness of the charges, and the fact you may make some attempt to get away. Anything else to say?"

"No."

The interview was terminated.

CHAPTER 16

The following day, all the detained persons had been charged.

John Biston was charged with the gunshop robbery, possession and supply of firearms and ammunition.

Patrick Parr was charged with the mobile bank robbery and possession and supply of firearms and ammunition.

Les Smythe was jointly charged with armed robberies at banks, jointly charged with the mobile bank robbery, possession and supply of shotgun, and handling a stolen shotgun. He was also dismissed as a serving police officer.

Billy Lowe was jointly charged with armed robberies at banks, jointly charged with the mobile bank robbery, possession of a shotgun and the murder of Michael Belking.

All were remanded into prison custody.

On his arrival at the prison, Smythe requested he be placed on the protection wing due to him being a former police officer.

Within twenty-four hours he was attacked by a fellow inmate, who had struck him in the kidneys whilst his back was turned. Smythe went down and rolled to one side. He kicked out at his attacker, kicking his legs from under him. He then straight finger jabbed him in the throat, kicked him as hard as he could in the testicles, then grabbed him by the throat.

He said, "I don't know who you are, or who sent you, next time you are dead. And anyone else who tries."

He threw him hard against the wall and went back to his cell.

The enquiries into the four men were going well, and a couple of days later, all four men were in a prison van being transported from the prison to Crown Court in Nottingham. As their van travelled down the A46, nearing the junction with the Flintham turn, a Transit van lumbered out of the junction to join the A46. As the prison van was about to pull out and overtake it, the van swerved across in front of it, forcing it to hit the central reservation and stop. A marked police vehicle had pulled behind the prison van, with his blue lights flashing. Officers got out and stopped traffic from passing.

Four men got out of the Transit van, pointing guns at the driver and his crew.

"Open the side door. Now."

The guard inside opened the door, two men went in, took the keys from him and opened the internal cell doors, releasing all four occupants. They were escorted out into a second Transit van, and driven away.

The guards were made to sit at the side of the road. Two men went to the van and the prison van, setting them on fire, then joined the bogus police crew and were driven off. The whole thing had taken about ninety seconds from start to finish. Following vehicles were unable to get past due to the blazing vehicles.

The van, containing the four now escaped prisoners, drove into the driveway of a large country house in the Vale of Belvoir, followed by the bogus police car. Once inside the large garage, the doors were lowered. The four prisoners were made to sit on separate chairs, still with their handcuffs on. A man wearing a facial mask came into the garage and stood in front of them.

Parr said, “Who are you? What do you want us for?”

“I want you to do a job for me.”

Smythe said, “And if we don’t?”

“You will be the first to die plod.”

The four men looked at each other. The masked man pulled his mask off.

Parr said, “Fuck me, Geoff Bull. I haven’t seen you for ages. How’s things?”

“Well I’m still around mate. Thanks for the guns and ammo by the way. Great pick-up idea. I’ll give you all ten minutes to think about my offer and make your minds up.”

Bull walked out.

The others looked at Parr. Smythe said, “So who is this guy, Bull?”

Parr replied, “He makes the Kray twins look like kittens. He’s a London gang boss, and ruthless.”

Smythe asked, “How do you know him?”

“Met him inside a bit back. He virtually ran the place, screws and all.”

Biston said, “What happens if we don’t go along with him?”

“He’ll probably find a motorway bridge to bury you under, or some bloke at the Crem to get rid of you. Believe me.”

Smythe said, “So I suppose we have no choice.”

Billy Lowe said, “I’m not with him.”

“You have to be Billy.”

“No I don’t. I’m in enough shit as it is.”

The door opened and Bull and two men walked in.

“OK you guys. No doubt Mr Parr has told you all about me. So are you in or out?”

Parr said, “I’m with you, Geoff.”

Biston said, “And me.”

Smythe said, “I suppose so.”

Lowe said, “I’m not sure, not very happy about this.”

Bull pulled a gun from behind his back and pointed it at him, "Will this help?"

"What job is it?"

"In or out. Your choice?"

Lowe said, "Out."

Bull said, "OK" and shot him between the eyes. "Out now my friend. Take him out, get rid of him."

One man left the room, returning shortly with a large plastic box on wheels. They put the body in and left.

"So you all know where you stand now boys. We'll get the cuffs off and get you settled in."

All three men nodded.

Bull said, "Right, you will all stay here until the job. I'll explain what it is later. If it all goes to plan, you should get around half a million each. Transferred to wherever you want."

Smyth said, "Is that guaranteed?"

"It is, unless you cross me. Then you get a plastic box like your mate. If you get caught, that's another matter. Just do as you are told, no fuck-ups and we should all be happy."

Speaking to one of his men, he said, "Jim, show them to their rooms. And by the way, the windows only open a couple of inches and cameras are watching you most of the time. Food will be bought to you shortly. Fresh clothing is in your wardrobes. You can walk in the gardens up to the white boundary posts; if you go beyond them the alarms will go off."

They were each shown to separate double rooms, which were large and airy, with king-size beds.

Looking out of his window, Smythe saw the house was set within a large area of land, lots of trees about. He could see Belvoir Castle, set on the hill, a couple of miles away.

He showered and changed, and decided to have a walk in the grounds.

CHAPTER 17

Shortly after the report had come through, Dick Jones, now Acting Detective Superintendent, was in a meeting with Paul Richard, his boss, and other senior officers.

Paul relayed to the meeting, "Ladies, and gents. If you are not aware, there was a prison van attacked this morning on the A46, near Flintham. All four prisoners were taken from the van, which was then set on fire, along with another vehicle, mainly in order to block traffic. A bogus police car stopped traffic whilst the men were being released. We don't know where they went after that, as the A46 has no cameras on it of any description. The prisoners released are ex-PC Les Smythe, his running mate, Billy Lowe, Patrick Parr and John Biston. All were en route back to court for hearings on their offences. Armed robbery, firearms offences, and Lowe, with murder. At the moment that's all we know. Anyone want to throw anything in?"

Det Insp Dave Nugent said, "Photos of all the men have been circulated countrywide. I suspect it's a matter of waiting and see what comes in from that, or any other information. Fortunately, no staff were injured in the incident.

CHAPTER 18

A couple of days into their enforced captivity, the three prisoners were escorted back to the large room.

Geoff Bull was there with a large flipchart and diagrams showing.

"Right lads, now you have settled in, here's the job we are doing." Pointing to the chart he said, "In two days' time, a bullion van leaves East Midlands Airport cargo centre terminal, bound for Coventry and Birmingham. That is our target."

Parr asked, "Out of curiosity, how much bullion, Geoff?"

"Between eight and ten million."

"Wow. Any armed escort with it?"

"No, but thanks to you, we all will be, or most of us. It's a monthly run, they take a different route each time. This time, it's the old A453, to join the A46 further down."

"What do you mean, guns thanks to me?"

"The guns we got from you at the tip at Calverton. You had no idea it was me, did you?"

"None at all, so he was a contact of yours then?"

"Anyway, the bullion van travels towards Ashby on the A453, we hit it on that road, just outside the garden centre. Plod, you will be dressed as a cop, with one of my men. John, you will be in a breakdown truck with one of my men. My men will be armed, but you two won't."

Parr said, "What about me?"

"You will be with me, Pat. We stage a breakdown, crash, just after the bend near the garden centre. This will cause a diversion. You cops will divert traffic through the garden centre. As the bullion van reaches you, you divert that, and the van behind it into the garden centre. You then stop any other traffic, as the breakdown will get cleared to allow traffic to the main road. John, your job will be to get that crash and breakdown truck out of the way as the vans go into the garden centre. You drive the truck into the first entrance on the right, which leads to the garden centre. My man with you will direct you. That's all you need to know at the moment. My men know the rest of the plan, and our getaway route."

Smythe asked, "Are you sure the van will take that route?"

"Positive. As I have just said, that's all you need to know."

Parr asked, "Why did you pick us, Geoff?"

"You all have nothing to lose, you gain half a mill each, and a get-out clause, to wherever you want to go, I can arrange that. Now that's enough. We all meet for dinner this evening, and you get to meet your men."

Later that evening, after dinner, they all sat around in the large lounge area, some were playing snooker in the adjoining room. Smythe was looking out of the French doors. "Nice place Mr Bull, had it long?"

"It belongs to a few of us, we've had it for about five years now. Comes in handy for jobs like this."

Smythe turned from the window and went and sat down in an overly stuffed armchair, just vacated by one of Bull's men. As he sat down, he noticed a mobile phone to one side of the seat, obviously it had slipped from the man's pocket. He put it into his own pocket. After a couple of minutes he stood up and said, "Just need to use my loo, it might be a smelly one."

***

Once in his room, he went to the bathroom and started flushing the toilet, whilst ringing the number for Trent Division. He asked to be put through to Paul Richards or Dick Jones urgently, as he had information on the escaped prisoners.

Paul Richards answered.

Smythe said, "Sir, it's Les Smythe. Please listen, I don't have long. Don't ask questions yet. In two days' time a bullion van leaves East Midlands Airport cargo centre, bound for Coventry and Birmingham. We've been pulled into help, not our doing. It's travelling from the airport along the old A453 towards Ashby. It's going to be hit the other side of Ashby near a garden centre. Bogus cops and a breakdown are being used. They are armed, we aren't. He got the guns off Pat Parr, at the tip at Calverton somehow."

"Where are you?"

"No idea, all I can tell you is, I can see Belvoir Castle from my window a couple of miles away, please listen. They have someone on the inside at the depot. The gang leader is a guy called Geoff Bull, a Londoner. He's ruthless. He shot Billy Lowe dead because he refused to take part. Look, I've got to go."

Paul said, "Hello, hello. Fuck he's rang off."

Smythe flushed the toilet again and made his way back to the lounge. The chair he left was still empty. As he sat down, he pushed the phone down the side. A couple of minutes later, the owner of the phone came in saying, "My phone's missing."

Bull said, "Search them three."

Smythe, Parr and Biston were searched. "Not on them," the man said.

"Any idea where you left it?"

"In here I thought."

Bull handed him his phone and said, "Ring it."

The man rang his number and heard it ringing where Smythe was sat. Bull went over and pulled it out.

"You left it, it slipped down the side of the chair. Just check it's not been used."

The man checked the log. Fortunately Smythe had the quick sense to delete his call. The man said, "No, not been used."

"In future, keep it safe," Bull warned him.

CHAPTER 19

At Trent Division, Paul rang and asked Dick to come straight up.

Walking in, Dick said, "What's so urgent?"

Paul said, "Just had a call from Les Smythe. They have evidently been sprung to do a job on a bullion van. It leaves the East Midlands Airport in a couple of days. He sounded genuine, and scared. The van is travelling from there to Coventry, then Birmingham. It's going to be hit en route, on the A453 near a place called Ashby. A guy called Geoff Bull is running the show, he's a Londoner and violent. He's already shot Billy Lowe because he didn't want to be involved."

Dick asked, "How does he know all this?"

"I presume because they have been told by this Bull character. He sounded under a lot of stress, and told me to listen, so I really couldn't ask anything. He was in a hurry I think. By the sounds of it, they have someone on the inside, so any approach to EMA is out of the question. Bogus cops and a vehicle breakdown are involved somewhere along the line, and near a garden centre."

"Did you check the number he was ringing from?"

"Yes, a burner phone I think, nothing came back. He said they were near Belvoir Castle, as he can see it a couple of miles away, but no real idea where he is."

"What do you intend to do?"

"Dougie is on his way in, he's only local."

A knock sounded on the door and Dougie walked in.

Paul related what he had been told.

Dougie said, "Sounds like an organised job. Can you trust Smythe?"

"Don't see why not. Sounds like he's trying to make amends for his previous actions. We have to act on it anyway. If we don't and it comes off, we'll be right muppets. What I want you to do Dougie is get a team together. No approach to EMA. We can't put men in the truck, because of inside information. Include two bikers, and I want all officers fully armed and with protective gear on. Dick, as the unit comes under you, is your firearms ticket up to date?"

"Yes."

"Right, I want you to ride with Dougie and his partner, but remember, Dougie is the surveillance commander, you are silver commander, regarding the firearms. Brief your lads the night before, and I want an early start. We don't know what time this van leaves. Can you do a recce on the route before? See how the land lies? Dick, get all the intel on this Geoff Bull guy. See if Greg can help. I'm off to see the Chief, put him in the picture. Keep in touch."

***

Paul travelled across to Police Headquarters and was explaining the bullion van information and plans to the Chief.

The Chief said, "What about crossing the border into a neighbouring force, carrying firearms? I'll speak to their Chief about that."

"Dougie has a great relationship with both Leicestershire and Derbyshire surveillance units. He is arranging for them to be on standby in case they are needed. Air support will be on standby at EMA."

"It sounds like this Bull character has no scruples for getting rid of folk who stand in his way."

"None at all, sir. I think Smythe has decided some information might help him at the end of the day."

"Our main concern is our own men. Let's make sure they are fully prepared."

"Dick and Dougie have things in hand, they work well together. All officers will be armed, suited and booted."

"OK Paul, good luck. I'll be on the end of a phone if needed."

"Thanks."

Back at his office, Paul met up with Dick who asked, "How did it go with the Chief?"

"He's backing us all the way. Any news on this Bull guy?"

"Yes. I spoke to your mate Greg, made DI now by the way. Bull sounds a right handful. Greg says he makes some of the older villains sound like kittens. He's got previous for firearms, armed robbery and is strongly suspected of gangland murders, but no evidence. According to Greg's intel, he is not to be trusted under any circumstances. Him and some of his gang, who are loyal to him, are ruthless."

Are you having a briefing with Dougie's team tomorrow?"

"Yes."

"OK, let's call it a night, quick pint and home my boy."

"Yes Boss."

CHAPTER 20

On the morning of the surveillance, Dick was at HQ at 7 am, joining Dougie and his team.

Dougie quickly ran through the job again. He warned his men to be extra careful, look out for each other. He warned them that Bull and his gang were ruthless. Photos were passed out of Bull and possible associates, plus Patrick Parr, Les Smythe and John Biston. Dougie was taking the first eyeball as Car 1, with seven other cars, plus Biker 1 and Biker 2. All officers were to be armed, weapons loaded and wearing body protection.

"All ready, let's go."

The unit made its way to EMA, where they plotted up on a couple of exits from the cargo depot. Radio checks were completed Dougie said, "Now we sit and wait. Keep your eyes open lads, no moving around."

At 10.55am, Dougie alerted the team, "From Car 1, standby, standby. Bullion van coming from the cargo terminal, down the exit road to roundabout. Vehicle at roundabout, not one, second exit, A453 towards Ashby. White Transit van, LG 13 ECT behind bullion van. We are behind that vehicle. All cars join up. They are up to the traffic lights, and straight through, still A453. I will only call up if any deviation made by bullion van. Call up in car order, to confirm you are in convoy?"

All cars replied, as did both bikes.

Dougie called through to the team, Car 1, "Tranny van is registered to EMA cargo centre, but may be on false plates. Still

A453 behind the bullion van, and Tranny. Now entering the village of Ashby, close-up team. Passing Quarry on right-hand side. Traffic slowing towards a left-hand bend, garden centre ahead. Looks like some police presence directing traffic. Standby team, this could be it."

The Bullion van was stopped by police and directed straight on into the garden centre, as was the Transit van. The police stopped Dougie's car and one approached him. "If you hang on a minute sir, the road will be cleared, you can go through."

"Where have they gone in front then?"

"They are in a hurry, so they are taking a short cut through the garden centre. They come out beyond the breakdown, it's like a horseshoe route."

Dick said, "The other cop is Smythe."

As he spoke, the police car moved off to follow the route the vans had taken. They saw the breakdown truck now entering the next entrance.

"Cars 2, 3, 4 and 5, follow me. Rest of you take the next entrance."

Dougie's driver gunned the motor and flew into the garden centre, followed by the team. As they rounded the bend at the end of the car park, they saw the bullion van had been stopped by the breakdown truck in front, the white van behind it. Armed men had surrounded it

Dick and his team were quickly out of their cars. Dick shouted, "Armed police, drop your weapons!"

It had happened so quickly, the armed gang were stunned when police came at them from both ends, guns trained on them. One of the gang raised his shotgun and fired at the nearest police officer. As he did so, the shotgun exploded in his hand, at the same time he was shot by police, hitting him in his shoulder.

***

Another member of the gang pointed his pistol at police and fired. His gun also exploded, as he was shot in the chest. Slowly the men started to raise their hands.

Dick had a megaphone and shouted, "You are surrounded by armed police. Very slowly place your firearms on the floor in front of you. Two of your men have already been shot. Do as you are ordered. Then take one step back from the van."

The gang complied. Dick said to Dougie, "Make sure we match the weapons recovered to the man as you arrest them."

The gang were all handcuffed and searched, as were the two injured men. The bogus police were searched, the gang member had a weapon, Smythe was unarmed. Parr had been one of the men covering the bullion van, although armed, his weapon was not loaded.

Dick called through to the control room, requesting uniform support and medical assistance for the injured men. He was checking the photos he had of the gang and picked out Bull, now handcuffed. Through his megaphone, Dick told all the gang members they were under arrest for attempted armed robbery and firearms offences. That done, he went to the crew of the bullion van. Although not injured, both were badly shaken.

"We have a relief crew coming out to take over, you will be needed for statements. I have arranged for airport police to come with them."

Dick walked up to Bull, who looked at him with intense hatred. "You are one fucking dead copper and your family."

Dick replied, "Only doing our job, which is to stop you doing yours."

Bull replied, "Fuck off."

Making sure all parties were secured, Dick went to Dougie, "Well done mate and your team. But your lads who made the shots will need to be questioned, they know that I hope."

"Yes, I've already spoken to them. That's no problem. Why did those guns explode though?"

"My thoughts are they are part of the haul from the gunshop raid. The manager was quick enough to pass on some old and wrong ammo for them. That guy there, Biston, and his brother did that job. He passed them on to Parr, as you know. Parr got them to Bull. I strongly suspect, when we check them, most, or all of them will be from there."

As more police support arrived, the gang were being taken back to Nottingham cell block with strict orders for ultra-tight security. The new crew for the van had arrived, with airport police, and they were to now act as escort to its destinations. The first crew were also taken back to Nottingham.

A short time later, in Nottingham, Smythe had requested to speak to Paul Richards and Dick Jones. He was escorted to their office.

Paul said, "Thanks for your help and information. How can we help you?"

"I have details of where the house we were held in is. I know I have done wrong, but if it helps with my sentence."

"I can't guarantee you anything, but I will let the sentencing judge know. If you had only done the proper thing in your career, you might have made a good cop, instead of a bad cop."

Before he left them, he passed over details of the house location.

EPILOGUE

John Biston was sentenced for the gunshop robbery and for his part in the mobile banking unit robbery. Also for supplying firearms to the criminal fraternity. He received 20 years in total.

***

Patrick Parr was sentenced for his part in the mobile banking unit robbery, and for handling and supplying stolen firearms. He received 15 years in total.

***

Les Smythe was sentenced for his part in the bank robberies, his part in the mobile banking unit robbery. Mention was passed to the judge, he received 12 years in total.

***

Geoff Bull was sentenced for the attempted robbery on the bullion van, firearms offences, and the murder of Billy Lowe, whose body had been recovered from the grounds of the house. He was also charged with two robberies in the London area. He received a minimum of 35 years in total.

As he was led away, he pointed his fingers at the judge and Dick Jones in the shape of a gun and shouted, "Bang."

The remainder of the gang were sentenced to various sentences ranging from 10 to 15 years.

All assets were seized.

BOOK THREE

THE END RESULT

CHAPTER 1

2018

The two helicopters dropped straight down into the centre of the prison exercise yard. Three men immediately sprinted towards them. Prison officers ran after them, but were forced to dive to the ground when shots were fired over their heads. The three men reached the helicopters and climbed in. As quickly as they had landed, they took off again. The whole thing took just 48 seconds. The prison was situated in Leicestershire and classed as 'maximum security'.

The prison break was circulated to all surrounding forces and countrywide.

Dick Jones, now promoted to Detective Superintendent, was sat in his office when the report landed on his desk. On reading it, he went next door to the Chief Superintendent's office.

Paul Richards was his mate of some years, his brother-in-law and his boss.

"Paul, just got details of a prison break from Leicestershire."

"And?" Paul asked.

"Three men got out in helicopters which landed in the exercise yard. Well planned."

"Anyone we know?"

Dick sat down. "One was Geoff Bull."

"The bullion van job, Geoff Bull?"

"Yes. The other two were Bob Teal and Joe Andrews."

Paul looked up. "Will those two men never get out of our lives? Did they track the helicopters?"

"No, they flew too low for staff at Flight Control at East Midlands Airport to track them."

"What's the latest update then?"

Dick said, "Newscast on about now."

Paul turned his television on as the headlines came on.

"In a daring prison escape earlier today, three men were taken from the exercise yard of a maximum security prison in Leicestershire, when two helicopters landed in the exercise yard. Prison staff were forced to dive for cover as shots were fired over their heads. The escaped men have been named as Geoffrey Bull, Robert Teal and Joseph Andrews. All three are classed as dangerous and have convictions for murder, firearms and violence. Police have warned not to approach them. If you have any information, please contact the police on the number shown below, under photographs of the men.

Paul said, "Notice all the photographs show them as clean shaven. Beards and moustaches could alter all their features."

Dick said, "Well until they are arrested, people's lives could be in danger, including ours."

"I agree. I wouldn't put anything past them, especially Bull. I think Julie, Alice and junior should be lodged at the flats at headquarters with armed guards. We should join them when we can, instead of going home. I'll speak to the Chief and get things arranged. The girls won't be happy, but their safety, and ours, comes first."

CHAPTER 2

On a large estate in Rutland, Bull, Teal and Andrews were enjoying their first meal on the outside for some time. Bull in a couple of years, the other two in five years.

"Well guys, have a rest for a couple of days, then we sort things out." This came from a man they now knew as Luke Bull, Geoff's younger brother.

Bob asked, "What happens after a couple of days then, Luke?"

Geoff butted in and said, "We plan our revenge on the fuckers that put us away. Cops, the judge and some other folk. But before that, Luke has a job planned."

Bob said, "Are you going to let us in on it then?"

"Tomorrow. Let's eat and enjoy tonight first."

***

Next morning, after breakfast, all four men made their way across the stable yard to a large outbuilding. Both helicopters were inside, but the livery on them was being changed, as were the registered numbers on them.

Luke said, "We are using them on our next job."

Bob said, "Which is?"

"A jeweller's van. There's a group of jewellery shops in the Nottingham and Derby area who buy old gold and silver, including stones. They collect these from the various shops, once a month, and take them to their main centre in

Manchester for sorting and melting down."

Bob asked, "What value are we looking at, do you know?"

Geoff said, "We reckon, about £5-million-worth a trip. We were going to do it as our next job, after the bullion job, but as you know, that caved in."

"So what's the plan?" asked Joe.

Geoff said, "For some reason the pickup never varies. The last two shops are in Bakewell and Matlock, Derbyshire. The van then travels back to Manchester, taking a route over the moors as one part of the journey. That's where we hit it."

"Is it a security van, Geoff?" asked Bob.

"No, a normal Transit van, one driver normally. We plan to do it tomorrow. You and Luke in one chopper, me and Joe in the other. Plus pilots. We have the van picked up by car, leaving Matlock. As soon as it clears Matlock for Bakewell, we get airborne. That's when the driver cuts across the moors here." He indicated on a large map, the A6 junction near Ashford on the Water. "He drives over the moors towards Wandlow to pick up the A623, and back onto the A6. We hit him on that moors road."

"Does the driver have radio contact with his firm?" asked Joe.

"No. Believe me, they don't take any security measures at all. After tomorrow they might. They've been doing the run for years, and never changed track," Luke said.

Geoff said, "Our plan is to put one chopper down in front of the van, the other behind it. There's no way he can get round us because of the stone walls. We'll be armed and masked up. We split the load between the choppers and head back here."

"What about other road traffic?" asked Bob.

"The road is very quiet, except for the occasional farm vehicle, but our choppers will have it blocked anyway."

"Sounds nearly foolproof," Bob replied.

Luke said, "I think it will be."

"What's the plan afterwards? Do you have somewhere to get rid of it all?" asked Joe.

Geoff said, "We have our own jewellery shop, fully equipped with smelter. We smelt the gold and silver down, then sell it on as bullion. Some of the stones will be reset, or just sold on. Don't worry about that side."

"Is the weather OK for tomorrow?" asked Bob.

Luke said, "Weather is fine for us."

Bob said, "Sounds good then. Can I ask what our cut will be, mine and Joe's?"

Geoff said, "We split whatever we get five ways. You and Joe each get a fifth, me and Luke each get a fifth. The other fifth is split for pilots and other expenses. OK?"

"So we all get around a million each?"

"If it's more, you get more, less you get less."

Bob said, "We've nothing to lose anyway. You OK with it, Joe?"

"OK with me mate."

***

The following morning, the weather as predicted was fine. After breakfast the gang did their final checks on the helicopters and other equipment.

They sat around playing cards, or at the snooker table. Luke got the call that the van was leaving Matlock, and that it was double crewed.

"That's our cue," he said. "Extra crew is no problem."

Bob and Luke climbed into one helicopter, Joe and Geoff into the other. The pilots knew the drill and were soon airborne, again flying as low as possible to avoid detection.

They reached their destination, with ten minutes to spare, putting down in a field close by, rotor blades just turning to keep noise down. They got word the van was onto the moor, and lifted off. A few minutes later they spotted the van, a red Transit van. As they got nearer, Geoff called the drop. His helicopter dropped onto the road a hundred yards in front, Luke dropped behind it as it stopped. The four men sprinted over to the van, two to each side.

"Open the doors!" shouted Luke.

The passenger made to pick his mobile off the dashboard, Luke shot the side window out, showering the occupants with glass.

"Open the fucking door," he shouted again.

Both doors opened and the men scrambled out. "Don't shoot!" the passenger said.

Luke said, "Do as you are instructed and no one gets hurt. Driver, open the side door now."

The driver unlocked the sliding side door and stood back.

Six boxes were stacked just inside.

Luke ordered him and his passenger to put three boxes in each chopper and be quick.

When they had finished, Luke said, "Now give me your phones!"

The phones were passed to him. Geoff shouted, "Come on, let's move it!"

Luke put both men in the back of the van and locked the door, taking the keys with him. He smashed both phones with his heels.

They were up and away within five minutes.

"Piece of piss, didn't know what hit them," Luke said.

CHAPTER 3

The following day, having read the crime circulation from Derbyshire police regarding the raid on the van, Paul and Dick were discussing the crime.

Paul said, "It's got to be Bull and company. Two helicopters, like the prison breakout, got to be them."

"I agree," said Dick. "That was the reason for the prison breakout."

"One reason, there were six people on the van raid, counting the pilots. All were wearing masks. Well planned. That jewellery firm has been doing that run for years, and never had any trouble. They used a plain van, rather than a security-type van, so as not to draw any attention to themselves."

"You have obviously spoken to Derbyshire police by the sounds of it," said Dick.

"Yes. I spoke to my counterpart over there this morning. He thinks the same as we do, now he knows about the prison escape. He's getting helicopter rental firms checked out, countrywide. Personally. I think they will have covered their tracks on that. By the way, the Chief has authorised us to carry a firearm, whilst this enquiry is ongoing. If we have to drive anywhere, we either use an ARV crew and car, or they follow as escort. The girls will be safe in the flats at HQ, we join them there when we finish work. They think they are on holiday."

"Not free to move around much, but safe," replied Dick.

CHAPTER 4

Back at the house in Rutland, the gang were sorting out the boxes of jewellery. The two helicopters had had all their fresh livery removed and were put back to their original state. They were being returned to different heliports, one in the north, one in the south.

The gold, silver and platinum were being separated, as were the various precious stones.

Geoff said, "The price of precious metals has shot up recently, so we'll use the latest prices to sort out the share-out amount, if that's OK with you guys? We'll do it by weight."

Bob said, "To be honest, I know nothing about prices nowadays, been out of it for too long."

Geoff said, "And me mate. Luke's the man, eh bro?"

Joe asked, "When do we get our share?"

Luke replied, "As soon as we've done the sums. We have plenty of cash to one side. When we know what your share is, just let us know where you want it paying to."

Bob turned to Joe, and said, "Swiss bank mate. It's one of the few accounts they don't know about. Can you transfer it straight in Luke?"

"Yes, we do it through a system that makes the transfer almost disappear."

Bob said, "So have you finished with us after that, or is there something else you want us for?"

Geoff said, "Don't you want to get even with the men who put you behind bars?"

Joe said, "In what way?"

"Kill them and their bitches, and the fucking judge."

Bob said, "At one time I think we felt like that, but not even given it a thought since."

"Well I have. I want them to suffer," Geoff said.

Bob said, "Let me think about it. What about you, Joe?"

"Like you mate, at one time we tried as you know, but not sure now."

Geoff said, "Well make your minds up quick."

Bob said, "What if we don't, Geoff?

"Down to you two. You both get your share anyway. But if you don't want to join in with me, when the jobs done, you are on your own, but not here guys."

***

Bob and Joe sat talking later in Bob's room.

Bob said, "What do you think about Geoff's idea?"

"A bit of an awkward situation. If we go with him, we could become cop killers, or killers. I know we did things earlier to harm them, but now I'm not sure. To be honest, I don't trust either of them, Geoff or Luke."

"I think if I had known about that plan, I'd have thought twice about escaping. The problem is now, what do we do? I'm stumped, I really am."

"What about going so far with them, getting our cash transferred, then do a runner?"

"We need passports though," Bob said. "I can get them, but we have to see the supplier. With us showing beards, dyed of course. We have to sit it out for a bit longer. I think we ought to get away from here, while we can. Then come back if they will let us."

Bob and Joe went downstairs to meet up with Geoff and Luke. Bob said, "We have had a chat. What we would like to do is get away from here for a few days, once our money has been transferred. We need to sort new passports out and other bits and pieces. Then we come back with our final decision."

Geoff said, "Can we trust you not to scarper for good?"

Bob held his hand out. "My word is my bond. We will get back I assure you."

Geoff took his hand and said, "If you don't come back, my word is I will hunt you both down and feed you to the fucking pigs. My word is also my bond. By the way, your share is £680,000 each. We bagged less than we reckoned."

Bob said, "That's good. When can we transfer?"

Luke said, "It's all set up, ready to go. I'll show you."

They went to a state-of-the-art computer, Luke typed some numbers in, then moved aside, saying, "Just type your bank and account numbers in, the money will transfer straight away."

"Can we do both to the same account? That OK with you Joe?" Bob asked.

"Fine with me, mate."

Bob typed in the details. Within less than a minute the transfer completed.

"All done," said Luke. "The transfer will wipe itself out in a minute."

"Thanks," said Bob. "We won't let you down."

"I hope not. When do you want to leave?"

"Tonight, if that's OK."

"Fine. We can provide you with a car, a top-of-the-range Audi. You will be driven out with hoods over your heads. Luke will drive you. You will be dropped off, then you are on your own. It's just that I don't want you knowing the way back to here. We'll contact you with a meeting-up point later."

***

Back in Bob's room, he said, "Don't worry Joe, the money is safe."

"Won't they know where it's gone through?"

"No, as soon as the bank received the money – and I was notified the money was in – it was moved out again through another system, to an account well hidden. When we are well away from here, I can transfer your share to wherever you want."

"Thanks."

"I suspect the car will have a tracker of some sort on it, but not to worry, we can park it up and use another car until we come back."

Both men packed their holdalls and went downstairs.

Luke said, "When you come back, ring us and we'll come and collect you."

Bob said, "I can understand you, but it's as though you don't trust us."

Geoff said, "I value my freedom. What you don't know, you can't tell."

Bob said, "Fair enough."

CHAPTER 5

Bob and Joe were taken to the leisure centre car park in the back of the Audi, where their blindfolds were removed. As all the rear windows were blacked out, no one could see them being removed. Saying their goodbyes to Geoff and Luke, they drove off.

Geoff said to Luke, "Not sure about them two coming back you know."

Luke replied, "They are very close and loyal to each other, like we are, that's all."

In their car, Joe was saying, "It's nice to be away from that Geoff. I really think he is a dangerous man, who would kill just for the sake of it."

Bob agreed, saying, "I certainly don't want to go on a killing spree, just to suit him. We have some serious talking to do, mate."

"Are we going back then?"

"Possibly, but if we do, we'll be prepared by then."

Bob was driving, and as they got to the outskirts of London, Joe made a call, signalling Bob to stay quiet.

"Fred, it's me, Austin. Are you OK mate?"

"Fine thanks. Are you on your way home?"

"Yes. Is the apartment all OK?"

"It's fine. I'll just nip round and put things on for you. How long will you be?"

"About an hour or so. Stopping off for a bite to eat. Leave the key in the normal place. Is the car OK?"

"Yes, all ready for you."

"Thanks Fred."

Bob looked at Joe. "Austin, apartment, car?"

"Lots you don't know Bob. Nobody knew where I was really living. Well Fred is my caretaker, he looks after everything for me. He thinks I work abroad a lot. We'll leave this thing in a long stay car park for a few days until we need it again, and taxi to the apartment. You OK with that?"

"Fine by me. Well sorted, you dark horse."

They eventually got to the apartment, which was situated east of London, a district called South Dikendon.

"Nice place, Joe, very nice."

"I've had it a few years now. It's dead handy for London and getting to the Eurotunnel, ferries and such things. Suits me, and not a crowded area. Completely private. I've got some spare cash and bank cards. Even a couple of spare passports. I took those ideas from you. The passports will want altering, but that's not a big job. Loose photos, just need refitting, get you a couple if you want."

"That suits me. The less people see us at the moment, the better."

"A couple of days complete R&R to get ourselves sorted out. Drink?"

"A very large scotch and ice, please Joe."

"Coming up."

***

Sitting in the quiet and comfortable surroundings of Joe's apartment, Bob began to think about the future, especially his relationship with Geoff and Luke Bull.

"Joe," he asked. "How well did you get on with Geoff inside?"

"I shared a cell with him for a month and was glad to get moved. He's a nutcase. A very violent man. I saw him beat two inmates up for ignoring him when he spoke to them. Not a big fan, but when he gave me the chance to get out, I agreed. How about you?"

Bob said, "Like you. I was glad to get out. I'm not a fan of his in any way, shape or form. I didn't mind doing the jewellery van job, but as I said back there, I've tapped a couple of men in my time, but killing cops is something different altogether. We'll never get any peace. I've got an idea but still working on it. I'll talk it through with you tomorrow."

"Talk it through now. At least the idea."

"Grass them up to the police."

"Grass them up?" Joe said. "We don't even know where they are."

"Get your iPad."

Joe got his iPad. Bob said, "Now put this phone number in the Find Your Phone app?"

After a few moments, the phone flashed up. Bob said, "That's where they are. I left my phone switched on in the bedroom. We pass that to the cops, who nick them."

"What about them tracing our call?"

"We use a call box, miles away from here, even abroad."

"Would you really do that Bob?"

"The guys that put us away were good. We got caught, that's what they get paid for, OK? We tried to fix them a couple of times, and failed. But cold-blooded revenge is not my style, and certainly not yours. I suggest we go over to France and ring from there. Use a burner phone, then dump it. We take their car across, and your car. Leave their car in one of the big supermarket car parks with the keys in. If it gets taken, they can chase it wherever. You take the ferry, I take the tunnel. You go a couple of hours before me. We meet over there and go where we want."

"Switzerland was good, but not Geneva, at least not to stay in."

"Let's get ready and move in a couple of days, plenty of places down there."

Crossings were arranged for a couple of days later. Bob had booked a tunnel crossing, Joe a ferry crossing. A couple of hours earlier, Bob was on the lookout for someone following him, and it didn't take him long to spot a likely tail. The man was in a similar car and seemed to be watching Bob. As he walked into the tunnel reception area to book his ticket, Bob had found the man's car and was removing the valves from all four tyres, fully deflating them.

Walking back to his own car, the man passed Bob. Bob nodded and smiled without speaking. With under 15 minutes to departure, Bob knew the man would not make it in his car.

The man got back to his car, started the engine and was then informed by the in-car information system that he had tyre problems. Getting out, he realised why.

"Fuck. Fuck and double fuck!" he shouted.

Realising he had been sussed out, and not wanting to run the wrath of Geoff Bull, he rang him to say he had followed the car to the Eurotunnel, but couldn't get on the same crossing as it was fully booked. He had booked the next one an hour later.

Not pleased, Geoff Bull had to accept this, saying, "Make sure you are on that one."

The man then arranged for new valves and the tyres to be re-inflated.

CHAPTER 6

Bob and Joe had arranged to meet in the giant supermarket complex near the port. Bob transferred his stuff from the Audi, into Joe's immaculate British racing green Jaguar. Although just over six years old, it was mint. "Fred keeps it right for me."

They left the Audi in the car park, keys in the ignition, and drove out. Bob told Joe about the follower he had picked out at the Eurotunnel, who would no doubt follow the tracker when able to.

"Hopefully, whoever takes it will lead him a merry dance."

"Let's hope so," said Joe, driving away.

***

The man who had been following Bob, sat in the giant supermarket car park. He had a glimpse of the roof of the Audi but was well away from it. He had rung Geoff Bull and updated him, he now had it in sight.

"Well don't lose it."

About an hour later, he saw the Audi moving off. He had the tracker switched on and followed at a safe distance. The Audi headed towards Paris, not rushing; the follower had no trouble staying with it. He followed it through the centre of Paris and out again. It was driven onto an industrial estate. When he reached the location, he still had a good signal, even though he couldn't see it, assuming it was inside one of the units. The follower sat for nearly three hours before the vehicle showed signs of moving. As it passed him, he realised the driver was not Bob, or Joe for that matter. He followed it to another freight centre where he saw it being loaded into a container and sealed up. When he was able to, he approached the container and saw that it was bound for Nigeria.

Not certain of what to do, he rang Geoff Bull, but Luke answered.

"Luke, I think Bob stuffed us somewhere along the line. I picked the Audi up at the supermarket and followed it. It's just been loaded onto a container bound for Nigeria. What do you want me to do?"

"Looks like he stuffed us all. Not your fault. Come home, I'll sort Geoff out."

"Thanks Luke," a relieved follower said.

***

Luke had found Geoff in the garden and told him about the phone call. Geoff was livid, but Luke managed to calm him down, and said, "Let's wait and see if they make contact, see what they have to say."

Geoff said, "They are dead. Both fucking dead."

***

Bob and Joe drove further into France, stopping off at a small hotel just outside Le Mans. The following day, they drove down to the Dordogne, staying for a couple of nights in Rocamadour, before cutting across towards Switzerland, staying on the French side of the border near the pretty town of Annecy.

CHAPTER 7

Bob and Joe were sat in the lounge of their rented house in Annecy. They put on the BBC news channel.

The announcer said, "A High Court judge was killed by a car bomb this morning. The bomb exploded a short distance from his house. He has been named as Justice George Proud. Police are investigating whether it was a terrorist attack or a revenge killing."

Bob said, "Looks like Geoff's started already. He was the judge that sent him down. He hated him. Nobody is safe now."

Joe said, "Do you think he knows about the Audi being abandoned yet?"

"No idea. We'll probably find out tonight when I ring him."

***

When Bob did ring, he put the phone on speaker. "Bob here, Geoff. How's things?"

Geoff said, "You let us down, you bastard."

"I haven't said anything yet."

"You don't fucking need to."

"You obviously didn't trust us, you had a man following the Audi, which must have had a tracker fitted. Your man deserved having his tyres let down at the terminal. You employ amateurs, that's what happens."

Geoff said, “Are you coming back? You gave me your word.”

Bob replied, “No. We don’t trust you. You killed Judge Proud, didn’t you?”

“He was the first one. Now you two fuckers are on the list.”

“You might be trying to trace this call, I don’t know, but you won’t because it’s a burner phone. When this conversation is done, so is this phone.”

Geoff shouted, “You two fuckers are pig food. Believe me, pig food. I’ll feed you to them myself if it’s the last thing I do.”

“It might well be, because we are not coming back until we hear you and your mob are back behind bars, or dead.” Bob rang off.

Geoff threw his phone against the wall, smashing the casing, shouting, “Bastards, fucking bastards. Get all our contacts working on them. Find the fuckers.”

Luke said, “We’ll try.”

“Not try. Do it.”

***

The next call Bob made was to Trent Division. He asked to speak to Dick Jones or Paul Richards. When asked who was calling, he replied, “Tell them it’s Bob and Joe, they’ll talk to us.”

Dick answered the call. “Superintendent Jones, how can I help you?”

“Bob Teal here. I need to talk to you and your pal Paul urgently.”

Dick sat still for a fraction of a second, then walked through to Paul’s office, saying, “Bob Teal on the phone. Go on Bob, I’m with Paul, speaker phone is on.”

"Just to let you both know, your lives are in danger, and your partners."

Paul said, "Are you threatening us, Bob?"

"Not me. Geoff Bull. He's said he's going to take revenge on those who put him away, and their loved ones. He's already had Judge Proud killed in a car bomb."

"Why are you telling us this? You tried to kill us a couple of times as well."

"That was then. Now we accept you were doing your job. Bull's not like that. He wants you and us dead."

Dick asked, "Why you two?"

"We left them a few days ago. We promised to get back to him, but we don't trust him, or Luke. He only sprung us to do that jewellery job in Derbyshire."

Paul said, "Is Luke Bull his brother?"

"Do you know him?" asked Bob.

Paul said, "I have heard of him. Where are they, do you know?"

"All I know is they are in a large house, down in Rutland somewhere."

"Where are you and Joe now?"

"That's for us to know and you to try and find out. You won't be able to trace this phone. It's a burner. We just feel you should know what's happening with the Bull brothers."

Dick asked, "Any further clue as to where the house is in Rutland?"

"All I can say, is it's within a five-mile radius of the leisure centre. That's where they dropped us off before they took the blindfolds off us."

"They blindfolded you?"

"That Geoff Bull is a very dangerous man, and trusts no one. Anyway, you have been warned. Hopefully we won't meet again, just be careful. If you trace the phone number I am about to give you, that might help. Not sure if it's still got battery life though." Bob reeled a number off and rang off.

Paul said, "That's a turn up for the book, Bob Teal helping us out."

Dick said, "Well we weren't wrong about taking precautions. I'll get onto the police at Rutland. By the way, this Luke Bull. Didn't you know he was Geoff's brother?"

"I never connected. He used to snout for me and Greg a few years ago in the Met. We did quite well out of him. He turned some good jobs in."

"When did you last have contact with him? I'm thinking he might turn his brother in."

"At least three to four years ago. Let me ring Greg, he ran him with me."

Paul got through to Greg. "Hello mate. How's things?"

"Still doing a lot and leaving a bit. How's Alice and the young un?"

"Both well thanks. And your mob, well I hope?"

"All fine, mate. You obviously need my help again, as you always did. What's up mate?"

"You remember that snout we had some time ago, Luke Bull? Have you heard from him lately?"

"Not for at least a couple of years. Why?"

"You remember we locked his brother Geoff up a couple of years back for a bullion van job and a murder up here? He was sprung from prison just over a week ago, with that Bob Teal and Joe Andrews. You remember them, don't you?"

Greg replied, "Very well."

"Since they were sprung, they have done a jewellery van job in Derbyshire, grabbing close on £5 million of used gold, silver and stones. Then that High Court judge, Judge Proud, was killed in a car bomb. That's all down to the Bull brothers."

Greg said, "I'm deputy officer in charge on that job. How do you know that?"

Paul went on to explain the phone call they had received from Bob Teal.

"Bob Teal, on your side? Can you trust him?"

"I think so. What about Luke?"

Greg said, "I have a number, whether he is still contactable on it, not sure. Let me try it and get back to you as soon as. Regards to all, mate."

Paul said to Dick, "Won't be long before he rings back, if it's the right number. If he has the bombing job, he'll want to get Bull potted for it."

A few minutes later, Greg did ring back. "I got a number for Luke. I've rung it, but it's gone straight to voicemail. I left a message for him to ring me back asap. He'll know it's me. I used our password."

"Thanks Greg. Keep in touch and vice versa."

Paul said, "Let's call it a day mate. Ring the girls and get a takeaway. OK by you?"

"Yes fine. Let me clear my desk and contact the control room, say leaving at 6pm."

***

About 40 minutes later, the two colleagues walked out of the police station to the rear car park. They still used their own cars, in the event one got a call out to an incident.

As they left the car park, the ARV car picked them up. All the vehicles were in contact via radio and with the control room.

As the convoy reached the roundabout, known as Redhill Roundabout, a car pulled out of the filling station, straight into the path of the following ARV, causing a collision. Over the radio, they heard the shout, "ARV in collision, Redhill Roundabout."

Paul quickly radioed back, "Do you require any help?"

"Not at the moment, no."

Paul said, "Well come back, just in case."

Both men went round the roundabout, pulling onto the filling station forecourt. They saw a white Ford Mondeo had pulled across the front of the ARV, causing it to broadside the Mondeo. One of the traffic officers were talking to the other driver, the other traffic officer on the radio, glancing round him, and observing the area for any other interference. As Paul and Dick started to climb out of their cars, a grey van parked on the forecourt opened its rear doors and shots were fired at them.

Both men fell to the floor, crawling behind their cars for cover, pulling their firearms out and returning limited fire at the grey van.

As the ARV crew heard gunshots, both officers drew their weapons, as did the driver of the Mondeo. He shot the officer he had been talking to, hitting him in the right shoulder, forcing him to drop his weapon. As he turned to the second officer, he wasn't quick enough. The officer double-tapped him in the chest, putting him down, killing him instantly. The officer shouted into his radio, "Shots fired, Redhill Roundabout. One officer down, others under fire."

He pulled his colleague to safety behind the crashed cars.

Looking across at the forecourt, he could see Paul and Dick returning fire towards a grey van. They were unable to return regular fire, due to the petrol pumps and members of the public in the area.

The ARV officer took aim and fired at the van, causing the side window to blow out. The van then started to move, although someone was still shooting from the rear doors towards Paul and Dick.

The doors were then pulled shut. As the van raced from the forecourt, a shot was fired at the ARV car as it turned right up to the roundabout, before racing off up the A614.

Both Paul and Dick got to their feet. "All OK, mate?"

"Yes, and you?"

"Yes, but the cars have taken a battering."

Both cars were riddled with bullet holes, neither appeared driveable.

Paul got onto his radio. "Control, grey van, driven off onto A614, north. Side window shattered. Occupants armed and dangerous. We need medical assistance, here, CID, SOCO."

"On its way sir. Any casualties?"

"One officer wounded, one gunman killed."

Hearing sirens, Paul said, "Dick, check the kiosk, make sure everyone is alright. Grab the security film before it goes missing."

Paul ran across to the ARV crew, just as the ambulance arrived. Paul waved the ambulance over to them.

The shot officer was ashen and in shock. The ambulance crew went straight to him. The dead gunman ignored for the time being.

As more police arrived and took over, Paul and Dick were conveyed to HQ to join their wives.

"Well," said Paul. "Bob Teal was right."

Alice said, "What's Bob Teal got to do with this?"

Paul said, "Bob Teal rang us earlier to warn us that Geoff Bull was out to get us. He wants revenge for being sent down. They've already killed a judge who sentenced them."

Julie hung onto Dick, and said, "Are we safe?"

"You both will be completely safe here, we'll get extra security, and until they are caught we are to work from HQ where possible."

"That's right," said Paul. "This Geoff bloke's a nutter."

The phone rang. It was the control room, telling him the van had been found near the old Calverton Pit, burnt out.

His mobile rang, "It's Greg. Just to let you know, Luke's rang me, he says Geoff's out of control. He was going up to Nottingham to sort you and Dick out."

Paul said, "They had a go a bit ago. Our cars got shot up, but we are OK. One of our officers was injured, and they had a man killed. From what you say, Luke wasn't in on it then?"

"He refused to go. Geoff wasn't a happy bunny with him and gave him a good hiding."

"Will he help us locate him?"

"He might when I tell him about today."

"Thanks for that Greg. Another one I owe you. When you get back to him, tell him if he comes up trumps, we can offer him some kind of immunity. This has now got us into the hunt for him as well as Leicestershire and Derbyshire police forces, and the Met. Are you going to contact him again?"

"I'll contact him asap. Look after each other. Speak soon."

CHAPTER 8

Back in the house in Rutland, Luke had sat nursing his cuts and bruises received from his brother earlier. He was watching the early evening news. A headline came on about a shooting in Nottingham, where a police officer had been injured and an attacker had been killed. At this time the details were a bit sketchy, and more was to follow on a later bulletin. Geoff wasn't home yet, so Luke gathered his gear together, got in his car and drove away from Rutland, not wanting any further involvement with his mad brother. He didn't want to be there when they got back. Driving back to London, he rang Greg from his car phone.

"Greg, it's Luke. Can we meet up sometime, as soon as possible?"

"Yes, sure. When?"

"Tomorrow, the place we used to meet. 11am."

"I'm OK for that, any objections to Paul Richards being there? It will be up to him to make any deal."

"I think after all these years I can trust you both. See you tomorrow."

Greg rang Paul. "Paul, Luke's rang, he wants to meet at our usual place, 11am tomorrow. He's agreed that you can be there. Can you make it?"

"I'll be there, don't worry."

***

The next morning, having spoken to the chief constable, and due to the seriousness of the crime, Paul was on his way to London in the police helicopter. Landing at a London hospital helipad, he was met by Greg. Shaking hands, they made their way to a waiting car.

The usual meeting place, where they had always met, was on the pavement, in the centre of Tower Bridge.

Paul said, "Are you armed, Greg?"

"No mate, are you?"

"Yes. Dick and myself are armed until Bull is either captured and put away, or killed."

"Let's hope we don't need it."

They parked near Tower Bridge and walked out to the middle.

Greg said, "I've got cameras trained on us all the time. One signal from me and the Bridge will be sealed off at both ends."

"Good thinking, mate. That looks like Luke coming the other way."

Waving to him, they met in the middle and shook hands.

"Long time no see, Paul, Greg. Staying well are you?"

"So far," said Paul. "And you? Looking at your face, you look like you've been in the wars a bit."

"Geoff didn't agree with me on something."

Greg said, "So how can we help you, Luke? I presume that's why you wanted a meet?"

"I can give you the house in Rutland where Geoff is. I can give you the jewellery shop where the stuff from Derbyshire is being smelted down. I can give you the pilots if you want them."

"What about Bob Teal and Joe Andrews?" asked Paul.

"I can honestly say, I have no idea where they are. All I can tell you is they left in one of our cars, which was tracked to France, just outside Paris. It's ended up in a container bound for Nigeria. Where they are now, I have no idea, over there, or back here, or wherever."

"OK Luke, what do you want from us?" asked Paul.

"I want immunity from any prosecution. You know I have a couple of pubs in the East End. I don't need this aggro from Geoff anymore. I only went along to make things easier for me and my family."

Looking at Greg, then at Luke, Paul said, "I think if you come up with the goods, we can certainly sort something out. You may have to face a charge of some sort, but I feel sure we can water it down."

"Can you promise me that?"

Paul held his hand out and said, "Yes."

Shaking Luke's hand he said tongue-in-cheek, "Would you agree to give evidence against him?"

Luke replied, "Don't push it mate. Do you want the information, or me dead?"

"Point taken. That's a no then. By the way, who did the shooting in Nottingham yesterday?"

"All I know was Geoff was going to shoot from the back of the van. A guy called Stan was driving. The dead man was on hire for the day, again all I know his name was Flavio. That's all I know. I got this face for refusing to take part."

Paul said, "Right tell us what you know then, we won't ask you to give evidence."

CHAPTER 9

Half an hour later, Paul and Greg walked back to their car. Luke went the opposite way.

Greg said, "Well what do you reckon to that?"

Paul replied, "If what he has told us is the truth, and good, he should be looked after. I've got it all down, recorded on my phone anyway."

Greg said, "And I came wired up."

"Great minds think alike. Let's get back to the office and go through it again. Get things organised. I'm stopping overnight, so no rush. Plenty to catch up on, mate."

During the evening, they discussed tactics and manpower needed. As the jewellery shop was in London, Greg's team would take that job on. Paul would liaise with Leicestershire police regarding the Rutland address, and hopefully have a joint operation with them, to include Derbyshire police.

Both addresses would be put under immediate surveillance and would be hit at the same time. All officers would be armed.

Paul said, "I'm thinking, a couple of days' time, gives Dougie and his team, and your team, to have a look. What do you reckon?"

Greg replied, "I think the sooner the better. Let the surveillance teams call it. I've already cleared it with my boss. She says, when we're ready, she will back us."

Paul asked, "Who is your boss now?"

"Rosie Potts, she came to us from Slough."

"What's she like?

"She's great. You are meeting her tomorrow, to go over things, being as you are stopping over. I arranged it, sort of knowing you would be."

The following morning, Greg introduced Paul to Detective Chief Superintendent Potts.

She was mid-forties, with striking red hair. Shaking hands she said, "Nice to meet you Paul, Greg speaks very highly of you."

"Greg never was a good judge of character." Digging him in the ribs. "If you ever want to get rid of him, I'll take him on my team anytime."

Rosie said, "Sorry, he stays here. Anyway, I know you both met up with Luke Bull yesterday. Have you two come up with a plan?"

Paul placed a recorder on the table. "This is what he told us, Rosie."

As she listened to the recording, she was taking notes, but saying nothing. When it finished, she sat back and said, "A lot of good information there. I fully agree, if it comes good he gets some help from us. Can he be trusted though?"

Paul said, "At the moment, we have to. His info always paid off in the past."

"Yes, but this is family. What's your plan of action?"

Paul said, "Surveillance, to check both properties. We leave the strike call to those teams and hit both properties at the same time. All officers will be armed, or the majority at least, and to be in full protective gear. We keep the operation tight, only those involved will be briefed and ready to go as soon as the strike is given. Remember, they have already killed a High Court judge, and had a go at my brother-in-law and myself in Nottingham, and shot a police officer. Until surveillance is started, we don't know how many persons are at any one property. We think air support and dog support should be included, or at least on standby."

Rosie said, "I've got that all down as well. Between you, you seem to have all angles covered. What about these Bob Teal and Joe Andrews characters? Will they be included do you think?"

Paul said, "As you heard from the recording, Luke has no idea where they are, and I don't think he has any reason to lie about that. We have dealt with them before, so will leave them on the back burner. In fact, it was Bob Teal who rang me to tell me that Geoff Bull was out to get us. If it hadn't been for him, we might not have been prepared for what happened."

"Right," said Rosie. "Get things organised down this end, Greg. Use my name where you want. Any problems, get straight back to me, or tell whoever to contact me. This job is a priority. Good hunting, you two."

They all shook hands and left her office.

Paul said, "She seems to be on the ball."

Greg said, "She is, trust me. She doesn't miss a trick."

The two men put their plan together with the various departments and arranged to keep in touch throughout.

Greg said, "So how are you getting back to Nottingham?"

"The Chief has arranged for the force helicopter to pick me up at 4pm at the hospital, so should be home around six. I can speak to Dick and Dougie on the way back to sort out any last-minute details. So we strike at 6am day after tomorrow, unless the strike is given earlier, so teams to be on standby from midnight."

"Sounds good to me. Let's eat, then I'll drop you off."

CHAPTER 10

The day before the planned strike, Dick was with Dougie's surveillance team and a couple from the Leicestershire team.

Although they couldn't get down to the house without being seen, they were able to get a good view from the church steeple close by, giving a good view of the side of the house and front and rear doors. The other side of the house was being watched by a CCTV set up. A team was to be in the steeple at all times. The only way into the property was through the main gates, as the back garden of the property went down to the edge of Rutland Water, but no landing stage was present. The CCTV was set up on the high wall of the garden centre next door. Two cars were parked outside on the drive.

Dougie said, "Looks like we go straight in through the gates. Leave the lads in the church steeple, if they see anyone making a breakout back for the water, we'll have that covered. Cars one and two straight to the front door, three and four to the left, five and six to the right. Super door rammers and straight in, no knocking."

"What are super door rammers, Dougie?" asked Dick.

"A bit like a bazooka. Hold it tight against the door, press the switch and the door's smashed open. Great bit of kit. Not much stops it, and looking at those doors, nothing special. We need to get back and get a relief team at the steeple."

"Already arranged," replied the Leicester officer.

Dick asked, "What if they leave the premises before we strike?"

The Leicester officer replied, "Already sorted as well, sir. Whoever leaves will be arrested away from the premises."

Dick said, "Please make sure all officers are armed and in protective gear at all times."

"They are," came the reply.

CHAPTER 11

On the morning of the raid, Dick joined Dougie and his team, plus the Leicestershire team. The strategy had already been worked out between them. As the house was in Leicestershire, they would take the lead. Dick as senior officer present would be on hand to make any tough decisions. They reached the gated entrance to the house, driving onto the drive. As they got within 50 yards, the cars split up and took their positions to the front, sides and back. A spare car covered the garage door. Officers were at the front and rear doors, super rammers were activated and the doors flew open.

Officers went in shouting, "Armed police, show yourselves!"

There was a blast from the stairs, towards the front door, where a window shattered. The leading officer looked up the stairs as the man was raising a shotgun. He put two shots into his chest before he could fire again. He ran up the stairs shouting, "Armed police. Show yourselves!"

As he was stepping over the shot man, a door opened and a second man came out, also armed with a shotgun.

The officer shouted, "Drop your weapon now, or we fire! Do it!"

The man dropped the weapon and put his hands up.

The officer instructed him to lie on the floor, arms outstretched. The man complied and was quickly handcuffed.

Dougie had now joined them. “Anybody else in the house?”

The man replied, “No, only me and him.” He pointed at the dead man.

“Where’s Geoff Bull?”

The man said, “He left last night. I came in with a pizza delivery. He went out in my place.”

Dougie turned to a Leicestershire colleague and asked in a low voice to check the log from the watchers in the steeple.

The officer came back a minute later confirming there had been a delivery recorded on the log, but he was in and out in 30 seconds.

“He must have been informed.”

Dick was now at the scene. “OK lads, search the rest of the house, make sure it’s cleared for SOCO.”

Dick rang Paul to update him about Bull.

“Fuck,” he said.

“Any news from Greg’s team yet Paul?”

“Not heard yet. Get that place secured and leave the Leicester lads with it. Get our teams back here.”

***

In London, Greg and his team hit the jewellers just as it opened. The staff gave them no trouble and were quickly taken into custody. At the rear of the premises they found a decent-sized smelter, just warming up on automatic setting. On the floor at the side of it were three boxes of mixed jewellery, one was completely full of and had the name of the Midlands jewellery firm on the side. They got the secured vault opened by a member of staff. Inside were various boxes containing different precious stones, silver and gold ingots, and larger bars. Also inside were forged passports, credit cards and thousands of pounds-worth in used currency from the UK and other parts of the world. There was also a number of firearms, including machine pistols, rifles and grenades, a quantity of drugs and a mountain of paperwork. SOCO were taking a video of the whole scene.

Greg rang through to Paul. "Mate, we've hit the jackpot this end. Never seen so much cash and jewellery, firearms, the lot. How's your end gone?"

"One of the gang shot dead, another arrested, but Bull got out last night. They had a pizza delivery, the delivery man went in, Bull came out in his place. Someone must have told him. There was only me, you and Luke knew what was going down. I reckon Luke's double-crossed us. We have to find that out. You have his phone number, can you get it checked out, see where he was, who he called, etc.?"

"I'll get someone straight on it. They've just told me they have found some explosives in the vault and looks like home-made bombs. We're all pulling out until the bomb squad get here. Will get back to you."

"OK mate, speak later. Tell your lads, job well done."

Paul rang Dick and updated him on Greg's raid.

"Sounds like a good bust in London. We're on our way back now. Leicestershire Officers will sort things out down here."

CHAPTER 12

Down in London, at the Whistle and Flute Pub owned by Luke, his brother Geoff was sat eating a full fry-up breakfast.

"Thanks for the tip-off, mate. How did you know they were going to raid the house?"

Luke replied, "Through one of our police mates. He let it slip that the police knew you were up north, where you were, and they were raiding it today."

They had got the mid-morning news on when the bulletin came on about the raids.

The police in the Midlands had raided a large house in the search for escaped gang leader, Geoff Bull. One member of his gang was fatally injured after being shot by police. Police had also raided a jewellery shop in London, believed to be owned by Bull. A large amount of stolen jewellery, cash, firearms, drugs and other items had been recovered. Bull was still at large.

Geoff said, "It's a fucking pity he didn't know about the raid on the shop. That's cost us a packet, one way and another. Strange, we've had it for years, and the cops have never bothered with it. What I would like to know is how the fuck they knew about it."

Luke looked away. After hearing from the police the night before, he had contacted Geoff. They had arranged for a fellow gang member to take a pizza delivery into the house. Geoff would put the man's jacket and cap on and leave the house, in case they were being watched. Luke had never mentioned he knew the shop was to be raided.

"So what now, Geoff?"

"I stay here for a while till things die down a bit, then dodge abroad for a bit."

Luke said, "No. I don't want you here. If the cops come sniffing round, which I'm sure they will, I don't want them to find you here. I've a legitimate pub here. Look, I have an apartment on Canary Wharf. I use it occasionally and no one knows I've got it. It's under a false name and company. You can stay there for a bit. Finish your breakfast and I'll run you over to the apartment. I'll put the feelers out, see if anyone knows anything."

Geoff replied, "If I find out we've been fucking grassed up, I'll personally feed them to the fucking pigs. Now take me to the apartment."

***

Luke drove them over to Canary Wharf, into the underground car park. "It's got its own lift to the top floor." Getting out on the top floor, Luke took him into the apartment.

Geoff said, "Fucking hell. This is magnificent. When did you get this? You never said anything about it."

"I didn't waste what I got pissing it up the walls or chasing after lame racehorses. This is my retirement fund. Where's yours Geoff?"

Geoff looked at him and said, "That jewellery shop and stuff was mine. That's all I had, and the flat above it. The two big houses we used, I had a share in, but they've both gone now. Really I've got fuck all, apart from you, and what you have."

"So for a change, listen to me will you? I'm going to get you out of the country. But you have to stay here for a few days, and I mean stay here. It's fully stocked with what you want."

"Can't I nip out to a safe club?"

"Not a chance. I'll call you later."

Luke left him to it and began to make his way back to the Whistle and Flute, when his car phone rang. "Hello," he answered.

"Luke, it's Greg. We need to talk, can we meet?"

Luke replied, "On the Embankment, near the Needle. Half an hour, or not at all."

"On my way."

The two men met as arranged.

Greg said, "The shop was good info, but Geoff wasn't at the house. Someone tipped him off. Any ideas?"

"Not a scooby mate."

"Have you heard from him at all?"

"No."

"Will you tell me if you do?"

"Depends," Luke replied.

"On what?"

"What's in it for me?"

"You are a callous bastard, you know. I reckon you could get five or ten per cent of any insurance money reward. That should be around £3–400,000."

"Not enough. I want full immunity from any prosecution. No charges."

Greg replied, "That's above my pay scale mate. I'll see what I can do. I'll get back in touch soon."

"You do that."

CHAPTER 13

Greg rang Paul. "Have just spoken to Luke. He reckons he says he has no idea where Geoff is, but I have a feeling he does, and that he tipped him off. He says he will only help us catch him if we give him full immunity from all charges."

"OK, Greg. Arrange another meeting with him. I'll come down and talk to him. Tell him I will see what I can sort out. A meeting place to suit him. Also, any chance of a surveillance team on him, like now?"

"I reckon Rose will run with that, especially as you suggested it. I think she fancies you."

"Fuck off, mate. Happily married and staying that way."

"Aren't we all!" laughed Greg. "Speak later."

***

Two days later, arrangements had been made to meet Luke at the usual place. Luke had agreed that Dick could be there, along with Greg and Paul.

Paul and Dick travelled down with Dougie and his surveillance team. On arriving in London, the two teams would meet up to cover the meeting with Luke. As all surveillance teams countrywide work to the same system, a Notts officer would team up with a London officer. The London team were to take the lead. Luke was still under surveillance, as requested. He would be followed to and from the meet. A further brief was that all officers would be armed, as would Paul, Dick and Greg. If anything untoward happened at the scene, the two vehicles at the back end of the team would come forward and assist; the rest of the team would follow Luke, until ordered to stand down, or strike.

The three detectives stood at the meeting place on Tower Bridge. Again, Luke walked from the opposite direction to where they had made their approach. After introductions were made, Paul said, "What happened? Geoff wasn't at the house when we raided it."

Luke replied, "I have spoken to him since. He says he was tipped off about the raid on the house, but not the shop."

Greg asked, "Do you know where he is now?"

"No idea. He said he was using a burner phone so it can't be traced."

"Have you any ideas where he might be holed up, or what his plans are?" Greg asked.

"I have no idea, and no idea what his plans are."

Paul said, "Luke. I have taken advice. We can offer you what you want, provided you turn him in and give evidence at his trial. Are you prepared to do that?"

Luke was standing with his back to the bridge railings, Dick stood to his right, Paul and Greg to his left. A grey Transit van approached. As it drew level with them it stopped. Luke saw the side door slide open and three men get out. As Paul turned to see what Luke was looking at, the three men started shooting. Dick and Greg were hit mid-chest and fell to the ground. Before Paul could draw his weapon, he was also hit mid-chest. Fortunately, one of the men's guns had misfired and exploded in his hand. He was bundled back into the van. One of the gunmen waved Luke across to join them, got him in the van, and it raced off. Passers-by were running and screaming in fear, in all directions.

Two cars pulled up at the scene, and armed surveillance officers ran to the prone bodies. Kneeling down, they were about to shout for medical assistance, when they heard someone say, "Can we get up now? Everyone OK?"

The three men gingerly got to their feet.

Paul said, "Thank goodness for bullet-proof vests. Let's get out of here."

The three of them had decided on the bullet-proof vests, as they felt – and it proved right – that Luke Bull could not be trusted. They got into the waiting cars and were driven off.

Paul said, "Let the teams know we are all OK, but keep it in-house. Where are they now?"

Dougie replied, "Looks like they are heading towards Canary Wharf, or that direction, but traffic is very heavy."

Paul said, "OK, keep at it, we're making up." Looking at Dick he said, "Well that's how much we can trust Luke. Apart from us three, no one else knew about that meet, so Luke set us up."

Dick replied, "And the surveillance teams. But I think, like you, Luke set us up. One of them had his gun blow up on him, so I reckon it's a gunshop gun and ammo. We need to check hospitals for injuries."

"No, I don't think they will take him to one. Somewhere along the chain they will have a doctor of sorts they can call on, or dispose of him their own way."

The radio came to life. "Car 12. The van is pulling into Canary Wharf and looks like it's parking up at a block of flats called Willis Court. Occupants out of vehicle. One man has a heavily bandaged right hand."

"Paul Richards to car 12. Can we identify any of the occupants?"

"Car 12. Affirmative. Luke and Geoff Bull, plus injured man and two unknowns. All into the lift. It's an outside lift. Standby."

A few seconds later, "Car 12. Lift now at top floor and occupants out. Now out of our view."

Paul said, "Well done team. Keep on the plot. We are listening, but we need to get some more info on that block of flats."

Paul then said, "I need to get back to the station and liaise with Rose. Greg, you come with me. Dick, make some discreet enquiries with the porter or such like. See if they can help with the flat details and floor plans. You know the drill."

***

Back at the station, Paul and Greg were with Rose in her office.

"Good call about the vest," she said.

Paul said, "Luck played a part at least. From experience, most untrained shooters aim for the body. Rose, what I would like you to do is put out a brief statement through your press office, to the fact the police in London are investigating a shooting on Tower Bridge. Early reports are that three police officers were shot. At this stage, police are not able to confirm what condition the officers are in. Leave it at that. If we go too far, some folks might jump on the social media wagon."

Rose picked her phone up, passed the message to the press officer and said, "Put this out for now. No phone number to ring, just that message. Thanks. So what do you intend doing now, Paul?" she asked.

"Well we know where they are to a degree. Luke, Geoff and a couple of others. Dick's doing some discreet enquiries to try and ascertain which flat it is they have. As soon as he can confirm, I want a search warrant for those premises, and Luke's pubs, and any other property he might have. I want them busting completely, and I want it asap."

Rose said, "As soon as you have the info, the warrants will be taken out. I take it the raids will be, as you said, asap?"

Paul said, "If we can get it done today, I can get some interviewing teams started."

A knock on her door and Dick walked in. Paul introduced him to Rose and said, "My deputy, my brother-in-law and mate."

As they shook hands, Rose said, "You have a full-time job then Dick, with him?"

"And babysitter," he laughed. "Anyway, the top floor of Willis Court is divided into four penthouse apartments. The one on the east corner, overlooking the river, is owned by a Kul Bulle. We reckon that's Luke Bull. The other owners are nothing like that. It cost a few quid, so he invested well. The porter is an ex-cop who confirmed it for us. The only access to the flat is by a lift, or a fire escape stairwell. CCTV camera are in the lift and also in all flats."

"What's the layout inside, Dick, do we know?" asked Greg.

"Large lounge and kitchen, all open plan. Three bedrooms, all en suite. Balcony to two sides."

Paul said, "So our only entry is the lift or stairs?"

Dick replied, "Looks like it. But cameras linked to the front doors and inside each apartment."

Rose said, "Can they be turned off at all?"

Dick said, "Having spoken to the porter, he has a master switch in his office. They are switched off for maintenance. As I said, he's ex-job, and one of your lads knows him, so that's not going to be a problem."

Paul said, "Right Rose. Warrants, are we good for them?"

"All typed up and ready for signing. Magistrate is waiting as we talk."

Greg said, "Told you she was super-efficient, didn't I?"

CHAPTER 14

Armed with the warrants. Paul and his teams met up in the basement of Willis Court; one crew were left to monitor the lift and van, with the porter present. He hadn't been told about the job, but had seen the van arrive and one injured occupant and had virtually sussed it out. He had agreed to disable the cameras, for 15 minutes, when they were ready to go.

The teams split up. Half made their way up the stairs, the rest in the lift, to the floor below Luke's flat. They would all then make their way to the top floor.

On arriving outside the door to the flat, the team spread out. On the signal from Paul, the door was busted straight through. Dick and Dougie were the first through the door shouting, "Armed police! Come out with your hands up!"

They were quickly followed by other armed officers.

Luke stood up from the sofa with his hands raised. "We heard you had been shot," he said.

Dick said, "What you heard, you heard wrong, no thanks to you."

Another door opened, and a man with one injured hand came out, the other hand in the air.

Dick said, "Where's Geoff, Luke?"

"No idea mate, not here." But indicating the closed bedroom door near to him. "He left a bit back."

Dick, Dougie and the team stood either side of the door.

Pushing it open they were met by a fusillade of shots, the only person hit by them was Luke. Killing him instantly.

"Come out, Geoff!" shouted Dick. "The only person you have shot is your brother."

"You bastards," he screamed. He carried on firing until he ran out of ammunition.

Hearing the click of an empty weapon, Dick entered the bedroom, backed up by Dougie. Geoff had gone towards the balcony.

"Give up Geoff, it's over," Dick said.

"Fuck you," he yelled and launched himself over the handrail, landing a few seconds later in an almighty thud on the concrete below, killing him instantly.

Looking down at the broken body, Dick said, "Good take off, shit landing."

Back inside, the team had the rest of Luke's team in custody.

Paul said, "Call it in, Greg. Rose will know what to do. Dougie, get your team to take the injured man to hospital. Leave two with him. Two to remain here for SOCO. The rest of us, Luke's pubs need doing. Let's go."

Between the teams, they searched the Whistle and Flute and the Brittany Arms.

At the end of the day, they had recovered around £200,000 in cash, plus a large amount of euros and forged, worldwide currency, a large amount of jewellery, drugs, and five firearms, two of which were identified as being from the gunshop robbery in Nottingham.

Paul and Dick shook hands with Rose and Greg.

Paul said, "Can't thank you both enough, and your teams. Greg, me old mate, you have never let me down yet. We both owe you. Any time we can help you and yours out, don't hesitate to shout. If you are ever up our way, please give us a call."

Rose said, "We certainly will, good luck to you both."

Paul and Dick, joined up with Dougie and his team. "OK boys. Back home. Great day's work."

CHAPTER 15

A few days later, sitting in his office, Paul's phone rang. "Hello, Paul Richards here."

The caller said, "Bob Teal here. Heard the news about Bull and his gang. Sounded like a good job."

"Yes, a bit scary at times, but a great result. What can I do for you? Do you want to give up?"

"No. Just to let you know, we always thought Luke was a double-crosser, that's why we never got back in touch with him. You won't be hearing from us again. I know we are still wanted, but we'll take that risk. If we ever do come unstuck, you and your mate will be the first to know."

"We won't stop looking, you know."

"I know that, but it's a big world, and you have to look in the right places. That will be the end result. Regards to all." Bob rang off.

Putting the phone down, Paul muttered, "Cheeky bastard."

ABOUT THE AUTHOR

Nottingham born and bred, joined the Nottinghamshire Police in 1971. Spent the last 27 years of service in the CID. Retired in 2001. Lives with his wife, East of Nottingham, and enjoys Golf, Reading and Antiques, and many other activities.

Printed in Great Britain
by Amazon

83012860R00181